THE COTTAGE ON BLUEBERRY BAY

BLUEBERRY BAY BOOK 1

ELLEN JOY

For my sister Carolyn. The best sister a girl could ask for.

Click HERE or visit ellenjoyauthor.com for more information about all of Ellen's books.

Beach Rose Secrets

*We cannot
direct the wind,
but we can adjust the sails.*

Dolly Parton

CHAPTER 1

*M*eredith stared at the sun's fading reflection rippling in the pool.

"I think I'm going to stay in the city for the summer," her son, Ryan, said over the phone.

"The whole summer?" Meredith's voice rose as her heart plummeted like an anchor falling. She felt slightly sick as she stared at the sparkling clean water. She'd spent most of her monthly earnings of piano lessons getting it professionally cleaned. She had hoped the lure of the pool would drag her youngest back home for the summer. "I thought you said you wanted to take it easy this summer before your last year in college."

"Yeah, I did. But Dad introduced me to a friend of his who offered me this amazing opportunity right downtown in Washington," Ryan explained.

Meredith did all the right *hmms*, and *ohhs*, and *ahhs* to sound as though she was listening, but her legs felt heavy, and she stepped down into the water on the stairs, sat on the edge of the pool she couldn't afford, and held back the tears.

"Have you been talking to Dad a lot?" she asked, immediately wishing she hadn't.

"Not a lot since the baby was born," Ryan said.

That's when she felt it. The heavy pain that fell on her chest at the mere mention of Phillip. She tried swallowing down the lump growing in her throat.

"You know you could intern here in Boston and live at home." Her voice squeaked, giving her emotions away. "Grandpa could help you out."

Would her father, a retired doctor, know someone in law?

"This is DC," Ryan said. "Besides, we live in Andover. It would take me an hour to even get into the city."

"It doesn't take that long." But she knew it could very well take commuters over an hour some days. "I just thought you wanted to come home for the summer."

"I did, but this is an opportunity I can't pass up."

Meredith knew her son was right, that it would be selfish to make him follow through on his promise to come home, and a mother shouldn't hold her son back for her own needs.

How could Phillip take this last summer away? Her last child, while he sits in his new home with his new child and new wife.

"I was just looking forward to you coming home," she said, making her voice peppy. "Can you come up for the Fourth at least?"

"I'll come up for a weekend," he said.

The vagueness made Meredith's stomach twist. "Sure, Ry. That would be great."

She squeezed her eyes shut, and tears fell down her face. She didn't want to lose it on the phone with Ryan. It wasn't fair to make him feel bad. This was a natural stage in his life, and he should be excited for this opportunity, not worried about whether his mother would be able to handle it.

Her baby would be leaving college and going who knew where. Her daughters had moved out a few years ago. Cora lived in the North End and worked as a waitress, and Muriel lived among the trees in New Hampshire, where she was a teacher. Meredith would officially be an empty nester.

She would have to sell the house.

Silence fell between them, until Ryan said, "Mom?"

"Yeah?" She almost tagged on her pet name for him but stopped herself. Her "pumpkin" was turning twenty-two this year. He no longer wanted to be referred to as a fruit.

"I love you," he said. "I'll make sure to come back for the Fourth."

But she could almost guarantee he wouldn't. A more important engagement would come up that he would just *have* to attend, and could she blame him? Why would her son want to come back home to just his mom and a pool?

"I love you, too, pump—" She took a deep breath. "Ryan. I love you, too."

"I'll be back, I promise," he said.

She hummed out an *mm-hmm* because she was about to lose it. "Oh, Ry, I've gotta go. There's a delivery. Love you! Good luck with finals."

And she hung up.

She looked out at the mountain pond pool Phillip had insisted on putting in when they'd built the house. The beautiful pool for her beautiful family.

Placing her phone on the tiled ledge, she dipped her hands into the cool water and wiped her face, promising herself that she wouldn't go on any social media. It was bad enough Phillip's second wedding had been a major event—his new wife came from a prominent family from Boston. His half of the guest list had been the same as for their own wedding. Even some of their closest couple friends were in attendance. Now, her same friends were visiting Phillip's new wife and new daughter and posting about it.

She held her hands to her chest, as if somehow, she could hold her heart together even though she could feel it tearing apart.

When her phone rang, she had no idea how long she had been sitting by the pool.

It was her dad. She went to silence it. She could crumble again at any moment, but she thought about how she'd feel if Ryan did that to her.

"Hey, Dad," she said, trying to sound upbeat.

"You busy?" he asked.

She almost laughed. She had a whole summer of nothing. "Nope."

"Good. I'm outside in your driveway."

She immediately stood up on the pool steps, turning toward the front of the house. "You are? I'm in the back."

She stepped out of the pool, wiping her eyes while checking herself on her phone's camera as she went around to the front of the house. She pasted a smile on her face as soon as she saw his car.

"Hi, Dad!" She bounced over to her seventy-five-year-old father.

"Hey, sugarplum," he said, walking up to the house.

"What are you doing here this late?" she asked, looking at the time. It was only six at night, but that was late for her father.

"I thought I'd come over with some ice cream." He lifted a bag with a pint-sized container.

Her heart dropped. Ice cream meant Gordon had something unpleasant to tell her. Throughout her childhood, her father would soften the blow of bad news with the sweet treat of ice cream.

"Why don't you come in," she said, gesturing her hand at the house.

He squinted as he got close enough to see her swollen eyes. "Looks like I came at the right time."

She shook her head, pretending she was fine. "I'm good."

He put his arm around her shoulder and squeezed it.

She led the way to the kitchen as he followed her inside the garage and up the few steps into the house.

Gordon walked to the table and pulled the pint of ice cream out of the bag as Meredith grabbed two bowls and two spoons, then put the small pint in the middle of them like they had when she was a kid.

"Do you want to talk about it?" her father asked.

Always a doctor, Gordon Johnson went right in with the talk.

When she'd gotten teased, he'd talked to her. When she'd had her first heartbreak, he'd talked to her. When she'd broken rules, he'd talked to her. That was what was so great about her father—she could talk to him.

But what else was there to say? She'd had nine months to talk about this baby. A year to talk about her divorce. Two years since she had lost her mom.

"I'm having a hard time not being happy about a baby being born," she said, laughing out her admission but feeling immediate shame. A renegade tear fell down her cheek before she could swipe it away. "I'm a fifty-year-old woman, and I should know better, but some of the greatest days of my life were when I had my babies with Phillip."

Her eyes teared up.

"You don't lose your memories because things change," Gordon said to her. "You can still have that and be sad and all of it."

She held her breath, pulling back the tears, holding a smile with as much force as possible.

"So what's going on?" she said, changing the subject. "What brings you by?"

Gordon reached inside the bag where he had the ice cream and pulled out an envelope with her maiden name written on top.

Ms. Meredith O'Neill Johnson.

"What's this?" she asked. She had not seen her name written with O'Neill except for on her birth certificate.

Gordon exhaled a long, heavy sigh. "It's from your father."

CHAPTER 2

*M*eredith hadn't thought of her biological father in years. He had been someone she'd thought about a lot as a child, especially in her teenage years, but once she'd become a parent herself, she had stopped obsessing about why a father would have nothing to do with his child.

"What does he want?" she asked, pushing the envelope back to Gordon. She had never once spoken to her father, and now he wanted to talk?

"Nothing," Gordon said, leaving the envelope where she had pushed it. "He passed away over the weekend."

"Jacob?" She looked up from her bowl. "He died?"

Gordon nodded. "Looks like a stroke."

"Oh," she said, calculating his age in her mind. He hadn't even reached seventy.

"Who gave you this?" she asked, gesturing toward the envelope. She noticed the name of the small fishing town that Jacob had lived in. Blueberry Bay sat on the edge of the Atlantic Ocean where the locals of Maine called Down East.

"An attorney named Quinn Michaud." Gordon handed her a card. "He only had your maiden name. I tried calling you when he came to the house, but I couldn't get a hold of you."

She picked up the card, thinking of Jacob. She didn't know how to feel about a man she had never met. A father's death should be significant, but she felt strangely normal.

"So he did know where we lived." She let out a single laugh as Gordon patted her hand.

"You're the sole beneficiary to his estate." Gordon pushed the envelope back to her.

What kind of inheritance could a fisherman have anyway?

She stared at the envelope, afraid only trouble lurked inside. "What is he giving me?"

He shrugged. "It's not mine to open."

She reached out and over the table, then pulled the envelope back to her. She held it in her hands, studying it. This was the kind of moment she wished she had Phillip here for, sitting by her side, encouraging her to make the next move.

She let it go, dropping it like it was hot to the touch.

"Don't you want to know what's inside?" her father asked.

"I don't know if I can handle more bad news today," she said, noticing her ice cream melting in the bowl.

"Meredith." Gordon leaned over the table, holding her hand. "Your mother was open about your father and his struggles. Maybe he left you something that can help with everything you're going through." He paused. "This might allow you to heal from the wounds his absence created."

"That's the thing about wounds," Meredith said. "They leave scars."

Gordon frowned. "I know this must be hard, but maybe it will give you the closure you need."

She inhaled. Gordon was right. Her *real* dad, Gordon. The dad who had stayed up with her looking at stars in the backyard. The dad who had held her hair when she got sick. The dad who had coached her games and given her pep talks. He was the dad who tucked her in at night and walked her down the aisle. Even now, at fifty, he still showed up for her. The guy in the envelope was just a sperm donor, for all she was concerned.

She looked over at him. Gordon looked more tired these days. The family physician had fallen head over heels for her and her mother. He'd taken them in when her mother had left her father and needed a place to stay. He always said he fell in love with both of them from the first moment he'd met them.

His girls.

"I think I'll wait until tomorrow." She shrugged. "I don't really want to know what he left me."

"Take your time," he said, but it was obvious that he wanted to know what was inside. How did Gordon feel about her father? She had no idea. He never spoke a negative word about Jacob O'Neill, the situation, about becoming her father, and adopting her. Did this bring up feelings about his relationship with Jacqueline?

She poked her finger through the small opening at the top and ripped it through.

Inside were thick papers with fancy ink letterhead.

Meredith pulled off a business card that was paper clipped to the letter. *Quinn Michaud* was written on top of the card, with Attorney at Law underneath it.

"You should call him," her dad said.

She looked at the return address—Blueberry Bay, Maine. She pulled the papers out. A quick glance revealed standard last will and testament documents. Like her divorce papers—cold, wordy, and without emotion.

"Okay, then," she said, stuffing the papers back into the envelope. "I love you, Dad, but I'm tired. Can we talk about this in the morning?"

Gordon nodded, not pushing her to call the attorney like Phillip and her mom would have.

"I'm just really tired and had a long day, and I…" She paused, then said, "Don't want to deal with this until the morning."

"Of course," he said, getting up from his seat at the table. He walked his bowl to the sink and put the ice cream into the freezer, leaving hers there. "You've had a long day." He stood next to her as she got up and hugged her for a long time. "I love you, sugarplum."

"I love you, too," she said as he kissed her on the cheek.

"You can always come back home and stay with me," he said into her ear.

"Dad, I'm fifty." She was not going to have a sleepover with her father. "I live down the road from you."

"We could combine households," he suggested. "Save some money."

Meredith had thought she'd reached rock bottom with Phillip having a baby with another woman, but she could not believe how bad things continued to get.

"Are you okay to get home?" She changed the subject, ushering Gordon toward the door.

"I'll be fine," he said. "I'm just glad there are streetlights."

"Yeah, those help at night," she said. Her father had not been particularly good at driving at night lately. Not that she was after she'd started needing to wear readers.

"Bye, Dad," she said, trying to sound upbeat, but her voice came out weak. She opened his door once they got outside.

He kissed her on the cheek once more before getting in. She shut the door and gave him a thumbs-up, a gesture they'd done with each other since she was a little girl playing soccer for the first time.

When she got back inside, she stared at the envelope. Her biological father was in that envelope. This was the closest she had ever been to him since she was a small child.

She thought about reading the papers, but instead she turned off the lights and went upstairs to bed.

By midnight, she had tossed and turned so much, she gave up and came back downstairs and decided to call her sister.

"Hey," Remy whispered into the phone. "Everything alright?"

Meredith could hear instrumental music playing in the background. Was she interrupting something?

"Sorry, is this a bad time?" she asked. Was her sister having a party?

"Joe's having a small thing at the house," she said.

Meredith could feel the pang of not being included. Did her sister not invite her to their fancy parties anymore because she didn't have a husband to bring? Or was it Phillip who they enjoyed? Was a divorced housewife who taught piano lessons not good enough for Remy's high society friends?

"I can let you go," Meredith said.

"No, no, Joe's happy entertaining everyone by himself," Remy said, oblivious to Meredith's feelings. "What's up?"

"It's nothing. I shouldn't have bothered you. I'll let you go." Meredith went to hang up when Remy called out.

"Mer, it's obviously not nothing. You're calling me in the middle of the night."

Meredith looked at the clock on the microwave. She got straight to the point. "Dad dropped off an envelope today."

"Okay...?" Remy asked.

"My real father died," Meredith said. "His attorney has been trying to contact me to give me his assets."

"Your dad died?"

"No, Jacob O'Neill died," she corrected her sister.

"Oh, Meredith. I'm so sorry. When did you find out?"

"Tonight. Dad told me." Meredith picked at the corner of the envelope with her thumb. "A lawyer dropped off paperwork at his house."

"How did he die?" Remy asked.

"A stroke," Meredith said.

"And he left something for you?" Remy asked.

"I guess so," Meredith said, staring at the envelope.

"But you don't know what he left you?" Remy sounded surprised by this.

"No, I haven't read the papers. I think I need to meet with the attorney," Meredith replied.

Remy was Gordon's first biological child and his "baby girl."

Even though Gordon had always treated Meredith like his own and she knew no other man as her father, something had always made her feel just slightly different.

She was his "sugarplum" and Remy was his "baby girl" and no matter how she rationalized their nicknames, Meredith could not stop that little part of her from thinking he loved Remy more because she was his own.

She wanted to pick up the phone and call her mom, but the stabbing realization that she couldn't pierced her heart.

"Do you want me to come with you to meet his attorney?" Remy asked. "I could bring ours."

She wanted Phillip by her side. Not her younger sister's attorney. "Thanks for the offer, but I'll be fine."

"I can drive up from the city in no time," her sister said. Then she heard a deep voice in the background. Joe said something that made her laugh.

"No, you don't have to do that," Meredith said.

"Are you going to be okay?" Remy asked.

She could feel her throat tightening up. "Yeah, I'll talk to you tomorrow."

"Love you, Meredith."

"Yeah, you, too."

There was only one other person Meredith wanted to call and talk to about this. But he was probably busy holding his new daughter in his arms like he had with all three of their children while she had rested, making her think he was a knight in shining armor. Not the one person who would hurt her the worst. Or had that been Jacob?

She grabbed her computer, and as soon as she opened a browser, she started with his name in the search bar.

Jacob O'Neill.

Pictures of different men littered the screen.

She typed in Blueberry Bay.

A photograph of a bronze mermaid statue came up next to another photograph of a man with gray hair and a beard—Jacob

O'Neill, her father.

She stared at his image. She had seen photographs in her mother's jewelry box. Her mother hadn't hid them, but she never encouraged her to look at them either. Meredith rarely did, feeling too many emotions, like she felt looking at his older image right now.

A sadness floated inside her as she stared at the picture—a sadness only an abandoned child could ever explain. No matter how much love the other people in Meredith's life gave her, and she'd had an exceptional childhood filled with tons of love from Jacqueline and Gordon, it never filled that empty feeling, a feeling of being tossed aside. Like something had to have been wrong with her for her real father to walk away like he did.

She clicked on the article about the mermaid.

Local Fisherman Sculptor.

She leaned closer to the laptop's screen and looked at the mermaid's face. The blur made her doubt herself at first. She grabbed her readers, and when the face focused, she let out a gasp.

It was her mother.

CHAPTER 3

"*T*hat's totally mom!" Remy said as she grabbed Meredith's phone from her hand. She looked closer, then sipped her coffee while studying the picture.

"It is." There was no doubt. The mermaid, from head to waist, was their mother.

Meredith hadn't slept a wink all night thinking about her mother's image.

"He didn't leave much to the imagination." Remy closed the screen.

"Yes, but he was very generous with her proportions." Meredith had noticed how voluptuous Jacqueline had been in the sculpture.

"It's kind of romantic," Remy said, returning her phone. "Now call the attorney."

Driving all the way from the city that morning, Remy had shown up with two coffees and homemade scones from a bakery on Commonwealth Avenue. Her baby sister was the epitome of Boston high society. Even in her loungewear, she looked pressed and ready for a yacht outing.

Meredith looked like she had slept in her clothes. She looked down at her leggings, which she *had* slept in.

Meredith took a deep breath. "Alright, I'll call."

She took the card, dialed the ten-digit number with a Maine area code, and waited.

"Is this the address?" Remy asked, pointing to the documents on the table.

Meredith nodded as the line began to ring.

"Hello. Quinn Michaud," a deep man's voice answered.

"Hi, my name is Meredith Johnson. I'm calling regarding my…" Meredith stopped. "Jacob O'Neill."

"Hi, yes, Ms. Johnson," the man said. "I'm sorry to have been the one who informed your family about Jacob's passing. I'm very sorry for your loss."

"Thank you," she said, but she didn't know what else to say.

An awkward silence hung on the line before he said, "It looks like he might've had a stroke and died in his sleep."

"My father gave me Jacob's papers, but I'm afraid I haven't had the time to really go through them." She felt silly now. She should have just read the papers. But something made her not want to know what her real father had when he died. What kind of life did he live without her and her mother? And what if he just left her a little nothing trinket?

Meredith hardly remembered the seaside village in Maine except for one memory as a little girl. Her mother had taken her on a long day's drive up the coast to a cottage on the edge of the sea. She was five or six, but too young to comprehend what all that meant at the time until that exact moment. An image of a man flashed through her head. A younger brown-haired man with a tattoo of a mermaid on the inside of his wrist.

"Yes," the attorney said. "I'm sorry I went to your father's house, but I had no current information for you. I could meet with you in Maine as soon as possible, but I'm afraid I can't make it to Massachusetts until later in the week."

"I was surprised to learn he left anything to me," she said, truthfully. Did this attorney understand the situation?

"Jacob left everything to you," the attorney said.

"He left me everything?" She whispered to Remy.

Remy's eyes lit up like she had won the lottery. "You're kidding!'

Meredith's mind started spinning and she asked the attorney, "Did he tell you why?"

"Excuse me?" the man said.

She covered the phone and said to Remy, "I don't want his guilt money."

"Jacob had his faults," the man said thinking Meredith was talking to him. "But he did a lot for our community and—"

"Mr…?" Meredith interrupted him.

"Michaud," he said.

"Mr. Michaud." She took a deep breath trying to hold in her swirling emotions. "I'm sorry, I was talking to my sister. What do I need to do?"

"Well, he left you his house. It's deeded to you, but you'll need to record it in the town registry," he said. "He also had a fishing boat."

The thought of going through Jacob O'Neill's things twisted her stomach. "Do I have to come to Maine to do all of this?"

"Yes, you will," the attorney said. "Dr. Johnson said he had a key to the cottage, and I have—"

"What?" she interrupted him. "Gordon? He has a key to the cottage?"

"Your mother had one, I guess," the attorney replied.

She looked at Remy, who silently mouthed, "What?"

Meredith covered the mouthpiece and whispered, "Mom had a key to Jacob's cottage."

This made no sense whatsoever to Meredith. "Are you sure?" she asked Quinn again.

"That's what your father told me, yes." Quinn sounded confused that she was surprised. "Would you like to meet, and I can go through all his assets with you?"

"How much are we talking about?" She didn't believe a fisherman would have much.

"Jacob had quite a nest egg at the time of his death," Quinn said.

"Really? A fisherman?" This shocked her. One of the reasons she had assumed he didn't want to be a father was the financial uncertainties that fishermen endured. She calculated his age in her head. He had been eighteen when she was born, so that made him sixty-eight at his death. Could fifty years of fishing bring fortune?

"He hadn't fished in years," the attorney said. "It was his artwork that had been his primary source of income. He has the house, the boat, the land."

The truth was she only wanted to see the statue. She had no interest in seeing the house of a guy who didn't want to be her father. "Could you recommend a real estate agent? Someone who deals with estate sales, etc.?"

"You're already thinking of selling?"

"Well, I live in Massachusetts," she said. "What would I do with a house in Maine?"

"Oh, wow!" gasped Remy, who showed her phone's screen to Meredith. "That's the house."

Meredith looked at Remy's phone, and sitting on the end of the earth over a blue horizon was a gray shingled cottage.

"It's gorgeous," Remy whispered.

"I guess I could make a few calls…" the attorney said.

Remy nodded her head. "Figure out all your options."

"Yes, that would be wonderful if you could do that," Meredith said into the phone.

"Sure," he said, but his friendly demeanor had changed. "There are many other items you'll have to go through, like his art, books, and other personal effects."

Remy whispered, "You should go up there."

Meredith shook her head…but she could use a day from doing nothing but perseverating on Phillip's baby, Jacob's death, and the fact that her mother had a key to his cottage. What else didn't she know?

"If you could get back to me about the real estate agent, that would be great," she said into the phone. "Otherwise, I'll have to check my schedule about coming to Maine."

"Okay." The attorney sounded surprised. "I'm happy to meet with you to go over everything if you'd like. I could come back down to Massachusetts in another week."

Meredith tapped her fingers against the table. Should she go up there? Figure this all out and deal with it like a big girl?

"Go up there," Remy insisted. "What else do you have to do?"

Meredith looked at her sister. The comment meant nothing to Remy, but it cut through Meredith. She had nothing in her life. No husband. No kids. Her summer was as free as free could be. None of her piano students wanted to continue through the summer. No one needed her around.

"I'll have to get back to you, Mr. Michaud," she said. "Have a nice day."

"Would you like me to call—"

She hung up.

Meredith put her phone down on the kitchen table and stared out.

"So?" Remy lifted her eyebrows. "Are you going to go?"

"He left me a house and a boat," Meredith said in utter disbelief. "And apparently our mother had a key to his cottage."

This man had enough money to have a cottage on the ocean, a boat, and more assets?

She opened the article again, staring at the photo of the artist in front of the statue. The byline read *Local sculptor, Jacob O'Neill, describes his muse for the mermaid.*

She closed the screen, unable to read more. She did not want to hear about his muse or inspiration to create her mother as a sea maiden. She'd been Gordon's wife for over forty years at that point.

She could not see if there was a tattoo on his wrist or not. But one thing she was certain about—it had been Jacob O'Neill the day they had visited Maine when she was a little girl.

CHAPTER 4

$\mathcal{M}$eredith stepped inside her childhood home. "Dad?"

"I'm in here!" Gordon called out from the kitchen. He poked his head around the corner. "I'm cleaning up."

Meredith had always known Gordon wasn't her *real* father. Her mother, Jacqueline, would talk about how Gordon had been her knight in shining armor. The doctor who had helped a single mom after Jacob had been "unable" to be a father. Gordon had adopted her after her parents had gotten married, giving her his last name. He did everything for her and loved her unconditionally. Meredith had always been grateful for Gordon coming into her life, and her loyalty ran deep.

So, what was Jacqueline doing with a key to Jacob's cottage?

Jacqueline had been open, to a point, about Meredith's father. He'd had mental issues and addiction, but she had never provided details. She'd never explained why her father couldn't be a father, but Meredith hadn't wanted to know. She only knew a few things about her real father through different conversations she had overheard throughout her lifetime. And she preferred it that way.

The facts she did know were slim.

Jacob O'Neill had been a fisherman due to family obligation but had wanted to be an artist.

Jacqueline's high-society, old-money family had disapproved of Jacob and their relationship.

He'd named her Meredith after his mother.

She could only remember that one time she'd met him at the cottage with her mom. Other than that, Jacob O'Neill could be a stranger.

She followed Gordon down the hall to the kitchen, holding the thick manila envelope in both hands.

"Hey, sugarplum," Gordon said, rinsing a plate under the faucet.

"Hey." She arranged the fruit in the bowl on the counter before asking, "Why did Mom have a key to Jacob's cottage?"

It didn't make sense.

Gordon turned off the water and sighed. He turned around and faced her. "Your mother visited him when she found out about the cancer."

"What?" She grabbed hold of the cold granite. This was unbelievable. "She visited Jacob?"

Gordon nodded his head. "Yes."

"I don't understand," she said. "She visited him? The guy who couldn't be bothered to be my father?"

Her hands started shaking, and an unexpected rage built up in her chest. "Why didn't she tell me? I had been with her at the end for months."

Meredith had basically moved into her parents' house once her mother had been placed in hospice care. She'd been by her mother's side throughout the whole sickness and until the end. Jacqueline had said nothing about Jacob.

"She had reconnected with him a few years ago, when she'd found out," he repeated, holding out his hands. "I guess he had been in and out of a mental health treatment center for years."

"Shouldn't I know this kind of stuff?" What else did she not know?

Gordon made a face. "She tried talking to you about him a few times, but you didn't want to hear anything at the time."

She could not believe her own words would come back and bite her. She had been so angry with her mother for even bringing him up in front of the kids; she'd told her she wanted nothing to do with Jacob. She hadn't planned to tell the kids about her real father, so why bring him up?

It just brought up a lot of pain from her childhood and confusion that lasted into her adulthood. She didn't want to rehash it all with her kids. Besides, the real issue for Meredith was that she didn't want Gordon to think he wasn't enough of a father for her. She felt like she would be betraying Gordon if she went looking for her "real" dad.

"Let me go get the key." Gordon held up his finger then walked to his office. When he came back into the kitchen, he handed over a velvet box someone would place jewelry inside, but as she opened its cover, she saw a brass key. She pulled it out by the silk ribbon tied through the key's hole. The ribbon had tiny shells strung to a piece of driftwood the size of a cork with *Le gîte en bord de Mer* written in her mother's cursive.

"The cottage by the sea," Gordon said, translating the French. "A lot of French Canadians around those parts."

"What am I going to do with a cottage all the way up in Maine?" she said, shutting the box and placing it down on the table.

"If you want to sell it, I would contact a real estate agent up there," Gordon said. "The sale of the cottage could help pay for your half of the Andover house."

She thought about the house she and Phillip had built together when they'd first gotten married. They had agreed she'd stay home with the kids and take care of the household, while Phillip worked as an attorney in Boston. It didn't make sense continuing her career as a pianist. She barely made enough to pay for daycare, let alone a household of five in Andover.

She loved being a stay-at-home mom, but now, at fifty, the

only career choices she had were in teaching piano lessons, retail, or local fast-food places. No one else wanted to hire someone with no work experience, besides cleaning and driving kids around.

Now she had a huge house with a bigger mortgage than she could afford without a lawyer husband.

"The pool is costly," she said. Her monthly alimony wouldn't cover all the chemicals she would need to dump into it if the kids spent the weekend. She knew she needed to sell the house. She just… "I love that pool."

She thought about the gardens. It took twenty years to design, dig, and grow those gardens and trails throughout the wooded lot.

The five bedroom, four bath, on a five-acre lot in Andover with a pool would sell in no time.

"It just doesn't make sense to live in that big house with all that yard," Gordon said and added, "By yourself."

It didn't. In fact, according to the divorce settlement, Phillip only had to pay the mortgage for one year, and then she had to either buy him out or sell their family home. And time was running out.

It didn't make sense to keep it, but she didn't know if she could let it go. She lost her mother, then her marriage, her children had all moved out, and now she was losing her family home.

"You could check out Jacob's cottage and fix it up, then sell it," Gordon said.

"I can't flip a house," she said.

"Why not?" Gordon gave her a look as though she was being unreasonable.

She picked up the velvet box and opened it again, pulled out the key, and pressed the teeth of the brass into her thumb, making indentations into her skin. Then she rubbed the smooth surface of the driftwood, feeling the contrast from the hard, cold key to the soft, warm wood.

"Remy thinks I should drive up there."

"That's a great idea!" Her father's eyes brightened, but a pain drifted in. "It gave your mother comfort to close that chapter in her life."

Something about the look in his eyes told her there was more to what he said, but she didn't push it. She loved Gordon, and to her, he was her father, whether she had his blood or not. Jacob was just a stranger.

"I can't believe she didn't tell me."

Gordon slanted his head in empathy. Jacqueline had not been the kind of parent who would confess her feelings or hopes or dreams. She had done that in her art. Meredith was almost certain Gordon didn't even know all of Jacqueline's story.

Meredith, on the other hand, had told Jacqueline everything. She would listen to her childish confessions and her darkest adult secrets. Her mother was the first person she told when she'd had her first kiss, her first and last cigarette, and the first time she had slept in the same bed with her husband. She was the first to know when she'd gotten engaged to Phillip and had been pregnant with her children, even before Phillip and Remy.

Her mother had known everything about her, but as she traced the jagged edge of the key with her thumb, she wondered what else her mother hadn't told her.

CHAPTER 5

*W*hen Meredith returned from her father's, she stood at her kitchen island, opened the velvet box, and stared at the key. She picked up the tiny piece of driftwood and ran her finger against the indents of her mother's handwriting.

Le gîte *en bord de Mer.*

The Cottage by the Sea.

Why hadn't her mother pushed her more to meet him? Why had she let one conversation stop her? Why hadn't she talked to Meredith about him before she'd died?

It had been Meredith's thirteenth birthday party when she had overheard Jacqueline talking to her friend's mother in the kitchen about Jacob. She had gone to find the mothers to let them know they wanted the cake, when she'd heard his name.

"Jacob had been the love of my life," she'd said to Mrs. Morrow. Meredith could see a look of sorrow across her face.

Her friend's mom had nodded like she understood. "That must've been difficult, what you two went through."

"Yes." Jacqueline had looked out the window. "But then Gordon took her in as if she were his own, and I will forever be grateful for him."

Mrs. Morrow had continued nodding her head. "Your first love will always stay with you."

"Yes, they always seem to hold a part of your heart, don't they?" Jacqueline had held her skinny hand to her heart.

Meredith had slipped away, ashamed of her mother for saying Gordon wasn't her true love, and vowed to always support Gordon, her *real* father, over some deadbeat who couldn't be bothered.

Why hadn't Jacqueline ever revealed any of this to her? What had he meant to her mother? Why go back there and see him? And why keep a key to his cottage?

For a full day, Meredith questioned what she should do. Should she go up to Maine and see what this man had left her? Or should she leave well enough alone? She could hire one of those companies to come in and sell Jacob's estate and assets. Not deal with any of it.

But something kept nagging at her. Questions filled her head as the minutes wore on. Questions that might be answered if she went to Maine.

As the sun faded away, she tried booking a hotel, but it seemed silly since she had inherited a beach house. She couldn't find one anyway. She packed an air mattress, a good sleeping bag, and a suitcase with more clothes than she needed, but she had no idea what the weather would be like on the coast in Maine. Summer or not, she had a feeling she needed more than one pair of pants.

She decided to leave first thing in the morning. If she got up early enough, she'd be able to get to the attorney's office right away and get all that over with.

She called the lawyer when she left the house the next morning. "The GPS says I'll arrive in Blueberry Bay in less than six hours."

She wished she hadn't drank all that coffee.

The drive was smooth at first, but then she hit traffic from New Hampshire all the way through Portland.

That's when Phillip called her.

Her stomach dropped. She hadn't spoken to Phillip since the baby was born.

"Hi, Phil," she answered and put it on speaker. "Congratulations!"

"Thanks, Mer," he said, causal like she had congratulated him on his softball league, not a new child in his family. "Did I catch you at a bad time?"

She put the blinker on, getting in the slow lane. "No, I'm just driving. What's up?"

She should make an excuse. Remy would give her grief for even answering his call. What was she doing talking to her ex-husband on the phone?

"Is there something you want to talk about?" She would stick to business. They shared three amazing children and needed to get along.

"Gosh, Meredith, I forgot how much there is to do with a newborn," he said, sounding overwhelmed.

"Yeah, babies are a lot," she said.

But she had loved that age. Those had been her favorite moments of her life—the first few days with her babies. Phillip acted like he remembered what it was like. He had been a wonderful father, but he had left the hospital hours after the birth of all their children and had to work. When their children were born, he was putting in extra hours trying to make partner. His firm had praised him in his annual review for doing so.

They had sold their condominium in Southie and moved in with her parents while they looked for houses. It had been bliss. Living with Gordon, a pediatrician, had been so helpful and gave her anxiety-free help. Gordon loved being a grandfather, and Jacqueline had adored her grandchildren.

Meredith's sister, being younger, still lived at home and had become a doting auntie for Cora.

Then a piece of land down the road from her parents had become available, and they'd put in an offer right away. It had taken a year to build, but they hadn't minded the wait to have exactly what they wanted for their growing family. She had Muriel next, then Ryan, and then Phillip had said he didn't want any more children when she'd said she wanted a fourth.

"You were such a natural," he said.

"Phillip, what do you want?" she asked.

"I just wanted to talk to you. Get some perspective, you know?" He groaned. "Sometimes I feel like I'm dealing with the girls with Rylie."

"Ouch," she said. "That's really not my business."

"I know, I know," he said, continuing with his complaining. "It's just a lot."

She tried biting her tongue, but as she sat in traffic, sweltering with a hot flash, she snapped and said, "She's at a totally different stage of life and you knew that going in."

"Geez, Meredith, I'm calling to thank you," he said. "You did all that work with the kids, and I just never knew how hard it was for you."

She sat there completely at a loss for words. Phillip had thanked her?

She moved the vents of the air-conditioning to hit her on the upper lip just perfectly, instantly cooling her off.

"I'm sorry. I should let you go," he said.

She should let him go. She should not talk to Phillip like everyone kept telling her. It was unhealthy. It was holding onto something that wasn't real. He wasn't her husband. He was someone else's, and he was using her.

"I'm headed to Maine," she blurted out, unable to let him go. "My real father, Jacob, died."

"Really?" he said. His voice immediately became sympathetic, and her heart pricked. "When?"

"Last week, I guess," she said. She shouldn't have brought Jacob up. It wasn't Phillip's business anymore. He wasn't her husband any longer.

"Are you okay?" he asked, and that was when she could feel the familiar comfort his voice gave her.

"Yes," she said, rolling her eyes at herself. Why was she so weak when it came to Phillip? "I didn't even know the man."

"Come on, Meredith," Phillip said. "Him dying ends that fantasy of him asking you to forgive him."

That was the hardest part about the divorce. Phillip knew all her secrets, even more than her mother. He knew the little things she'd never told anyone else, like how she had wished her real father would come back and beg for forgiveness. How she had wished he would tell her how much he'd missed by not being her dad.

Now she felt like a fool for trusting Phillip with those secrets.

"Well, he left everything to me, so there's that," she said.

"He left you an inheritance?" Phillip sounded as shocked as she had been.

"A cottage, too," she said. "I haven't talked to the kids about it yet, so please don't say anything."

"Like a house?" he asked.

"Yes," she said. "I'm going up there right now to check it out."

"Oh, Meredith, that's great news."

"What?" she said, confused. "My father dying is great news?"

"No, but now you have a little cushion, and we can sell the house."

She started seeing red. "What?"

"I really need to sell, Mer. Now I have another kid to get through school and college." Phillip rattled off all the huge expenses he would have to pay now with a baby and a new wife and alimony to her.

"Phillip, I haven't even met with his attorney," she said.

"Do you want me to go up there and meet his lawyer with you?"

She needed to see a therapist. "No, you have a baby and a new wife!"

Phillip sighed into the phone.

"I still care about you, Meredith," Phillip said. "We were married long enough that I know this must be hard for you."

Having a baby with another woman closer in age to their daughters was hard, she thought, but instead, she said, "It's not your business anymore, so I should go…" Then she shot out, "Take the baby as much as you can when you get home."

"What?" he said.

"When you got home, you usually ate and relaxed, leaving me all day and night with the kids," she said. "The best thing you can do for that baby, and for Rylie, is to come home with food, help clean up, play with the baby, and put her to bed."

"So now we're unloading on what a bad father I was?" he said, his voice rising in a defensive tone.

"You wanted a friend," she said back.

"Okay, I guess I deserved that," he said. "Let me know if I can help in any way with everything."

And this was where she hated Phillip, because she loved him so much. Why was he so agreeable? Why was he so kind and thoughtful, yet willing to leave her and ruin everything? Had she been that horrible as a wife? Had he gotten tired of the old model? Traded her in for a newer version?

And why did she love herself so little to let him sneak back in like she was doing?

"I should get off the phone," she said. "You should be with your wife and new daughter."

"Don't be like that, Meredith," he said. "We were always better as friends."

The gut punch was immediate and took her breath away. "I've got to go."

She threw the phone into the console. Instead of taking the interstate the whole way, she decided to slip off onto the route that followed the edge of the ocean. She needed to see the ocean right about now.

When she reached the exit, a green sign with white lettering saying, *Welcome to Blueberry Bay, Home of the Blueberry Festival* greeted her.

She cringed at the cheesy name.

She checked the time. Ugh, she was already late for her meeting with Jacob's lawyer. Her plan had been to see the cottage before talking with him, to see what they were going to be talking about. She pulled over on the side of the road and decided to text him that she would be even later than she already was, but her phone had no service.

She continued to drive through the small town, passing a school and a fire station as her GPS made her follow the public beach signs.

Suddenly, off in the distance, she could see the shimmering blue sparkling sea ahead. As if there were an invisible rope dragging her toward it, she had to get to the water. She hit the window buttons and rolled them all down, inhaling the briny sea smell. Along both sides of the road, seagrass and winding waterways meandered in and out of tall grass. Above her, a flock of white birds swooped through the air, soaring in unison above the tidal waters.

She drove down the main strip of tiny, shingled clapboard shops with touristy trinkets displayed in the windows. People lined the streets in sunhats and sunglasses, wearing bright beach attire and swimsuits. Beachgoers pulled wagons and colorful umbrellas. Window shoppers lined the streets, with husbands waiting on perfectly placed benches. Window boxes hung on every storefront and hanging flower baskets swayed in the sea breeze from the streetlights. Brick sidewalks lined each side of the street with granite street curbs.

Blueberry Bay was perfect, in a postcard-perfect kind of way. The village was impeccably clean. The people walking around looked happy as they talked and laughed together along the streets. She saw some waving at each other and exchanging pleasantries.

It would be the kind of town she would drag Phillip to for a weekend away.

Her heart pained at the thought she would never have a weekend away with him again.

And that was when the street opened to a large grassy square with a public garden, where a pier sat at the end. She didn't even hesitate when she saw a parking spot. She knew this was the square from the pictures she'd seen online. She got out as soon as she turned off the car and walked straight to the statue.

At one end of the public garden rested the bronze mermaid sculpture lying on top of a granite pedestal.

Meredith gasped as soon as she saw her mother's face looking back at her. She reached out to touch it and jumped at the cool touch. The statue smiled, her eyes half-closed as though she had been laughing. Her hair was down, pulled behind her shoulders as she looked off to the side toward land, toward Meredith.

She almost wanted to say hello—the statue looked just like her mother.

She read the inscription on the bronze plate attached to the pedestal.

Lady of the Sea, artist Jacob O'Neill.

She stared at the mermaid. Her father's hands had created that statue. Working with bronze was a tedious task that took months, if not years, to finish.

And there was no doubt this statue was not of the young woman he'd had a baby with, but the older version she knew as her mother. Had her mother posed for her real father?

The statue was discreet enough. It wasn't exactly a nude, but like Remy had said, Jacob O'Neill did not leave much to the imagination. Her mother's full figure was the centerpiece of this beautiful garden and the first thing visitors saw when walking from the pier—her mother's chest covered in seaweed.

She looked up at the face, the expression one she had seen so many times throughout her life. Pure happiness. Jacqueline never got defeated, even in the face of adversity. Her mother went from riches to rags with a baby on her hip and nothing stopped her.

Here Meredith was, falling apart because she had to sell her house.

She took a picture of the statue and sent it to Remy. **Well, there's no denying it. It's definitely Jacqueline.**

She looks radiant! Remy sent a heart emoji as though seeing your mother as a bronze statue wasn't haunting. **When did you go up there?**

She felt like she was looking at a ghost, and one she didn't know. **Just now.**

Have you seen the cottage? Remy texted.

Not yet.

Send pics when you get there! Bubbles appeared underneath. **I'll come as soon as you say the word!** And she sent a kissing face emoji.

Meredith walked to the pier, and took a deep breath, closing her eyes as she listened to the sounds around her. She wished she had Phillip there by her side, someone that understood her like he did.

Yes, Remy understood, but Phillip had gotten to the heart of it. She'd wanted an apology all her life, and now he was dead and just a name on a statue. The irony was that the person she really wished she could talk to about all of this was memorialized in bronze just a few feet away from her. She wanted to scream at the statue.

How could you die without talking to your daughter about her past? How could you carry on a relationship and leave your daughter in the dark?

Did Gordon know about the statue?

She found a bench and sat down, facing the bronze piece, and stared out at the water. The Atlantic Ocean sparkled in the sunlight as far as the eye could see. If she had not been visiting her dead father's home, it would have been a perfect day—blue skies, no clouds, just enough of a breeze to cool from the sun's heat.

She looked back at the statue. Her mother looked happy, which at the end of her life, Meredith hadn't seen. The end had been hard for her mother, and she had been drugged up so much she had hardly been cognizant of what was happening. When Meredith had finally gotten enough bravery to ask the questions she wanted to know, Jacqueline had been too sick to answer them.

Maybe Jacqueline had wanted closure, and so did Meredith, by coming up here. There were so many what-ifs. What if her mother and Jacob had stayed married? What if she had grown up in this beautiful small town?

Taking another deep breath, she collected herself and headed back to the car. Leaving the pier, she took a few more photos of the little village square lined with potted plants and different pieces of art. The mermaid had been one of a dozen or so different pieces displayed in perennial flower gardens.

Meredith couldn't deny the beauty of the New England seaside village. The quaint clapboard buildings, the easygoing feel everyone gave off, the simple feeling of nature being the center of everyone's attention. It had been the reason her mother's family had bought a summer home there and how her mother had met Jacob, the local fisherman's boy. That much she did know about her parents.

She pulled back onto Main Street and drove toward Blueberry Bay Lane. On the GPS, it looked as though there was only one road in to get to Jacob's house.

She drove down the long, narrow road, following a winding waterway. Soon, houses lined the sides—small Victorian fishing houses with front porches. The road curved along a sandy beach. She followed the GPS as the paved road ended and turned to seashell gravel. There at the end sat a cottage that appeared to be hanging over the Atlantic Ocean. She stopped the car in the middle of the road and looked at it.

With a deep breath, she got out of her car and walked up to the cottage.

The tiny gray cape looked even quainter than the Google Street View photo Remy had shown her. But as she got closer, the quaintness gave way to a look of neglect. Pink beach plum rose bushes grew over the windows and hid a porch she hadn't even noticed until she got closer. The paint had peeled off the old porch that held one broken rocking chair. Overgrown brush covered what may have been the front yard. Window boxes sat empty, and broken pots sat in what appeared to have been a flower garden but now looked like a patch of weeds.

But none of that mattered when she saw the view.

The sparkling blue water dazzled, as if millions of diamonds shimmered the sun's reflection back at her. The sight was over-whelming, and without warning, Meredith started to tear up for no reason.

She remembered the man who had chased her in the gardens.

Jacob.

She turned around before reaching the porch, deciding she wanted nothing to do with Jacob O'Neill. She wasn't even going to bother going inside the house. She would take a quick pic for Remy and meet with the lawyer.

Then she would sell it.

CHAPTER 6

Quinn Michaud waited outside Blueberry Bay High School, watching all the other parents sit in the pickup line. Parents—well, mostly, the moms—of Blueberry Bay sat in their minivans or mini-SUVs. Quinn realized there were only two fathers in the pickup line waiting for their child to finish their sports practice. Back in his day, his father had made him walk.

Always a fisherman, John Michaud believed in three things— God, family, and hard work. Along with making your kid walk home from sports practice.

"Hey, Dad," Kyle said, getting into the truck.

"Hey, bud," Quinn said, shifting the truck into drive.

"Didn't you have a meeting?" Kyle said. "I thought Grandma was picking me up."

Quinn shook his head. For two hours, Quinn had waited in his office for Jacob's daughter to arrive. "She hasn't shown up."

Quinn understood this woman hadn't had a relationship with Jacob, but to just blow off a dead man and his attorney rubbed him the wrong way.

But just as he pulled out of the parking lot, he got a text.

Stuck in traffic with no service. My GPS says it will be another hour.

He moaned to himself. He had forgotten how badly the highway got clogged up by tourists during the summer. He hadn't had to drive up to Maine since he'd lived in the city.

Take your time, he texted back.

"Dude, can I borrow the car tonight?" Kyle asked him as he typed on his phone. "I finally got Brianna to go out with me."

"Dude, no," Quinn said, shaking his head. "I have to meet Jacob's daughter tonight."

"I thought you said she wasn't coming," Kyle said.

"That's not what I said." Quinn looked at Kyle's shaggy hair and noticed two white earbuds. "How do you even hear with those things in your ears?"

"Because I can multitask," Kyle said with a smirk on his face. "Do you think Grandma will lend me her car?"

"You could ask." Quinn's mother had been a bit reluctant to let the new driver behind the wheel of her car. "Maybe if you give her the exact details of who you're with and where you're going."

"She loves Brianna," Kyle said. "She goes to church on Sundays."

"There you go," Quinn said to his son. "You know Grandma loves a girl who attends church."

Kyle pointed his finger at Quinn. "You know, Dad, you're smart sometimes."

Quinn laughed. "Gee, thanks. I think."

Grandma Ginny didn't really like the idea of her grandson dating in high school. Too young was her excuse, but she was really afraid he would do something stupid.

"He forgets his jacket every day," she said to Quinn as Kyle had gotten ready for the prom last spring. "Have you had the talk with him?"

"Of course I've had the talk with him," Quinn had said, but it had been more like a science lesson than a father-son heart-to-heart about falling in love and dating girls and all the other stuff that came with it like Lisa would have done.

"Well, he still needs to be reminded of things, if you know what I mean," his mother had said to him.

He heard his mother loud and clear when Kyle showed him the latest pic of Brianna.

"I thought you said she goes to church?" he asked, looking at the scantily clad girl in a belly shirt.

"That's her *at* church," Kyle said, pointing to the people in the background.

Quinn needed his glasses to see better. "That's what kids wear to church?"

He would have gone to church more often if it had been that way when he was a kid.

"You can't be late tonight," Quinn said to him.

"Why? It's summer."

"Because you promised Uncle Bobby you'd work with him tomorrow," he said, waiting for the imminent complaints.

"Ah, come on," Kyle started. "I hate working with Uncle Bobby's crew on his boat. They're all so lame."

"You could work for me," Quinn said, but he wasn't even paying himself these days and could hardly afford his secretary, who was his mother. But he wasn't paying for Kyle's spending money and gas and all the food the kid eats at this point.

"Chris continuously rags on me," Kyle complained. "Why can't I just get my own license and take Jacob's boat out?"

"He doesn't know how to act around you. You're the older cousin he just wants to impress," Quinn reminded him, but also ignoring the boat comment.

"Can't I just take Jacob's boat?" Kyle begged. "Please? She won't even know."

"She's coming to town today. She'll know," Quinn said. "And no going on her property anymore. It's not ours to use."

He could tell his son wasn't going to listen to that one. "Kyle?"

"I know," Kyle said, annoyed.

"Work for your uncle," Quinn said, "and we can negotiate your curfew for the summer."

"That's so unfair." Kyle muttered, then gave Quinn the silent treatment all the way back to Quinn's childhood home, which he had moved back into after Lisa had died.

Kyle dragged his feet up the drive until he reached the stairs to the front porch, then he stomped up each one and slammed the front door closed before Quinn reached it.

"We're home!" Quinn said, walking in with a bag of groceries.

His mom stood in the kitchen, fixing lunch. "How was practice?"

"Good," Quinn said, setting the bag on the counter. "He's just mad because I'm making him work tomorrow with Uncle Bobby."

"Ah," Ginny said, tapping a wooden spoon on a pot. "He says he isn't going to be home for dinner tonight?"

"He's got a date, I guess." Quinn waited for his mother's comment.

"Yes, that Brianna is a darling," Ginny said, wiping her hands on a dishtowel. "Nice family, the Pattersons." Ginny pointed out the window. "She's in town."

Quinn stopped unpacking the groceries, not sure who his mother had referred to until he saw the woman out the window. "Jacob's daughter is here?"

His mother pointed out the window again at Jacob's cottage, which sat on the end of Blueberry Bay Lane on a little peninsula that crept out onto the Atlantic Ocean. One of the best views in all of Harmony Bay—in all of Maine, in Quinn's opinion. Most of the houses had been built by fishing families back at the turn of the century and were now mixed with big summer homes built by families with *lots* of money or a family that had inherited the house that had been handed down for generations.

And then there were the Michauds, who had been fishing

lobster for decades. The family of seven had five boys, all willing to help the family business, including Quinn. It had been Quinn's teacher who had told his parents his talents would be wasted fishing lobsters for the rest of his life, even if it had made their family a good living.

His mother made his father take him off the football field, and in his senior year, he applied himself more than ever and got a full ride to the local university. He went to law school after that and graduated at the top of his class. He'd had offers from prestigious law firms right out of school and had worked at one of the top-earning firms in Maine.

Then everything changed when Lisa had died.

"She said she was stuck in traffic," he said. He peeked out the window, and sure enough, there was a fancy automobile sitting in Jacob's driveway.

Ginny walked over to Quinn, and the two of them watched as the woman stood staring at the house. "Looks like she's leaving."

Jacob's daughter marched back to her car, got in, and drove away.

Had traffic suddenly moved, and she made it faster than the GPS had predicted?

She'd made it to the house before he had made it across town.

"We better get down to the office," Ginny said.

Quinn had promised Jacob that he would make things right for him before he'd died, when he wrote up his will. The old man had lived next door to his family as long as Quinn had been alive. He'd helped the Michauds out more times than Quinn could count and had ended up being family. It wasn't until a year or so back that Jacob had asked Quinn to represent him and his estate.

"I want to leave her everything," Jacob had said to Quinn when he'd showed up at his dinky office in the village.

"Who?" Quinn had asked.

"My daughter, Meredith."

"You have a daughter?" Quinn had forgotten since Jacob never spoke of her.

He'd nodded. "Give it all to her."

Now, as Quinn stood in the window watching Jacob's daughter drive away toward the village, he wondered two things: How did Jacob have that beautiful of a daughter? And what kind of woman would he be dealing with?

CHAPTER 7

$\mathcal{A}$fter an hour of circling town and working up the nerve, Meredith finally stood outside a little shop front that adorned the words *Quinn Michaud, Attorney at Law, Family Practice, L.L.C.* Meredith assumed this lawyer couldn't cut it at a big firm, but still wanted to charge an arm and leg while representing people going through the worst moments of their life.

Meredith hated lawyers.

When Phillip had first become an *attorney*—his choice of title— she'd been expected to attend parties and gatherings with *the other wives*. Just like Tom Cruise's character in *The Firm*, Phillip had wined and dined and played golf with the partners, kissing up and doing their favors without asking any questions. He didn't work for a crazy crime-filled mafia drama like the movie's firm, but the intensity to show loyalty, devotion, and sacrifice was there just the same.

She had been naïve at first. She would let Phillip guide her through introductions with each of the attorneys in the room, whether it was the annual Christmas Eve brunch, or the company trips, or fancy dinners. He'd whisper in her ear what she should say—things of interest and what they had talked about last time.

"Marshall and his wife, Heather, just went to Hawaii," he had whispered as one of the senior partners came close.

Then she had come in with the perfect personable question. "How was Hawaii with Heather?"

They had been the perfect couple at the firm.

When Phillip had become a partner, they had mentioned Meredith in his yearly review as a positive to his character and a fit for the firm.

At first, Meredith had loved being part of this "family." She'd hosted events at their house and gotten along great with the other wives. Their families celebrated holidays and vacations together.

Then, the firm's founder divorced his wife, Marcia. When Phillip had told her the news, he'd explained how she couldn't be friends with her any longer.

"You're kidding?" she'd said. "Marcia came to the hospital when the kids were born. Of course I'm going to stay friends with her."

She could not believe the firm would ask her to cut off communication.

But the other wives had agreed and followed suit.

"They'll cut you off, too," Marcia had warned her when they'd met for lunch. "You better watch it."

Meredith had thought Marcia was being dramatic, but as she'd continued to see Marcia as she always had, the other women had stopped inviting her to things for the wives. That was when Phillip had come to her.

"I don't want you hanging out together anymore," he'd said. "It's going to ruin my career."

She'd gone to argue, but he'd stopped her.

"I worked really hard for this, Meredith. I wouldn't ask you to ruin your dream for a casual friend."

And that had somehow made enough sense for Meredith, and that was that. She'd stopped hanging around Marcia. The wives had started inviting her back to parties, and the firm had made Phillip one of the senior partners.

The irony came when Phillip had divorced Meredith, and she had been excommunicated from the wives immediately. No one fought their husband like she had for Marcia. All the invitations to events and parties she had once planned and sometimes hosted had ended immediately.

The worst part, Phillip's new wife, Rylie, had slipped into her place perfectly, right where Meredith had left it. Rylie attended the parties with the wives and asked questions to the big partners and clients and got to be part of the "family."

"You must be Meredith!" An elderly woman stood at the door out of nowhere. The woman looked as though she wanted to go in for a hug, but Meredith stepped back.

"Yes, I am," Meredith said. "I'm afraid I'm late for a meeting with Mr. Michaud."

"Heard there was a bit of traffic," the woman said, opening the door. "He's on his way, so come on in."

How old was his secretary? Meredith guessed the woman had to be at least seventy.

"Can I get you something to drink?" the woman asked.

"I'm good, thanks," Meredith said, walking into the office.

"I'm Virginia, but folks around here call me Ginny," she said, holding out her hand to an empty chair in a sitting area. "Feel free to make yourself comfortable."

"Thanks," Meredith said, placing her purse in the chair next to her. She sat crossed-legged, bobbing her foot up and down, nervous about what was about to come.

"I'm sorry about your loss," Ginny said from behind the counter.

At first, her mother, flashed in her mind, and she became confused, but then Meredith realized the woman was talking about Jacob.

"Thank you," she said, hoping that would be the end of it.

"Jacob had his faults, for sure," the woman continued, "but he was a good man deep down."

Meredith forced a smile and nodded her head, focusing on her foot bouncing up and down. She didn't want to talk about Jacob or how good a man he had been. She wanted to get this whole thing done and over with so she could go back to her life.

"That's what alcohol can do to a man," the woman said.

Great, her dad was a drunk. What a cliché—Jacob was a drunken sailor.

That's where all my child support went, she wanted to say, but she bit her tongue. The woman wouldn't understand the sarcasm and would think it disrespectful to make fun of the dead. She obviously thought higher of Jacob than Meredith did.

"So do you live in Blueberry Bay?" Meredith asked, changing the conversation like a natural. Meredith had learned how to talk to anyone through the firm. Her secret weapon was to let other people talk about themselves. People loved talking about themselves. "It's such a beautiful village."

"We do love our tiny seaside village," Ginny said. "We take great pride in our community."

"The public garden by the pier is gorgeous," Meredith said, and she meant the compliment. "It's done beautifully."

"That's all our gardening club, the Queen Bees," Ginny said.

Meredith smiled at the woman. She seemed friendly enough but older than what Meredith would expect for someone working as an assistant in an attorney's office.

"You'll be glad to be a resident soon enough," Ginny said. "You'll love living here, even if you only stay during the summers like most people."

"Oh, no." Meredith started shaking her head. "I'm selling Jacob's place."

"What?" The woman's face dropped. "That piece of property has stayed in your family for decades."

Meredith looked at this woman. Obviously, attorney-client privilege was a real thing, but small-town gossip was, too. This woman had to know Meredith's situation, and to flat out say that to her was a bit tacky.

Meredith wasn't sure how she could state the obvious politely. "That's not my family."

"Right." The woman frowned at that, then she shook her finger at the ceiling. "Well, if you want to know more about Jacob's family, I lived next door to him my whole life. I used to babysit him."

Meredith sat there, not sure how to reciprocate. She didn't want to carry on this conversation. "Neat."

"I remember when he first met your mom," she said, which jolted Meredith.

She had forgotten her mother's connection to Blueberry Bay.

"Does the Cote family still live there?" Meredith asked. Her mother's maiden name felt weird to say.

"In the big house?" Ginny asked, and Meredith nodded. "I believe there's a cousin or someone that owns it now."

Meredith wondered how much this woman knew. More than Meredith, obviously, but did she understand that Meredith knew nothing, absolutely nothing, about her father and her mother's family?

The only family she'd ever shared time with had been Gordon's family.

Not once had Jacqueline's family sent a birthday card, Christmas card, or even an acknowledgment of her existence, but neither had her birth father. Remy had looked up the family, did the whole DNA family tracing and tried to connect with some of their mother's family, but she'd had no luck.

And Meredith felt perfectly fine with that while sitting there in the office of Quinn Michaud.

"Did you say he was coming?" she asked as the door to the office opened.

"Ms. Johnson," a man said, coming through the front door and into the space. "Nice to meet you. I'm Quinn Michaud."

Meredith took a double take at the man standing in a

tailored three-piece suit that hadn't come off the racks of L.L.Bean. He looked like he'd stepped out of a cologne commercial. She'd expected a lumberjack in a flannel, not some hot Hugh Jackman.

The elderly woman smiled at him.

"Yes, sorry about the confusion," he said. "I thought you were stuck in traffic."

"I had been," she said, but his forehead creased when she said it.

"Well, you're here now," he said, holding out his hands. "Would you like to discuss the contents of the will?"

He pointed to a table with a few chairs around it at the other end of the space. The building looked like it had once been someone's house, not a store, and definitely not an attorney's office.

"I ran into a friend who's a real estate agent, and she said she'd be happy to meet with you about selling the house, if you'd like," he said.

She noticed Ginny make a side glance at him as he spoke.

"Thank you." She held the envelope he had left with her father in her hands. "I understand there's art as well?"

Quinn nodded. "Yes, Jacob had a large collection in his barn."

"There's a barn?" She didn't remember seeing a barn, but then again, she wasn't looking for one.

"It was a blueberry farm originally," he said. "But a buyer will most likely tear the place down and use the land for something else."

"He had a farm?" That place was a farm?

"It's not much of a farm," he continued. "More of a garden, really, and a lot of wild blueberries."

"People from all over come to pick 'em," the secretary said from the other side. "Brings in a lot of business to the little town."

Meredith turned to look at the secretary.

"Mom, please," Mr. Michaud said, then he turned back to Meredith. "Jacob opened the land to the public."

Mom? Meredith thought. What kind of law office is this?

Then an image of hunting for blueberries with her mother on the edge of the earth flashed through her mind.

"Did you say there was a boat as well?" she asked.

"Yes, a commercial fishing boat," he said. "It's old, but still in working condition."

She would sell the boat. She didn't even know how to drive a small boat, much less a commercial fishing boat.

If Phillip were here, he would tell her what the next steps were. He would advise her just like some billionaire client, but Phillip wasn't here, and she wasn't Phillip.

"What are the next steps?"

"I can file with the registry of deeds to transfer the house into your name as soon as town hall is open," he said.

"They're not open?" she asked.

He shook his head. "Bonnie takes Fridays off."

He passed a packet of papers across the table.

"You'll have to sign a few things now, but I can give you the keys to the house and the boat." He got up and walked over to a file cabinet, where he pulled out another manila folder, then handed it to her. "Here's the boat slip information."

He pulled a set of keys out of the envelope and placed them in front of her. "These are to everything."

She stared down at the keys—brass, silver, all varying in sizes and clipped together with a ring.

"Thank you, Mr. Michaud," she said, but she didn't take the keys. "I was hoping to just leave the estate for the agent. Find someone to appraise everything and sell."

The attorney shifted in his seat. "I was hoping you would reconsider. At least, until you have a chance to meet with the town's selectman."

"Town selectman?" What did the town of Blueberry Bay have to say about her selling a cottage? "Why?"

His eyes flickered over to his secretary—or mom—then back to her.

"Because it's been a part of the town for many, many years!" she called out, rushing from her desk and over to Meredith.

He held out his hand. "Ginny, calm down. This is her property."

Meredith sat there. She could feel the energy in the room change. The friendly secretary talking about her quaint town now looked upset.

"How much land is there?" Meredith asked.

He looked at his mother. "Thirty acres."

"Thirty acres!" Meredith's jaw dropped. Thirty acres! On the water. It had to be worth at least her portion of the house, if not a little more. Maybe. "How much is it worth?"

The secretary frowned. "It's a piece of our town. Jacob has always opened his land to the public—"

"Mom," the attorney cut her off. "I'm not sure the current estimate of its worth, but a few years ago, it was appraised for slightly over a million."

"A million!" She couldn't believe it. "The land is worth a million?"

"Yes," he said, shifting some papers.

The secretary's face dropped in disappointment as she looked at her son.

"It'll be torn up and destroyed." The secretary turned to her. "Wildlife, the shoreline, the blueberries—all of it will be destroyed by builders if you sell it to the wrong hands. Jacob hoped you would want to continue the family tradition and allow the town to use the farm."

Meredith thought of the liability of having strangers walking along the ocean's edge plucking blueberries.

"Mom, seriously, you need to leave now," the man said.

The secretary shot him a look in shock.

He gestured his head to her desk and widened his eyes. "Please."

She turned her attention to Meredith. "You seem like a very lovely woman. I apologize if I come across pushy, but I'm just deeply passionate about my town and keeping some of it untouched."

She shot her son a look before she walked to her desk, opened the bottom drawer, pulled out a purse, hooked it on her shoulder, and headed toward the door.

"I'll have the leftovers in the microwave," she said to him as she pushed the door open.

And with that, she walked out.

Meredith watched through the office windows as the woman walked to a station wagon and got in.

"I apologize for that," he said once she turned back around. "She doesn't want to see the land sold to developers."

Meredith folded her hands together and placed them on the table, wishing she had taken Remy's offer to come up with her.

"Mr. Michaud," she began.

"Please, call me Quinn," he said.

"I never knew Jacob O'Neill," she said, beginning with the most glaring fact. "Who I just recently found out has died. To say I'm a bit overwhelmed by all of this is an understatement."

"Yes, I apologize for my mother," he said. "She shouldn't have interrupted our meeting. I'm sorry for that."

"Am I walking into a town dispute about land?" she asked. She remembered when a house at the other end of town had wanted to build an addition and the town of Andover had the poor couple jump through hoops and cut tons of red tape to no avail.

But, if she did sell, she could keep her home in Andover. "What do I need to do next?"

"Jacob's art is still in a few galleries," he said. "I talked to all the owners, and they'll keep them until they sell for now."

She thought about her mother's artwork. After she had died, Meredith hadn't been able to look at her mother's stuff. She hadn't even been able to go into her art studio above the garage. The regrets filled her when she looked at her mother's paintings. From the little questions of her muse to what she felt about life's purpose. How she felt as a single mother and if she'd been proud of her accomplishments of motherhood.

So many questions she hadn't asked.

"The rest of his artwork is up to you," he said. "But I'm sure we will find buyers for at least some of it."

"How long does this kind of thing take?" Meredith asked. She hadn't had to go through and distribute someone's whole life before. After her mother died, they all just kept her things like she left it. "And will I have to pay an inheritance tax?"

He shook his head. "No inheritance tax in Maine for property. However, that could change with Jacob's artwork."

"Oh, right, the art." She sat there quietly, wishing she could calculate all of this in her head, but she didn't know the numbers. Hopefully with the price of the house and what she may receive with Jacob's art and boat, she could very well save her house. "Will I have to pay you for all of this?"

He shook his head. "Jacob took care of it."

Meredith nodded, staring at the name. She should call her attorney, but the only attorney she knew was the one who helped her with her divorce.

She could call Gordon. He would suggest someone he knows from somewhere. She could call Remy and ask for one of her fancy attorneys, though Meredith wouldn't be able to afford hers.

And to her horror, that was when her throat started to tighten, and her hands started shaking, and her eyes started filling with tears.

"Do you have a bathroom?" she asked, but the tears had already fallen.

"It's in the back," he said, standing up and pointing to a narrow hall. "On the right."

She didn't look at him as she hurried to the bathroom, hoping he wouldn't connect this emotion to the loss of Jacob. She carried no grief for a man who had deserted her. She'd become emotional because she realized just how alone she really was.

CHAPTER 8

*A*s a family lawyer, Quinn had been in plenty of meetings with clients and their family where emotions ran high. It wasn't easy watching people go through the hardest times in their lives. It was another reason why he hated his job so much. No one in a small town ever went to his office for good things.

Usually, in a small town, people *had* to go to a lawyer, *had* to give their money, because something terrible had happened to them.

He thought, naively, that this meeting with Jacob's daughter would be different. She had no real ties to Jacob, and to inherit a windfall should've seemed like a dream come true.

When she returned to the table, he passed her the box of tissues and started to move on with the meeting.

"I have an art appraiser in Portland that will be able to help you," he said, handing over the packet he'd created with some of Jacob's art.

She drew a tissue out of the box, twisted it in her hand, and stared at the cover.

"Is this Jacob's work?" she asked, her finger tracing the rectangular shape of a picture of one of his paintings.

"Yes." Quinn waited as she opened the cover to the table of

contents. "He had quite a few pieces that I'm sure would go for a good price."

"Really?" She slanted her head, as though the idea surprised her. She shut the cover before even going through Jacob's work.

Quinn shrugged. "Jacob had no trouble selling his stuff."

"Are you serious?" she asked, almost appearing angry, and it took him by surprise.

"Excuse me?" he asked.

"He made money on his artwork?"

"Yes," he said.

She let out a huff and leaned back in her chair, shaking her head. "I can't believe he had all this"—she gestured with both hands to the papers covering the table— "and not once did he try to reach out to his daughter."

Quinn felt that one. He wished he had an explanation, but Jacob never provided one, and he didn't ask.

"After the accident, he was never the same," Quinn said. He had heard all the stories about the storm of the century. The boat capsizing. All the crew dead, except for Jacob.

"Accident?" She looked confused.

"Years ago." He calculated the time. "Maybe right before...?" He looked down at the papers, calculating the time period. "Yes, right before you were born."

She stared at him.

He nodded, wishing Jacob had done exactly what she had said and reached out. Told her about everything. He only knew what Ginny had told him, and knowing his mother, it was only half-true.

"There was a storm that came out of nowhere," Quinn said. "No one survived except for Jacob, but he suffered multiple injuries and had a difficult recovery. Afterwards, Jacob was never the same."

Her eyes scattered around the room. "I didn't know."

Quinn had never been one to tell another's story, but this

woman was in the dark about everything. "Did you know much about your father?"

"Jacob?" she asked, shaking her head. "Just that he was a fisherman, basically."

"Ah," he said, trying to navigate this carefully.

"Did you know him?"

Quinn sat there, not sure what would be the best thing to say. "Yes. I grew up next door to him."

"Oh, right," she said, pointing to his mother's empty desk.

He would not divulge the fact that Jacob had never once talked about being a father. Even living next to the odd man his whole life, Quinn had never known he had any family at all. The recluse rarely came out of his house. Jacob had no visitors other than random neighbors checking in with blueberry goods, but no friends or family. Well, except for them.

"So, the house is mine?" she asked.

"Yes, you're the owner," he said. "But we still need to record the deed."

Her forehead wrinkled in disbelief. "I can just go into his house and start removing things?"

This was when being an attorney was difficult for Quinn. He was being paid to represent Jacob and his needs, not the needs of his family. Could he make up some law that would make this woman think she couldn't do what she wanted with the land? Say that Jacob wanted it made into a preserve? Fudge the documents? It would be so easy…

Quinn sighed. He could never break a rule, especially the law. "Yes."

She pushed back her chair. "Do I take all of this?" She waved her hands out at the papers.

He nodded, pausing before getting up, trying to think of a way to explain Jacob's wishes that he hadn't put in his will. "The town is also interested in having his land become conservation land."

She looked at the papers before picking up all the documents he had painstakingly worked on. "The town's willing to buy the land?"

He wished Fred had listened to him. "I'm sure they're willing to offer you something in return for the land."

"At market price?" She looked doubtful.

He shook his head. "I'm afraid not."

The last time the town offered to buy a farm, they'd paid a dollar for it. Blueberry Bay could barely afford things as it was. What would they do without Jacob's land?

"I have everything on a flash drive as well," he said, handing the drive to her. "I'm happy to help you with anything you need." Jacob had promised to pay him to help put all his affairs in order. "I promised Jacob to help you."

"What?" She looked even more surprised.

"I promised Jacob I'd help you until you figure out what you want to do with the estate." He passed the final and last booklet he'd created. "This was what he had hoped you would do with the inheritance."

He had promised Jacob that whatever his daughter wanted to do, he would help her through the process if needed. Now he wished he had quit being a lawyer and did some mindless job instead. Why had he promised Jacob he'd do this? Especially since the man died before paying him.

Because his mother had wanted him to.

Ginny had that way of making him do the right thing, even if it meant the wrong thing for him.

"It's the largest property on the shoreline here in Blueberry Bay," he said. "Lots of developers have been hounding Jacob to sell, but he wanted to leave it the way it was."

"Why didn't he make it into conservation if he had been so worried about it?" she asked.

How many times had Quinn tried to persuade him to do just that? Jacob had always refused. "Because he wanted the next generation to keep it in the family."

She laughed at this. "He wanted to keep it in the family?" She laughed again but suddenly stopped cold. "I'm sorry, Mr. Michaud, but I want nothing to do with this piece of property."

He closed his eyes for a split second as he felt the blow. All that work, and she didn't even open the book.

"It's not just a piece of property, Mrs. Johnson." He stopped, knowing he was crossing into gray area as an attorney. "It has become a special place for our community."

"It's Ms. Johnson. I'm divorced." Her voice came out hard, like a schoolteacher correcting a class clown. She got up, taking the booklets and packets of information Quinn had stayed up all night preparing and piled it up in front of her. "I'm sorry Mr. Michaud, but it's just a property to me."

Quinn stood from his seat as Ms. Johnson collected everything, along with Jacob's keys, and walked out.

CHAPTER 9

"*K*eep it in the family," she said to herself in the car as she started it. "Are you kidding me?"

She reversed the car, then put it into drive. Then she stopped. Where was she going?

If Jacob's attorney hadn't come out of his office at that exact moment, she might have pulled back in and looked through the documents. Maybe called Remy and talked this through. She really wanted to call Phillip. Talk to someone who knew something about law besides Jacob's lawyer who wanted her to hand over a piece of land for the good of the community.

She drove through the intersection and back up the road where she'd come from, heading in the direction of home. She would go back to Andover, where she could take her time and figure out what to do. Find a real estate agent willing to work with her from Massachusetts, because she'd had enough of this place already.

She threw on her blinker to take the next turn toward the highway, when she looked in the rearview mirror and saw her mother's face. The statue stared back at her. When the light turned green, she didn't turn. Instead, she pulled over into a parking spot and sat there, looking into the mirror. She cut the engine, studying her mother's expression.

Grabbing the handle, Meredith got out of the car and faced the bronze statue. Her mother looked as though she floated on the water behind her. She slammed the door and walked back to the park, ranting off questions to her mother inside her head.

Why didn't you tell me about him?

Why didn't you say he had been in an accident?

Why didn't he reach out if he had all this money?

When did you come back and visit besides the time you brought me?

Did Gordon know any of this?

She walked straight up to the statue, ready to scream at it, when a mother holding two little girls' hands walked up to it.

"I want to be a mermaid," one of the little girls said to her mother. She wore a pink polka-dot bathing suit.

"Are they real?" the other girl asked her mother.

The mother smiled. "Only in fairy tales."

"I'm going to believe they're real," the little girl said, closing her eyes shut as if she were making a wish.

"Can I be a mermaid?" the little sister asked.

"No." The mother shook her head, then picked the little one up. "But you can take care of the people we love, like mermaids."

Meredith looked at the mother, wishing her own mother could answer her questions.

"Ms. Johnson?" a voice said behind her.

She turned to see the elderly secretary sitting on a bench next to the statue.

"Mrs. Michaud?" Meredith couldn't hide her surprise.

"Call me Ginny," Mrs. Michaud said, placing her hand on her chest. "I can't imagine how you must be feeling right now." Ginny didn't move from her seat. She looked up at the statue. "I know it doesn't feel like it right now, but believe me when I say that Jacob always wanted to do what was best for you and your mother."

Meredith almost laughed but realized this woman was serious. "Leaving your wife and child is best?"

"Of course not." The woman shook her head, then slanted it at Meredith. "But that's what he felt would be best. Whether I agreed with him or not was none of my business, but there's more to Jacob than just this statue and that house."

"It's a bit more complicated for me," Meredith said, looking up at the statue.

"I know Quinn told you about the storm," Ginny said. "It was covered by the local paper. You can look it up at the library. I was just a young mother at the time, but my father was on the boat."

Meredith frowned. "How horrible."

"There was only one survivor," Ginny said. "Quinn was two at the time. Never thought there would be survivors after they found some of the wreckage, but then Jacob washed up on shore the next day." She shook her head. "My husband was one of the volunteers looking for them. It wasn't pretty."

"I'm sorry about your father," Meredith said.

"I'm sorry to hear about Jacqueline." Ginny looked up at Meredith. "I can't ask you to forgive Jacob for his decisions, but I can ask you to take your time before you make your own."

Meredith looked at the statue again.

"Your mother was just lovely," Ginny said.

"What?" Meredith hadn't expected that. "You knew my mother?"

The woman nodded. "Jacob always loved her."

If Remy had been here instead, she would have delved into this woman's past, asked the right questions and made the woman feel comfortable talking. But that only made Meredith more uncomfortable. Who else knew her horrible situation? Did the whole town of Blueberry Bay know about the abandoned girl of their local hero?

"Thanks for giving me some insight, but I think it's best if I get going," Meredith said, stepping a few inches away from the strange lady.

"I would hate for you to leave here not knowing where you came from," Ginny said.

"I come from outside of Boston, Mrs. Michaud." Meredith appreciated what Ginny was doing, but she didn't want to be a part of this world, because it just reminded her of how much she didn't belong—in any of her families. Not Jacob's. Not Phillip's. Not her children's or Remy's. That's when the realization of Gordon's inevitable death twisted her stomach. She would be alone, alone.

Did she even belong in Andover seeing as how she couldn't even afford to live there?

"Thank you for your time," Meredith said.

"Have you seen inside?" Ginny called after her. "You should see inside Jacob's house before you leave. It's quite lovely. Needs some work but could really be a nice beach cottage."

Meredith wondered what was at stake for them being next door. Would a big developer be interested?

Meredith looked back at the statue. There would be more paintings inside the house and the barn. Would there be more paintings of her mother?

"Maybe I'll head over there before going back home," Meredith said, changing her mind.

"Would you like me to come with you?" Ginny said. "I can help you go through some of Jacob's things."

Meredith looked at the older woman, whose gray hair had been pulled back into a bun. "I should be fine, but thanks."

Ginny sighed at this. "There's something you should know before going inside."

"What's that?"

Ginny grimaced. "Jacob had a bit of a hoarding problem."

Meredith didn't like the idea of stepping into this man's mess. "Like those people on television?"

"No, like art," she said. "He rarely sold his art, and he painted all the time."

"You know, maybe you should come," Meredith said, changing her mind. "I'll feel strange walking through his house without someone else." *Who knows him.*

"I'll head back to the house now," Ginny said. She stood up and held out her hand to Meredith.

With a bit of hesitancy, Meredith held out her own, and the older woman embraced it with both her hands, shaking as she held Meredith's.

"He'd be so happy you came."

CHAPTER 10

*M*eredith stepped out of her car and met Ginny on the front doorstep of Jacob's cottage. She couldn't deny the beauty of the location—a panoramic unobstructed view on the cliffs of the Atlantic Ocean. Granite walls lined the sandy beaches, and Jacob's cottage clung to their ledges. The cold gray stone softened by the overgrown blueberry bushes scattered among beach roses and purple lupine. If it had been anyone else's property, she would be amazed by the beauty. Now she only saw a cold gray house.

"Do you have a key?" Ginny asked as Meredith stood staring at the front door.

"Yes." Meredith pulled out the small piece of wood first, which she realized she'd been rubbing with her thumb as she stood there. Meredith paused before putting the key into the hole. "Why a mermaid?"

"Excuse me?"

"Why did he sculpt a mermaid for the town?"

"Don't you like it?" Ginny asked, as if she were offended.

"It's beautiful," Meredith said, sliding the key into the hole. "But why a mermaid? Are there legends of mermaids here?"

"You could say that." Ginny looked out at the water—a stunning view one would find on a calendar, not in their backyard—and ignored Meredith's question. "But I think he believed someone saved him from drowning like the rest of the men."

Meredith didn't ask any more as she twisted the key into the lock and swung the door open. A set of stairs greeted her, along with a smell of oil paints. The distinct fragrance sent her back to her mother's art studio above the garage, sitting still and quiet while she painted the sea.

"My mother also had a thing for mermaids," Meredith said. And that was when she saw the painting. Her mother's familiar strokes hung above the fireplace. "I guess he knew that."

Sitting perfectly on the mantle was a framed oil landscape. Like a fingerprint, her mother's style of painting was unique. No one could replicate it. And like most of her mother's signature pieces, a whimsical mermaid shadow hid in the background like an *I Spy*, but Meredith could find the hidden mythical creatures right away. She smiled as she saw her mother's signature of three letters JCJ.

She went to walk through the living room but stopped short when her foot knocked over a pile of framed art. Like a deck of cards, the stack fell along the floor. Art lay everywhere—on top of each other, against each other, underneath each other, stuffed among other things. Everywhere, there were paintings after paintings after paintings. Landscapes mostly, ocean scenery, backdrops with granite cliffs. They all looked as though they had been painted from his own back yard. Fields of lupine and sea roses and seagrass and white flowered bushes—were they blueberry bushes?

"These are all his?" Meredith asked, counting quickly at the area by the front door. There had to be at least a couple dozen in the corner alone, and the room was packed full of canvases, framed art of all assorted sizes placed all over the room.

"Some are local artists he supported." Ginny let out a heavy sigh. "But it's mostly his."

Ginny shook her head, pointing to more paintings, distinctive styles of Jacob's. Portraits, abstracts, watercolors, even his shelves were filled with pottery and sculptures.

"Did you know my mom painted?" Meredith asked Ginny as she stepped over a stack of paintings, going deeper into the room.

"Yes," Ginny said. "She's a bit of a local legend around here."

"My mother?" Meredith had no idea. Did Gordon know?

Ginny nodded. "One of her paintings hangs in town hall. She donated it after she received her lifetime achievement award."

That shouldn't have surprised Meredith. Her mother's talent had been displayed in The Museum of Fine Arts in Boston and other galleries around the world. Her bold imagery of landscapes rivaled the best. Unlike Jacob, Jackie hadn't produced this amount of work. Meredith glanced into another room, which she suspected would be the dining room. Just like the living room, artwork filled the space, cluttering the table and chairs. The cabinet filled with more pottery. Then she peeked into what looked like an office with even more art.

Meredith followed the only path through the living room into the kitchen. Unlike the living room and dining room, the kitchen hadn't been filled with art. The wood floors shined. The counters gleaned. The sink sat empty and dry. Jacob took care of this room.

She walked up to the small round table and froze when she saw the two photographs. One she had seen before—her mother's senior picture. And the other was of a little girl standing at the edge of the ocean, letting the waves touch her toes. She had to have been five or six. Meredith may have never seen the photo, but she was certain it was her.

She stared at the photograph, not moving.

"Is there a hotel or an inn where I could maybe stay a night or two?" Meredith asked Ginny, not wanting to stay in the stranger's house.

Ginny frowned as she shook her head. "Not in town, but if you head out by the highway, you'll find something."

"Any B&Bs?" Surely, something had to be available in this beach town.

Ginny tapped her chin with her finger. "There are a few, but this time of year it's real hard to find any vacancies. Let me make a few phone calls, and I'll be right back."

Ginny walked back toward the front door and out of the house, leaving Meredith alone. Carefully stepping over to the sink, Meredith looked out the window—the ocean seemed endless from that vantage point. Blue as far as she could see sparkled under the high afternoon sun. Triangular white sails quivered in the distance, slowly blowing along the horizon.

She turned back to the picture sitting right at the center of the round table. Picking it up, she closed her eyes to retrieve the tiny bits of memories she had of that day so long ago. All she could remember was the ocean and her mother sitting while watching her.

Exactly one placemat had been carefully arranged, along with a napkin holder and salt and paper shakers. The rest of the old oak table was free of any kind of clutter. A juxtaposition to the rest of the house.

A recliner sat in the corner of the room next to a woodstove. Kindling piled in a wicker basket. Quaint came to mind as Meredith walked the thick honey pine floors. She admired the wood beams that crossed the white spackled ceiling. The anti-quated New England cape was adorable.

She stepped over a threshold into another section of the house that looked as though it were a later addition but still very dated. And it was beautiful. The A-frame interior made the room feel like a cathedral, with its beveled glass above the windows and French doors. Tiny rainbows scattered across the walls and ceiling. At the other end, a tall stone fireplace dominated the room from floor to ceiling. Smack in the middle sat a long rectangular table with no accompanying chairs. Only a wingback chair and what looked like a Turkish rug sat in front of the fireplace.

The rest of the room was filled with easels, paints, brushes, tools, papers, canvases—the space crammed with even more art and pottery. A door beside the fireplace led to another room beyond. Then she saw a porch ran along the whole backside of the house.

She reached out and unlocked the doors. The sounds of the ocean were amplified by a hundred as she stepped outside onto a covered porch. Beyond the porch was a small patch of blueberry bushes and beach roses that grew up to the edge of the granite shoreline. A wave pounded against the rocks below, spraying droplets into the sky. They hung suspended in the air, then splattered onto the rocky shoreline.

It was breathtaking. She inhaled the tangy, sweet scents, when an energy swept through her body, stealing her breath and stinging her eyes.

This place was hers?

Meredith had to catch a loose tear and started to laugh. She took in the scene, watching as one wave after another splashed against the rocks.

This place was hers.

"Hello?" a man's voice called out from the other end of the house.

"Hello?" she said back, unsure where it had come from. She wiped her face with her hands.

"Ms. Johnson?" the voice said.

As she turned to find the voice, Mr. Michaud walked onto the porch.

"Sorry to startle you," he said, holding out his hands.

She shook her head, crossing her arms against her chest. "It's fine. Do you need something?"

He pointed back toward where he came from. "My mother said you were looking for a place to stay."

"Yes," she said, looking around the house. Did she need a place to stay? Or should she stay at Jacob's? Or should she go back home and figure this all out?

What did she have to go home to? Phillip wasn't coming back.

The kids were gone doing their own things. Her father had his friends and his own life. She didn't even have a dog to go home to.

"Just for a few nights."

He frowned at that. "Look, what if I turn the water on and help clean it up enough for you to be comfortable for at least tonight or until you can find a better arrangement? It's cramped, but Jacob took surprisingly good care of the place."

She looked around the porch. She didn't even think about the water being turned off. Would she have to start paying the bills? What else would she have to do?

Then she looked out at the water. Waking up and having her coffee here, listening to the waves, and watching the seagulls float in the water didn't sound like a bad idea. When was the last time she had watched a sunrise?

"I think that might be a good idea," she said, looking out at the water. What did she have to lose at this point?

"Great," he said. "Let me run next door and grab some hands to help."

She held out her hands. "Please don't do this just for me," she said, wondering how much an hour the attorney charged.

He stopped when he opened the screen door, the hinges creaking as the rusted springs turned. "We all want to help."

Meredith almost laughed at the idea that these perfect strangers would want to help her. They wanted something from her more likely, but she hushed herself because of the way Quinn Michaud looked at her. He was serious.

"Well, thank you," she said. "But I just need to figure this all out. I don't plan on staying more than a night or two."

CHAPTER 11

Quinn pounded twice on Kyle's door, then opened it. There on his bed lay his son, with his earbuds stuffed into his ears.

"What?" his son shouted, not shutting off whatever he was listening to.

Teenagers, thought Quinn. "Turn off your music."

With an eye roll, Kyle did what he was told. His only son had his moments, but overall, he was a very good boy.

"I need your help with something," he said, not giving the details yet.

"What is it?" Kyle grumbled.

Quinn silently groaned inside his head because he knew he'd get a hard time from his son. "I need to get Jacob's house cleaned up. Just enough for someone to stay the night."

"Like, clean toilets?" Kyle scrunched his face as if he already had his hand down a drain.

"No, I'll take care of the bathrooms, though it wouldn't hurt if you did clean some toilets around here," he said.

"What do I need to do?" Kyle cut him off.

"I'll probably need help with moving things around," Quinn

said. He knew Jacob had his idiosyncrasies, the way he lived being one of them. "I need you to run some errands."

Quinn handed him his credit card. "Run to the hardware store and get a couple boxes of heavy-duty trash bags and all the cleaning supplies you can."

Kyle nodded, taking the card. "Anything else?"

"Grab dinner from Parker's." Quinn would probably regret all this wining and dining. "Enough for four."

Kyle made a face.

"We're inviting our new neighbor," Quinn said.

"Must be some neighbor," Kyle said.

Quinn looked out Kyle's bedroom window, which faced Jacob's place. The woman had been sitting on the porch talking into her phone since he'd left her. He wondered if she was calling her fancy attorney in the city or setting up appointments with real estate developers. She would be crazy if she weren't. The property alone was worth selling.

Why hadn't Jacob made the land conservation when he'd had the chance? He could've given the house to his daughter but saved the land for the community.

Quinn had no faith that this woman would do right by Jacob. She obviously had been hurt by him. And could he blame her? Being a parent himself, he couldn't imagine choosing to never see Kyle. All the things that Lisa missed with Kyle haunted him at night.

"Where did Gram go?" Kyle asked, grabbing his phone from the bed.

"She's out gathering the ladies." Quinn watched as Ms. Johnson stuck her phone in her back pocket.

"That's Jacob's daughter?" Kyle said, and so loudly, Quinn saw Ms. Johnson turn to face the window.

"Yes." Quinn stepped away from the window.

"She doesn't look like him at all," Kyle said.

Quinn couldn't believe how beautiful Jacob's daughter turned out to be.

"I'm headed back over there," Quinn said, pointing out the window. "When you get back, I want you to help me."

"This sounds like a lot more than an hour's worth of work," Kyle began to whine, but he stuffed the credit card in his back pocket.

Quinn watched Kyle leave the house and jump into the truck, blasting music as soon as he turned the key. He missed the days of wasting time, wishing the best days away for something better in adulthood. What he wouldn't do to go back. Even in his dreams.

He never dreamt anymore.

The truck's engine revved up as Kyle pulled out of the driveway and onto the road, kicking up some of the seashell dust. He flinched, waiting to hear pieces of shell hitting Ms. Johnson's car, but he only heard the waves and Kyle driving away.

Quinn grabbed every cleaning supply he could, along with his mother's rubber gloves, and headed over to Jacob's.

He went to cut through the lawn like always but stopped himself. Technically, he would be trespassing. This wasn't Jacob's property any longer.

And it really hit him. He just stood there for a minute, thinking about how things would change if Jacob's daughter sold. The farm was Blueberry Bay's last piece of untouched land along its beautiful shoreline. Real estate developers had been bugging Jacob for years, hoping he'd sell some of the farm, but he never did.

How fast would it be sold? Quinn wondered. How long would it take to tear up the land and build tacky mega mansions or worse, a hotel or some gross condo complex like other coastlines in Maine?

If Jacob's daughter sold, would Quinn be a fool for holding onto his parents' century old cottage just because it has been in the family for generations?

He walked down the driveway toward the road and went the long way. When he reached the front porch, he took a deep breath and put his smile back on his face. He would have to be as sweet as honey over the next twenty-four hours, no matter what this woman from the suburbs said about Jacob and their town, because he wanted to get the rest of what he was owed.

"Hello?" he called out toward the house. He was about to step onto the porch when a car pulled up the driveway.

"Fred…" he mumbled.

"Excuse me?" a woman's voice said from behind.

He turned to see her coming around her car, but her attention was on the man getting out of the car that had just pulled in.

"Hello!" Fred's voice boomed over the sound of the ocean. "Mrs. O'Neill!"

Quinn closed his eyes at Fred's blunder. She didn't use her father's last name, and she did not like being called Mrs.

"Do I know you?" she asked, looking from Fred to Quinn.

"My name is Fred Kimball." Fred held out his hand and shook hers with gusto. "I'm one of the town selectmen."

"Oh," she said, taking back her hand. "Can I help you?"

"I wanted to welcome you to Blueberry Bay!" Fred's usual overly boisterous voice came out extra energetic. "The prettiest coast is the Blueberry Coast!"

Quinn cringed at the cheesy town slogan. "Ms. Johnson is here to finalize a few things after Jacob's death."

"What a great man." Fred placed one hand on his chest, closing his eyes and taking a moment of silence. In his other hand was a plastic food container—most likely Fred's wife's famous blueberry scones. His mother had already got to them.

Meredith Johnson looked horrified. "It's nice to meet you."

"The missus made something to welcome you to town." Fred didn't move or hand over the goods.

"That's very kind of you," she said, waiting for Fred to do something, but he just stood there looking at them.

Fred scrunched his forehead when he saw the vacuum. "You're cleaning something?"

"Just the house," Quinn said.

"I'm sorry, Mr. Kimball," she said. "But I have to discuss some matters with Mr. Michaud."

"Ah, yes, our best and brightest!" Fred patted Quinn on the back hard, his stature big due to eating too many free meals and drinks as selectman. "Well, of course, not counting your own parents!"

Fred laughed at this, totally not reading the room. Ms. Johnson's eyes widened as he continued to laugh at himself. He finally handed over the container he held in his hands.

"Thank you for stopping by," she said, but then she walked inside and closed the door, leaving Quinn behind.

"Feisty, just like her ol' man," Fred said to Quinn, patting him harder on the back before he left for his car. "You're coming tomorrow for the committee meeting, right?"

"Do I have a choice?" Quinn said as Fred's car beeped to unlock.

Fred laughed. "See you there!"

Quinn walked up the driveway toward the house. "Hello? Ms. Johnson?"

She stood in the middle of the kitchen with her hands on her hips. "You can just call me Meredith."

He nodded, hoping she wasn't upset by Fred's behavior.

"Is he always that way?" she asked.

"Loud?" Quinn said.

"Very." She looked behind him to see if Fred was gone.

"Yes." He nodded. "But he means well. Loves his town."

"I can see why you all do," she said, looking back out at the water. "It's a gorgeous spot."

"This spot in particular," Quinn couldn't help but say it. He noticed she didn't disagree.

He looked behind him at his own place. "I grew up here my whole life, looking out at this view." His mother wanted him to keep the house for Kyle, keep it in the family for more generations to come. But what would be left around their small postage stamp yard once she sold? He looked up at her. "Sorry, I'm not trying to pressure you."

"You really lived next door to Jacob then," she said, as though she hadn't believed what he'd told her earlier.

He nodded. "Yes."

"Huh," she said.

He wondered if he should throw out some Jacob facts. "We used to call him, Ol' Man Jacob because he didn't leave his house much. I never heard him talk more than a hello and a few mumbles before he came to me about the will."

He stopped talking when her face went from horrified to alarmed.

"He was a mute?" She now looked shocked.

He shook his head. "Just quiet. He kept to himself after the accident."

"Right, the boat accident," she said, walking deeper into the house.

He followed behind, carrying the box of cleaning supplies and balancing the vacuum at the same time.

"Thanks for bringing all this over." She held the door open for him and pointed to the corner. "You can put it all over there for now."

He stood up, straightening his back, wishing he hadn't worked out that morning. "I've got dinner coming if you're hungry."

"You don't have to do that," she said, shaking her head. "I should be fine."

Quinn looked around the kitchen. Jacob wasn't necessarily dirty or messy, but the place smelled stale, old, closed up. He could see a layer of dust on the things that Jacob didn't use on a daily basis.

"I'm happy to help," Quinn said. "I promised Jacob I would."

This seemed to make her scowl.

"I'll start with getting rid of any trash." Quinn grabbed a trash bag.

Meredith stared at him. "A lawyer that cleans. How much did he pay you?"

Not enough, Quinn said in his head, but then aloud, he said, "I just want to help make your stay as comfortable as possible."

She looked like she didn't believe him, but she pointed her phone at the plastic container of blueberry scones. "Is this safe to eat, you think?"

"Linda makes the best blueberry scones this side of the Saco," he said, gesturing in the direction of the cabinets. "Let me grab a plate for you."

He pulled out a cooler he had packed. Cream, milk, a bit of sugar, a container of freshly picked blueberries, a box of crackers, and his mother's own famous blueberry jam. After setting it on the table, he went to the cabinet before realizing she hadn't given permission. He stopped in his tracks.

"I mean, if that's okay?" he asked, wincing as he looked at her.

"That's really nice of you," she said, sitting down at the table. "Would you care to join me?" She held out her hand.

He hesitated for a split second. Did she really want him there or did she feel obligated? He set the container down between them, and sat, placing the plates down. "You can't keep me away from Linda's scones."

"How well did you know Jacob?" she asked while opening the lid.

"Not as well as you would think living next door, but well enough." Quinn rolled his eyes at his answer. Could he be more vague?

He didn't want to tell the whole truth yet and scare the woman off. Jacob had been a bit of a recluse while Quinn had been growing up. He had been Ol' Man Jacob back then, and he'd stayed in his house, no matter how many times Quinn had dropped off baked goods and treats from his mother. Quinn never saw Ol' Man Jacob come out of his house more than a handful of times. He'd been a legend during Halloween. A real live Boo Radley.

When Quinn came back, a widower in over his head with a curious little boy, that was when Jacob had come out of the house. He'd liked Kyle. Kyle would knock on Jacob's front door and ask to play in his yard. Jacob had never said a word, just gave Kyle a nod and retreated into the house.

Quinn hadn't even known Kyle had started talking to Jacob until years after playing in Jacob's yard.

"He said he'll teach me to fish!" Kyle had said one day after coming home from the beach.

"Who?" Quinn had asked.

"Jacob!"

Quinn hadn't liked the idea of the village drunk spending time with his son on a boat, alone, and Ginny hadn't liked it either and told Jacob so.

"You can't be drinking and take my grandson out on the water," Ginny had said, sticking her finger in Jacob's chest.

Quinn had been certain Jacob was afraid of Ginny, because he'd sobered up after that.

He turned to Meredith. "You don't know anything about him at all?"

She shook her head, taking a scone and biting into it. She closed her eyes. "This is good."

He got up. "Coffee?"

She looked pleasantly surprised. "Yes, please."

He pulled out the familiar coffee grounds he had purchased for Jacob a few weeks ago.

"My mom probably knew him best," Quinn said, scooping out the grounds into the coffee filter.

"Was he mentally disturbed?" she asked, her eyes glancing at the photograph that sat on the table.

Quinn shook his head. "He suffered a severe head injury in the boat accident, but he had a serious problem with alcohol as well."

"Your mom said I should look it up," she said, breaking the scone apart with her fingers. "The accident."

He shut the coffee maker lid and turned it on. The water hissed as it spurted out of the opening.

"You could, but it's like any other tragedy." Quinn understood what his mother was trying to do. Meredith didn't understand the degree to which the accident had damaged Jacob. The reason why he'd drank himself into oblivion and couldn't be a father. "He was the only survivor."

"I'm sorry about your grandfather," she said.

He shrugged. "It's more my mother who suffered."

He glanced over at her and that was when he felt her pain—a grief that hung around her like the fog in the morning. His first instinct was to go to her, and it surprised him.

A feeling he hadn't felt in a long time swept up inside him as he looked at her, and he went back to the coffee.

What was that?

"How do you take it?" he asked, turning his back to her.

"I'll take some cream," she said.

He rubbed the back of his neck, feeling a bit flushed as he poured the coffee.

"I can answer anything," he said. "I mean, if you have questions."

"Was he really this great man?" she asked, picking up the photograph of Jacqueline, the love of Jacob's life.

"Yes." Quinn didn't even hesitate. "He was one of the greatest."

CHAPTER 12

"Wow," she said, looking at the cup of coffee. She swallowed down the bit of irritation that brewed every time this town defended her absentee father. "The greatest."

"Yes," he said, nodding. "I know that must be hard to hear, and I'm not trying to dismiss what you've been through, but the man we knew was very generous."

Meredith never went searching for her father like a couple of her adopted friends had done when they'd turned of age. She'd never had the longing to find that missing father in her life. She had Gordon and her mother, and they had been enough.

She tried not to show her annoyance, but he must have seen through it, because he began to defend his answer.

"He helped his neighbors, always," Quinn said. "And my son adored him."

She blinked at this. What was she supposed to say? Yay, the man who left her as a baby took care of his neighbors.

"Mr. Michaud," she began.

"Quinn, if you don't mind," he said. "I always feel like people are talking to my father when they call me that."

"Quinn," she corrected herself. "I think it's best if we leave Jacob out of all of this."

He frowned. "You don't want me to talk about Jacob?"

She so badly just wanted to lay it all out. Explain how she felt like that little abandoned girl every time he mentioned something about the supposedly great man, Jacob.

But her phone began to vibrate. It was Gordon.

"I need to take this," she said.

She had texted everyone to let them know she would be staying the night in Maine—the kids, Remy, and Gordon.

She had thought about Phillip but decided against it. Remy would kill her if she had.

She got up from the table and walked outside onto the back porch. She didn't know the house well enough to find a private spot, but the waves pounding against the shore would hide her conversation well enough.

"Hi, Dad," she said, grateful he had called.

"Hey, sugarplum. How's it going up there?"

"Good, good," she said, looking around and wondering how much she could tell him. "When was the last time you came to Blueberry Bay?"

"Not since your mother and I were first married," he said, he stayed quiet for a second. "I remember it's gorgeous."

She looked out at the endless blue sky. "It is that."

Should she tell him about the statue?

"What a nice way to start your summer break," he said, with the same enthusiasm as if she were headed on a tropical vacation and not going through her dead biological father's house. "That's one beautiful spot, but are you sure you want to stay there tonight, all alone? I could leave now and make it up before it gets dark."

She checked the time. He would just barely make it.

"No, Dad. Thanks, I'll be okay," she lied.

If she could ask for anyone to come and figure this whole situation out, it would be the one person she couldn't have. Her mother would've turned this whole situation into an adventure. Even when they had lived in a one-room studio, broke, with barely any furniture, she had made it cool to sleep on the floor in a sleeping bag.

Then Jacqueline ran into Gordon, and the rest, they say, was history.

"It's just weird, that's all." Meredith paused as a wave broke against the shore. "His lawyer is helping me clean the place tonight."

She looked through the kitchen window and saw Quinn jump from his chair and rush to the front door. He swung the door open quickly, then dashed out. Meredith watched as Quinn met a woman standing in the field of blueberries with a wicker basket in her hand. They kept looking back at the house and pointing.

"Hey, Dad, can I let you go?" she said. "I'll call you back when I have a free minute."

"Sure thing, sugarplum," he said. "But do me a favor, will you?"

"What's that?" she asked.

"Use this as a way to reevaluate," Gordon said. "You don't have to rush out of there, you know?"

Meredith stared out at the front yard at the interaction between Quinn and the newcomer. The two of them were deep in a heavy conversation, hands moving, basket being used for dramatics. Whatever they were talking about, the woman wasn't having it.

"I will, Dad," she said.

Meredith stood watching the exchange, wondering if she should go back inside or see what was going on, when the woman saw her and began to wave.

Quinn's hand went to the top of his head, his face horrified, and Meredith gave a slight wave back.

Who the heck was this woman?

"Excuse me!" the woman called out, using her free hand to magnify her voice. "Excuse me, Ms. Johnson! Jacob's daughter!"

Meredith stood stock-still. She couldn't very well ignore the woman who stood there pointing at her, knowing her somehow but not knowing her enough to know her actual name.

Meredith thought about ducking around the corner, pretending she didn't see her, but she didn't move quickly enough these days.

"Hello, Meredith!" she called out.

Meredith looked at Quinn, who had obviously told this wild woman her name.

She took a deep breath and stepped off the porch to meet her.

"My name is Hazel," she said, holding onto the basket. "I've been picking blueberries here since I was a little girl."

She smiled at Meredith. The basket appeared empty.

When Meredith didn't speak, Hazel continued, "Blueberries have grown wild here for over ten thousand years. One of the last spots along the coast like this." She reached into the basket and pulled out some hand pruning shears. "But only if someone takes proper care."

"Are you asking permission to pick blueberries?" Meredith asked.

Hazel shook her head. "No, to take care of them."

Quinn stuffed his hands into his pockets. "Hazel is one of many people in town that helped Jacob take care of the bushes."

"You can't plant them," the short woman said. "They only grow wild."

"So, you come here to care for Jacob's blueberry bushes?" This place kept getting crazier by the minute. "Why?"

"Because he was too busy painting," Hazel said in a huff.

"Would you mind them on your property, taking care of the blueberries?" Quinn said.

"If I miss one day, it could throw off the whole crop," Hazel said, though it felt like a demand.

Meredith didn't know much about blueberries, but she did understand lawyers. Hazel didn't seem as ripe as the blueberries, and what if she fell?

"What would happen if she or someone else were to get hurt in the process of shearing blueberries?" she asked Quinn.

Hazel's mouth dropped. "I'm not going to get hurt."

Quinn closed his eyes as if Meredith were the one being unreasonable. "We could have them sign a waiver."

"All I want to do is help," Hazel gaped at her. "To keep the crop going. Over half the blueberries for the festival are picked here."

"The festival?" Meredith asked Quinn, whose head swept back and forth like a referee.

"The town has an annual Blueberry Festival," Quinn said.

Of course it does, she thought to herself. "Look, Hazel, I don't have any feelings one way or the other about you picking blueberries—"

"Taking care of the blueberries," Hazel corrected her.

"Yes, that," Meredith said, exhausted. She didn't want to deal with this new stranger. Not that she wanted to deal with any of this. Her pool back in Andover sounded better and better. She remembered she needed to call a real estate agent. "For now, if that's what Jacob let you do, then feel free."

She made a mental note to talk to Quinn about stopping that once she put the house on the market.

She turned around to go inside the cottage and opened the door, and that was when she saw something that made her catch her breath. On the doorframe, lines showing height were scratched perpendicular on the wood's surface. The few lines had Meredith's name written in her mother's handwriting—age two, age four, age five. No other lines or names. Just the three lines.

She *had* been here.

Meredith's mind spun. Had she been here three times or more? She tried to locate these lost memories, but only the man standing on the beach holding her hand flashed in her head.

She didn't hear what else Hazel had to say about "taking care" of the darn blueberries. She gave a little wave, said a quick goodbye, and shut the door behind her. Once inside, she grabbed the plastic gloves, stuffed her hands inside, and took out all the cleaning supplies. She needed to do something, anything other than perseverate on all the things she can't change. Like why her mother never told her about these memories.

A knock on the door stopped the spinning inside her head, and Quinn waved from outside.

"Sorry, I didn't mean to kick you out," she said, opening the door. "But I'm okay. You really don't need to help."

"I want to." Quinn grabbed a bucket, along with some rags. "I'll start upstairs in the bathroom."

Meredith didn't argue this time. Instead, she focused her attention on the kitchen.

She would wait until she was alone to go explore the house. Until then, she would clean. She looked around the kitchen, which was in better shape than the rest of the house, but still needed a lot of work.

The first thing she did was open all the windows and doors to let the ocean breeze come inside. She dropped the drain into the sink, turned on the hot water, and looked out at the ocean as it filled. She stopped what she was doing and pulled out her phone to take a picture of the view.

She sent it to Remy.

INCREDIBLE! Remy wrote back immediately. **Send more pics.**

But Meredith didn't want to send more. She wanted her sister to call her, so she could explain that she was about to have a nervous breakdown. Everything was starting to pile up.

After scrubbing the counters, she cleaned the cabinets, ran the dishwasher, and removed all perishables from the fridge. As she was taking out the trash, a pickup truck pulled up.

A teenage boy jumped out of the driver's side, holding bags in his hands, and walked up and into the house. She could smell something fantastic coming from one of the bags. He came back out as fast as he went in.

"Um…Ms. Johnson," the boy said. "I'm Quinn's son, Kyle. My dad wanted me to bring this stuff to you."

"Hi, Kyle," she said, looking down at the garbage bags in her hands. "Do you mind bringing it into the kitchen?"

"Sure thing," he said. He pointed at the trash bags. "You can leave those by the garage if you'd like, and I'll take them."

"Oh, um, where will you take them?" she asked.

"To the dump," the boy said. "We don't have trash pickup around here."

She thought about that for a moment. They didn't have trash pickup.

"That's really nice of you," she said.

"We always took Jacob's garbage for him," he said with a shrug.

Kyle walked up to the porch and inside like he had been there many times before, easily walking through the mess of things.

She was impressed with the young man. Would her children offer to take the trash across town for a stranger?

Meredith thought about the time Ryan had dropped a whole bag of garbage and it exploded all over the kitchen floor. As it had happened, she'd almost lost it—a great big mess that she would have to clean up. But Ryan hadn't asked for help, like usual. Instead, he'd done what he had to do to clean it up. She watched in amazement as her son, who she had thought knew nothing about housework, had pulled out the bucket and mop. She'd been so proud at the time—of Ryan for taking ownership of his mistake and of herself for raising a young man who cleaned up after himself.

When Phillip had come home that night, she couldn't wait to tell him. But rather than share in her small victory, it actually upset him. "You're excited about Ryan cleaning up, and I barely want to come home," Phillip had complained.

At first, Phillip had thought he was depressed, that his unhappiness was him needing more free time, and then even more free time. Then her mother got sick. Phillip suddenly had all the free time in the world with her taking care of her mother.

Then a year after her mother's death, he asked for a divorce.

It wasn't until later that she knew what Phillip was doing in his free time.

"Ms. Johnson?" Kyle said.

"Oh, sorry. Were you saying something?" she asked, realizing she was still standing with the garbage bags in her hand.

"Would you like me to take them for you?" Kyle asked.

"Yes, please, that would be wonderful," she said. "How far is the dump?"

"It's a good drive," Kyle said, looking behind him. Then he said, "But it beats mowing the lawn, so I'll take the trash anytime you want."

He plucked the trash out of her hands and walked toward the truck.

"You hungry?" Quinn said, coming out of the house. She noticed the bags with a lobster on it. "We'd love for you to join us tonight."

Was this guy for real? Or was it all an act to get her to continue to work with him on Jacob's estate? Maybe he continued to get a fee the longer he helped?

But by the way he held up the bag, and how badly her stomach growled, she didn't see a better option.

"Sure. That sounds great."

CHAPTER 13

"There's a difference," Quinn's mother said to Meredith after they had all finished their lobster rolls. "Maine coats their lobster in a cold mayo, where Connecticut serves it warm and dripping with butter. Very messy."

Quinn wished he could tell what Jacob's daughter was thinking as his mother continued talking about lobsters and blueberries and everything wonderful about Blueberry Bay. She wanted to win Meredith over, but Quinn had a feeling it was a lost cause.

And could he blame her?

He could see the pain on her face as she walked through a complete stranger's house that he kept calling her father's.

He found it so crazy that Jacob didn't at least try to have a relationship with her. He may have thought he was doing the right thing for her by staying away, but what child doesn't need their father?

"Thank you so much for dinner," she said. "But I think I'm going to head back."

"Let me help you get the bedroom set up," Quinn said, getting up from his chair.

"No, no, I think I'm going to be okay," she said, placing her napkin on the table.

Kyle got up and grabbed her plate for her.

"Thank you," she said, surprised by the gesture. "That's very nice."

Kyle nodded. "Gram would kill me if I didn't."

"Yup." Ginny gave a wink to her grandson. "He does the dishes, too."

"He'll make a good husband for sure," Meredith said, and she looked away suddenly.

If she hadn't corrected her last name from Mrs. to Ms., he never would have noticed the uncomfortable look on her face. Even after years of not having Lisa by his side, he was still hit with feelings of grief time and time again.

It never went away.

"It's the least we can do to make this whole situation easier for you. Jacob certainly didn't do the right thing by you while he was alive, but I do think he thought leaving you the house and farm would be a sort of olive branch." There, he said it. No more tiptoeing around the dead man in the room. "But he should've done better, obviously."

Ginny's eyes widened by the acknowledgment. "Yes, well, Jacob had his demons, but he would've been so pleased to know you are as lovely as you are."

Meredith's fingers played with the edge of the linen napkin his mother hadn't used since Christmas in the late nineties.

Meredith opened her mouth to say something, then stopped herself. After a brief pause, she got up and said, "Thank you for dinner."

Ginny didn't see the writing on the wall, but it was clearly written all over Meredith's face as she sat through endless Blueberry Bay fables. She wasn't changing her mind about staying.

"Let me walk you back," Quinn said, getting up from his seat.

"That's okay," she said, holding her hands together in front of her. "I'm good."

She pushed her chair back and got up before he could help. He walked Meredith out as Kyle turned on the water in the sink. Stepping out on the porch, he didn't push it but, rather, stayed behind as she walked down the steps.

"I can come back in the morning. Help you catalog some of Jacob's paintings." Quinn had recommended Jacob take care of cataloging years ago.

Meredith shook her head. "I'm all set, thanks."

She began to walk down the driveway when Quinn called out to her. "You can take the shortcut through the yards."

He pointed to a sandy path running between beach plum rose bushes in full bloom. Their signature fragrance hung in the humid summer air.

She looked at the beaten path worn down from generations traveling back and forth.

"Would you mind letting your mom know that I'm going to sell?" she said to him. "I don't want to get her hopes up."

He nodded. "Sure."

Meredith turned and walked down the driveway and took the long way back to Jacob's place.

His heart sank as Ginny smiled when he walked back into the house.

"So? What did she say?" Ginny asked.

"She's going to sell." Quinn just said it.

Ginny's smile dropped. "What?"

Kyle shut off the water. "Can't we buy it?"

Quinn laughed at his son's naivety. "We don't have that kind of money."

Quinn needed to work for a Something, Something, and Associates, to afford that property, not a one-man show whose biggest client was dead.

"Let's not freak out yet," Quinn said. "I mean, she may find a buyer who wants what we do."

"To keep a million-dollar piece of property a blueberry field?" Kyle said, rolling his eyes.

With each of her grandson's words, Ginny's expression of worry deepened in the lines on her face.

"It's not the end of the world," Quinn said. "This is just a piece of property. We'll be fine."

Ginny sat down at the table, rubbing the wood under her hand. "This is more than just a piece of property."

Quinn didn't want to speculate. "Maybe someone will buy it as a farm. Let's not worry yet."

To Ginny, Jacob's property was more than just a blueberry field. It was tradition. A piece of land that tied a community together. It was a way of life that would immediately change if Meredith sold.

"What if we help her find a buyer that wants to keep the place?" he said aloud but not sure why. Who would want to buy a dilapidated, centuries-old cape?

The rest of the night, Quinn stayed awake thinking of business ideas to pitch to Meredith before she left.

Could it be turned into a quaint bed-and-breakfast? Could she turn it into a wedding venue? Could a fine art museum buy it for Jacob's work?

With every idea that came to Quinn, so did all the ways it wouldn't work.

Just when the dust had finally seemed to settle in his life, now this.

Worst-case scenario, she would sell to some developer, and the whole place would be torn down, ripped apart, and built on. Blueberry Bay would be a place known for the blueberries they once had.

There weren't many places like Blueberry Bay left in Maine, where the coastline hadn't been touched like Jacob's property.

And there were plenty of people who wanted to get their hands on Jacob's property, no matter the consequences to the landowners around them.

As he watched the nightly news with Ginny, he peeked through the windows to Jacob's, noticing the lights were still on.

How could this day have gone so bad so quickly?

If he had known she was going to show up, he would have asked permission to clean the house and get it ready for her.

"I'm sorry I messed up," he said to Ginny. "I should've stayed down there in Massachusetts and told her about everything."

"How would you know she'd react this way?" Ginny said. "Jacob had been a pretty lousy father."

"I just can't imagine him choosing that for himself." Quinn still couldn't believe Jacob, who loved Kyle so much, would choose not to know his own daughter.

"His mind wasn't well," Ginny said.

"The fact is, we were lucky he didn't sell years ago," Quinn said. "If he hadn't been a hermit, he'd be gone by now."

"Let's just hope this doesn't jack up the taxes on our house."

Quinn could barely afford his life right now. Between saving for college, paying back his own college loans, and helping with the house expenses and mortgage left from his parents, he was barely in the black. "Maybe there's some historical housing rule I could find somewhere."

Ginny turned off the television.

Ginny's eyes watered. "What will happen to the Queen Bees and all our work we do for the community? What will happen to Kyle's inheritance after they tear apart the view and build in front of us?"

"Mom, it's going to be fine," Quinn said. "Don't worry."

But the truth was, Jacob's daughter would be crazy not to sell.

CHAPTER 14

*M*eredith sat outside all night. She found a few blankets, washed them, and set herself up on the porch so that she could wake to the sunrise.

As the night got colder, she went inside to look for some more blankets, when she noticed a flicker of firelight out on the beach. Jacob's beach. No one should be having a fire on the beach, well, besides her.

Because it was her beach.

She grabbed a flashlight and put her sneakers on. She didn't have a clue how to get to where the light was, but she wanted to see what was going on. She didn't even know what she was going to do if she got there. Did it even matter if someone was using Jacob's beach? He didn't seem to mind anyone on his property. Just because her name was now on the deed didn't mean people were going to stop using a piece of property they believed they were allowed to use.

Besides, the idea of a fire on the edge of the Atlantic Ocean appealed to her.

Had she ever had a fire on the beach before?

Phillip didn't like the beach or lakes or sand. He preferred the clean water of the pool. They had gone to Mexico for their honeymoon, but after that, they'd traveled to Europe.

Seaside villages like Blueberry Bay, with its bric-a-brac store-fronts and touristy restaurants, were tacky to Phillip. He preferred the exclusive areas or cities. She couldn't even remember the last time she'd gone to a beach.

With the flashlight in hand, she noticed a couple sitting by the fire. The two were tangled together like the branches of the bushes that she tried to carefully walk between, yet still scraped every part of her leg with its thorns.

"There's someone coming!" The girl said loud enough that Meredith could hear, and her first instinct was to duck.

She turned the flashlight off and listened.

"That's Jacob's daughter."

Meredith recognized Kyle's voice.

"That crazy old guy had a daughter?" the girl said.

Meredith couldn't hear what Kyle said back, but she wasn't going to wait around to hear more of their opinions of Jacob or her. She hurried back through the bushes, scratching up her legs even more, and ran into the cottage before they saw her.

She stood inside the house and laughed at herself. Why was she running from a couple of teenagers making out on the beach?

Her phone began ringing in the other room, and she saw it was her sister.

"Hey," she said as she answered, looking at the time. "It's late."

"Hey," Remy said back. "I waited for you to call, but...How is everything?"

Meredith looked around the small room she stood in. If she were to guess, she would say it was Jacob's studio for painting or pottery. Splatter from all kinds of art materials scattered the walls and floors. For a split second, she imagined it as a music room. But she shook the idea as quickly away as it came.

Her music room was in Andover, where she once could get lost in for hours if not days at a time. She hadn't thought about her and her music room as a refuge in a long time. When was the last time she'd played the piano and gotten lost in the music?

In her prime, Meredith had lived and breathed her music. At times, she'd seemed haunted by it. At one point in her life, there had never been a passing moment where she hadn't been thinking about playing or working on her music or creating it. Every free moment had been spent in her music room. Many nights she'd stay awake finishing a piece she couldn't stop thinking about. She'd had extreme highs and lows with her music to the point it had concerned Jacqueline.

Meredith looked at the paintings stuffed around the rooms. Was Jacob the reason her mother was worried about her waves of euphoria and devastation? Would Meredith's highs and lows become like her father's? Would this dark shadow that hung over her ever lift? Or would she end up like Jacob, stuck in her house and dying alone?

"Fine. It's going fine," she blurted out on the phone.

"I'm coming up," Remy said, reading the situation like only a sister could. "I'll leave first thing in the morning."

"You don't have to do that," Meredith said. "I think I'm coming home tomorrow anyway."

"What?" Remy said. "Why?"

"Because I don't belong here," Meredith said before even thinking. But it was the truth. She didn't belong here. "This man didn't want me to be his daughter until he died."

She could feel her throat closing, and she stopped talking.

"He couldn't be your father," Remy said. "He was unwell."

"What?"

"He was unwell."

"No, what do you mean?" Meredith said. "How do *you* know he was unwell."

"Because I talked to Mom about him," Remy said.

A strong wave of betrayal hit Meredith. "How could Mom talk to *you* about him but not me?" Meredith squeezed her fingernails into her palm. How could her mother tell Remy things she didn't even know.

"Because *you* wouldn't talk to her about this stuff, and when Mom was sick, she wanted to get things off her chest." Remy made it sound as though this was no big deal. But it was a huge deal.

"What else did she say?" Meredith immediately wanted to know the answers.

"I don't know, just some stories and stuff here and there." Remy paused for a second. "She didn't talk about it a lot."

Why did it bother her that Remy knew so much about this? Jacqueline was her mother too.

Maybe because Remy only had to hear about this man as a story; he wasn't her actual father. She had Gordon for that.

Meredith cleared the lump in her throat. "I'm just going to leave in the morning. I will need that real estate agent you mentioned."

"Meredith." Remy said her name hard, and for a split second, she sounded like their mother. "Mom wanted *you* to know your father."

Meredith couldn't hold back the tears at that point. Her throat tightened up, and she just sat there, waiting for Remy to continue the conversation.

"Meredith, stay there and let me help," Remy said. "You have the whole summer to figure things out. Why are you rushing?"

"He didn't want to be my father, Remy." She said it. The truth. Jacob could have been unwell, but the fact remained that he didn't make any effort to be a father.

Remy sighed into the phone as though Meredith was being unreasonable. "It wasn't that he didn't want to be a father, Meredith. He couldn't."

Maybe it had been that simple. Maybe his mental health had deteriorated after the accident. Or maybe not. She didn't know because he hadn't let her know.

"Whichever way you want to look at things, Remy, it's still not *your* father," Meredith said. "*Your* father loved you."

The long silence from Remy's end was uncomfortable for both of them.

"Meredith, I understand this is a lot for you," Remy said, her voice calm. "But this doesn't affect just you, it affects everyone in *our* family, whether the man's *your* father or not. We love you and we want to help."

Meredith went to argue but stopped before she made herself look like even more of a jerk. Her sister was right.

"You don't know what it's like to live with this feeling, okay, Remy? You don't." Meredith didn't mean to be harsh, but it was the truth. "I feel like I was tossed out like garbage."

"You're right, I don't," Remy said softly on the phone. "But I'll never know if you don't let me. You never want to talk about things. You never want our help."

Meredith exhaled hard. "Alright, come and help me deal with all of this."

"Finally," Remy said. "I'll leave straight away in the morning." Then just after she said goodbye, Remy said, "I love you, Merry."

"I love you, too, Frodo," Meredith said, their sibling joke from when they read *The Lord of the Rings* on a family vacation.

Meredith sat down on the daybed on the back porch, looking out at the inky black sea under a blanket of stars. The waves drowned out her thoughts.

Why didn't she want Remy to come up? Was she ashamed? Would Remy look at her differently when she found out her father's mental state was folklore among the teenagers in town? Would it further alienate Meredith from the family?

She lay down, counting the waves as they pounded along the shore. One after the other, they crashed against the rocks like the thoughts inside her head. She thought about leaving the cottage and going back to a house she couldn't afford. She thought about the cottage and oceanfront property she could sell to pay for a big empty house that no one even wanted to come back to visit, and about Gordon's offer to move back in. She flinched at the thought of living with her father again. She felt the pang when thinking about Remy's happy marriage and fabulous life. Then she felt the suffocation of losing her mother and the drowning of divorcing Phillip.

Her thoughts kept coming again and again, and she felt like the rocks below as the waves kept hitting, over and over.

CHAPTER 15

*M*eredith hadn't slept a whole night since Phillip had left, so she was pleasantly surprised when she woke up to see the sun rising over the horizon. She sat up, rubbing her eyes. Seagulls called out, landing along the water's surface. A lobster boat cut through the water and headed east toward the golden light.

Squinting, she raised her hand up to cover her eyes. The sun's rays raced across the water straight into the porch, its warmth hitting her cool cheeks. She inhaled and the scent of beach plum roses wafted through the muggy air. She could already tell it would be a warm one.

That was when she smelled the musky scent of campfire. A strange wanting to have her own campfire hit her again.

She wrapped the blanket around her shoulders and got up from the porch's daybed. She needed some coffee and a plan for the day before her sister came.

When she opened the door to Jacob's studio, that was when she saw the hundreds of prisms of light dancing along every surface of the room. Her eyes followed along the south wall where wooden frames sat without canvases. They all appeared to be handmade from old wood and reused frames or large pieces of driftwood for frames. In the corner, an antique standing radio. On the other side of the room, stood a copper sink.

She walked to a long wooden table set up in the middle of the room to the pile of canvasses that sat on top. At first, she just stared at them. Would there be something in there that would reveal something to her, a clue to her life?

Then, she leafed through, scanning each one, mostly landscapes of the ocean, but as she reached the end of the pile, she came across a portrait of a woman standing along the water's edge, looking out at the endless ocean before her. Meredith knew exactly where that had been painted because she had looked out at the same scene and she knew exactly who the woman was. She could recognize her mother from anywhere.

She pulled the canvas out of its place slowly and set it on top of the pile.

Her mother looked young—mid-twenties; her long auburn hair hung below her shoulders back then. She stood alone, her neck straight, her shoulders pulled back with her hair blowing in the breeze.

He painted her in a sundress, but Meredith didn't remember that one—not that she remembered all her mother's things, but Jacqueline had a classic style, not frilly or colorful, whereas the dress in the painting billowed out around her and had deep shades of blue like the blueberries around her.

Only the silhouette of her mother's face had been painted, but it was enough to feel the happiness radiating out of her as she looked up at the sun. And that's when a wave of empathy washed over her.

She knew exactly why it was on the bottom of the pile because she had done the same thing with her family photos. Stuffed the ones with Phillip in the back of the pile. Tried to forget what life was like before he'd left her.

Had Jacob lost everything he'd loved, just like her? Or let it go?

She stared at her mother's face.

And did Jacqueline?

Meredith looked out the window as the sun crept higher in the sky. She walked back out to the porch, getting a better view, looking for the exact spot where her mother had once stood happily.

She grabbed a sweatshirt from her luggage and her phone, then pushed the screen door open and walked toward the beach. It was much easier getting there in the daylight as she noticed a sandy path that Kyle and the young woman must've used. The path had been easy to follow as it meandered through beach plums and blueberry bushes. As it reached the granite ledge, she stopped.

Standing on the edge, she felt like she was at the end of the earth. Nowhere else to run away from her problems.

Boom! A wave crashed into the rocks below, spraying seafoam up into the air and splattering on the rocks below. She jumped for a second, then laughed at the abrupt sound. Like a well-trained orchestra, waves came up against the coast, hitting it one right after another like a percussionist pounding the drums. The steady rhythm filled her chest, and she inhaled the air from the briny, salty sea as it sprayed around her.

She didn't leave that spot until she saw someone waving their hand at her.

"Meredith!" Remy yelled from the trail. "I'm here!"

CHAPTER 16

*M*eredith watched as Remy unlocked the windows in the living room and opened them up. Her sister had started in the kitchen and went around opening the shutters, then each window, letting the stale air escape.

"I love the clapboard," Remy said as she ran her hand against the wall.

"The whole house has it." Meredith folded her arms against her chest, watching as her sister explored the room, carefully touching Jacob's things as if they were in a museum.

"You could really fix this place up," Remy said, running her finger along a table's surface, then inspecting the dust residue built up on the tip.

Meredith shook her head. "To turn around and sell it?"

"You really want to sell this place?" Remy said.

"I don't have the money to keep both houses," Meredith pointed out the obvious. She wasn't married to a fancy attorney anymore. She didn't have a husband to share the finances like Remy did.

Remy pointed to Jacqueline's painting on the mantel. "That's Mom's."

Meredith nodded. "There are a lot of Mom's paintings here."

Remy's forehead wrinkled. "Really? What's upstairs?"

"I haven't been up there yet," Meredith said, feeling silly she hadn't explored the whole house.

"Why not?" Remy asked, as though something bad might happen if she went up there.

"I don't know, I just..." *Don't want to lose it again*, she wanted to say. But then she said, "I just didn't feel like it."

Remy didn't hesitate and climbed up the narrow staircase to the second floor. She disappeared off to the right where Meredith assumed there was a bedroom.

"There are three decent sized bedrooms," Remy called down. "And a smaller room that you have to cut through another room to get to."

Meredith felt weird going up into the more private areas of the very private Jacob.

But when she heard Remy opening and shutting doors, she went up.

Four bedrooms were up there, two on one side of the cottage and two on the other. All had a view of the water. The rooms on the right looked out at the crescent bay, where Meredith had walked that morning. The rooms to the left looked out toward the other end of the beach, where the cliffs towered over the water.

Remy walked to the right, opened the window, and leaned out.

"This place is so beautiful!" Remy said as she leaned out further. When she came back in, her face radiated the same happiness Meredith had seen on her mother's face in the painting. "Meredith, you can't sell this place."

"Well, I can't hold onto it." Meredith shut the window and locked it as soon as Remy moved from the area.

"At least go through the place and take some time before making any decisions," Remy said. "I mean, there's probably a lot you can learn about your dad here."

"I have a dad, remember?" Meredith said.

"Come on, Merry, you know what I mean."

"Do you have to call me that?"

"When you're acting ridiculous, yes, I do." Remy opened the window again. "Where do you have to go?"

Meredith clenched her jaw. Of course her sister wouldn't understand. She didn't need to. She was happily married and financially stable.

"I'm about to lose the house, okay?" Meredith didn't like discussing what a disaster she was, but there it was. "I don't have the kind of lifestyle I used to. I need to sell this place so I can keep mine."

Remy's jaw dropped. "Phillip is making you sell the house?"

Hadn't Gordon told her?

"Yes, he wants me to buy him out or sell." Meredith looked away from Remy.

"How could he do that to you?" Remy flung her hand out. "He wants you to just leave the house you raised your family in?"

Meredith sat on the bed, wondering if Jacob had slept in here, though she doubted it. The room had a woman's touch and looked as though no one had stepped into it in years.

Then she wondered where Jacob had died.

Was his soul still hanging around? Watching over them? Was her mother's? What did Meredith even believe anymore?

She didn't believe in trust or marriage or family. She could only trust death. Everyone dies.

"Have you thought that maybe you're not supposed to keep the house?" Remy asked.

"Don't start with the whole *set your intentions and make a vision board* thing." Meredith got that from her sister when she'd first gotten divorced. "They don't work. I'm still not married to Denzel Washington."

"I'm serious, Mer." Remy circled the room and stopped at the dresser, looking at a black-and-white photograph. "Why are you holding onto that big house?" She picked up the framed picture. "This could be like your grandmother or something."

Meredith looked at the picture. "It probably is."

Remy looked at the photo, then went back to Meredith. "She has your eyes."

Meredith got up and looked at the photograph. Then before she could stop herself, she blurted out, "I think Mom was having an affair with this man."

"You mean Jacob?" Remy asked.

"Yes." Meredith didn't know how else to say it.

Remy put the photograph down. "I think she never stopped loving Jacob, but I know she didn't have an affair."

"How do you know?" Meredith asked.

"Because Mom loved Dad. She wasn't having an affair with Jacob."

Meredith noticed Remy make a face as if Meredith was being ridiculous. "What do you mean she didn't? She's got paintings all over this house. He's got pictures and portraits of her. And not just when she was younger. Stuff well after meeting Gordon and getting married. She posed for a statue."

"Look, I know this is all a lot," Remy said.

"You're right this is all a lot." At least they could agree on one thing.

"But Mom was still Mom," Remy said. "She loved Dad, and she may have also loved Jacob, but she died with Dad by her side."

Jacqueline had held Gordon's hand at the very end, not a slight ounce of fear on her face.

"She loved Dad." Remy put her hand on Meredith's shoulder. "And Dad loves you. And he'll still love you if you have this other father you want to learn more about. He wants the only thing any parent wants."

For his children to be happy, Meredith answered in her head. She knew the answer because she wanted her own children to be happy. The same reason she didn't want to hold Ryan back because of her own insecurities and loneliness.

"This could be your chance to start something just for you,"

Remy said, sitting next to Meredith. "That you can share with the kids."

Meredith looked around the room. Could this be a fresh start? Could this be her time to figure things out?

Then something caught Remy's eye, and she walked to the window. She pointed at something outside. "Ah, Mer?"

Meredith looked over. "What is it?"

"There's a group of people meeting in front of the house." Remy craned her head closer to the window.

Meredith got up and walked next to Remy. She recognized Hazel from the other day standing in front of a group of elderly women.

"We only have until she sells to get this place in order," Hazel said loud enough that Meredith and Remy could hear through the windows.

Remy turned to Meredith. "You already told everyone you're selling?"

"I told Jacob's lawyer." Meredith looked next door as Quinn came outside. Meredith saw his mother, Ginny, in the crowd.

"Alright, ladies, let's make some magic!" Hazel held her straw hat on her head as she shouted to the group of women. "We need to see that our blooms are being taken care of by our ladies."

That was when the others put their hats on, too. Then they pulled what looked like netting over their faces and put on matching white suits. They looked like beekeepers.

"Look, there are beehives down the field." Remy pointed out the other window now. "Look at that!"

Meredith walked to the window Remy had opened and hung out. Out the back, beyond the blueberry bushes, Meredith saw the women talking and opening the hives.

"Should they be doing that?" Remy asked as Hazel carried a tin can with smoke billowing out.

Meredith watched in horror as all the women followed suit. Some moved around the hives and took off the covers. Soon, all six women stood in front of the hives, pulling out frames from inside. Small black dots flew around them, but lazily, not aggressive like Meredith expected.

"Should I tell them to leave?" she asked Remy.

Remy waved as one of the women looked up at the house. "I think you should at least say hi."

Meredith looked out the window. "I'm not going out there."

From the corner of her eye, she saw Quinn walking down the road and then up the drive. She expected him to go to the women, but instead, he walked up to the house.

"Who's that?" Remy jerked her chin toward Quinn.

"That's Jacob's lawyer," said Meredith. She pushed herself off the windowsill and started leaving the room to meet Quinn.

When he rang the doorbell, Meredith was already walking down the stairs, with Remy right behind her.

"Good morning," he said as he handed her a newspaper.

"Good morning." Meredith turned to Remy. "Quinn, this is my sister, Remy."

Quinn held out his hand to her, and that's when Meredith noticed how different Quinn looked that morning from the other day. He hadn't shaved, wore a casual flannel button-up, and a pair of jeans which made him look less pompous and stuffy than the three-piece suit he'd worn before.

Remy took his hand, and Meredith could see the look in Quinn's eyes that all men had when meeting her younger sister. He, too, was mesmerized. Remy had all the good features from both Jacqueline and Gordon. Long cheekbones, and long, shiny hair. Petite yet perfectly curvy in the right places, Remy's natural beauty was stunning even to Meredith.

Meredith somehow didn't get those genes.

She wished she'd had time to shower.

"Nice to meet you," he said to Remy. Then turned to Meredith. "How did you sleep?"

"Good," she replied, still surprised she slept so well. Meredith nodded at the women. "So, Jacob allows beekeepers, too?"

He looked back behind him, where the women were gathered

around one particular hive. "They're looking to see if they have queens."

"I'm beginning to become uncomfortable with all these people on the property doing whatever they want," she said.

His eyebrows burrowed at this. "The bees help with the production of the blueberries."

"Yes, but someone could get hurt." Meredith looked out at the women, where Hazel now held a frame with bare hands as bees buzzed around their heads. "Have you seen *My Girl?*"

Quinn looked in the same direction. "Hazel has been taking care of those bees for years. I promise she knows what she's doing."

"Well, I just think—" Meredith began.

"Would you like to come in?" Remy smiled at Quinn and stepped back.

Quinn's eyes moved to Meredith before accepting Remy's offer.

"Sure, come on in." Meredith stepped inside, letting Remy do what she did best—socialize.

"I wanted to let you know I talked to the town, and they have a proposal for you for some of Jacob's art," Quinn said.

"You're selling his art?" Remy turned to Meredith. "Why are you selling?"

"What am I going to do with all this?" Meredith gestured at the rooms filled of art. She had a legitimate point.

"How long does that sort of thing take?" Meredith asked.

Quinn shrugged. "I don't know much about the art world, but—"

Remy put her hand on Meredith's arm. "You should get someone from Boston to come up."

Quinn grimaced at the comment. "Of course, it's up to you, but the town has a proposal as well."

"The town is willing to pay for this?" Remy asked.

Quinn coughed at that. Then said, "The historical society would like a chance to discuss it with you."

Meredith didn't care who bought Jacob's art if she got the money. "When can they meet?"

Quinn looked down at his phone.

"Unfortunately, one of our selectmen's on vacation for the week, but I know the town would really like to propose—"

"You know, Meredith, this place could really be turned into something amazing," Remy said, going through the stacked pile of framed art. "We could go through all his work together and find the stuff you want to keep."

"I don't want any of it," Meredith said, suddenly irritated that Remy was going through the art, that this man wanted her to wait another week to hear a proposal, that no one asked what she wanted.

"No, I think it's best you get the women off my property, and I go find a real estate agent."

"You want the Queen Bees to leave?" he asked.

"They call themselves the Queen Bees?" Remy asked, looking out the window. "That's adorable. Come on, Merry."

"The bees will suffer." Quinn's forehead creased. His hand began to rub it. "It'll take some time to relocate them."

"Fine, let the Queen Bees finish what they're doing, but they'll have to sign a waiver or something, like now, if they want to continue," she said. She could hear Phillip's attorney warnings shooting through her head.

"I guess I could draw up some kind of waiver for you," Quinn said.

"Don't be silly," Remy said, waving her hand at Quinn. "Meredith, they're fine."

Suddenly, all of it felt like too much. She just wanted to go home. She wanted to have her babies little again. She wanted her husband to be in love with her again. And she wanted her mother to be alive again.

Her hand went to her chest as the air restricted in her throat at the thought that she wouldn't have that again.

"Meredith, are you okay?" Remy asked.

Meredith hadn't realized that tears had formed until the two of them were looking at her. She shook her head. "This is all…" She looked around the room stuffed full of art made by a man whose mind had been clearly unraveling. Was hers? "This is all just a lot."

She rushed out of the room and headed toward the kitchen, not sure what she was doing, just getting away from them. She walked out the back door and onto the porch, the ocean air hitting her. She leaned against the railing and looked out, wiping her face with the back of her hand.

What was she doing here? She needed to go.

"Merry?" Remy asked.

"Enough with the nickname, Remy," Meredith snapped at her. Would her sister ever start being helpful?

Remy stepped slowly onto the porch but went back to the wooden threshold. "I'm so sorry."

"What for?" Meredith rolled her eyes at the litany of things her sister should be sorry for.

"You lost Jacob," Remy said.

"He wasn't my father. I didn't even know him." Meredith sighed. "Goodness, Remy. Leave it be."

Remy didn't move. "Do you want *me* to leave?"

Meredith hesitated for a split second, not sure what to say. "I don't want you to insert yourself."

"Wow, okay." Remy crossed her arms. "So you just want to do whatever you want with our mother's history without even thinking about my feelings?"

"Are you kidding me right now?" Meredith said. "Are you making this about you?"

Remy sighed as if Meredith was being the ridiculous one. "No, Meredith. I'm stating a fact. The fact is, Jacob loved *our* mother. He painted her and sculpted her and kept her picture where he ate. This isn't just about you, but all of us. *Your* family." She stepped up to Meredith. "Have you even told the kids?"

Meredith didn't answer because she hadn't. What was the point?

"All I want to do is help," Remy said. "But if I'm in your way and inserting myself where I don't belong, then I'll leave."

Like when she was a little girl not getting her way, Remy turned to leave in dramatic form, heading for the house.

"Stop, Remy. I don't want you to go," Meredith said. She looked back at the water. She knew Remy was right. Jacob was as much a part of Remy's life as he was Meredith's. "We should probably start cataloging his art and make sure anything to do with Mom stays with us."

CHAPTER 17

Quinn walked toward his mother as the Queen Bees did their work with the hives. All that time and effort they had put into getting the crop ready for Blueberry Bay's annual festival, and they might not even make it that long. For years, the women of the Queen Bees Society had worked in Jacob's crop, one of Maine's most abundant blueberry crops, the most picturesque spots, and they were about to lose it all.

How long would they have until everything ended? How long would he be able to convince Meredith not to sell? How long did the town have to get their act together?

Why had Jacob not followed through on his end?

Because Jacob had never promised anything in writing. Rather, he'd assumed his daughter would do the right thing for the town.

From what he could tell, the discovery of Jacob's fortune hadn't changed her mind about him. And he certainly blamed Jacob for that. He just wished he could somehow show her why that piece of land was so important to Blueberry Bay.

Ginny held a tin smoker in her hands, puffing the smoke out at the hives as she checked on things.

He waved at her from afar, not willing to get too close to the bees, even though they may be less likely to sting. He didn't want to take his chances.

She put the tin can down and started walking over to him.

"Good morning," she said, looking at the time. "I see you got Meredith to stay."

"Not exactly," he said. "She's not happy you're all here. I thought we said you'd give her some space."

"We can't neglect the bees," she said. "It's been a week since we last checked on our girls."

Quinn looked back at the house, waiting to hear a car pull out of the drive, but he got a text.

He looked at his phone, and his heart sank. "She wants a real estate agent to come by, and her sister sounds like she's"—he used air quotes—"'an expert' to appraise all of Jacob's art."

Ginny put her hands on her hips. "Well, then it's time to do it my way."

Quinn dropped his head. "That's not going to work."

"What's not going to work?" Ginny said, not expecting his answer. "Showing her everything we have to offer is exactly what needs to be done in order to make her understand she's a part of this place just as much as you and me."

He looked back at the house. The shingled cape symbolized everything about Jacob—old, weathered, beaten by the sea, abundant beauty everywhere, and completely alone.

"You know I'm right," Ginny said.

Quinn groaned. "Kyle has football practice this afternoon. But don't go and bother her and her sister."

She puffed smoke at him.

"I'm serious, Mom." He groaned again. That's like telling his mother to stop working the land. Look how good that had turned out.

He had no control. Wasn't that what the family therapist had said after Lisa had died? Control was just an illusion. He had no control over anything. Not his feelings or his son's. Not his wife's accident or her injuries. Not over her wish not to be resuscitated or to donate her organs. His need for control had been his ultimate downfall.

He'd spent years revisiting what he could have done. He could have been like most normal couples and not have had a living will, but instead he'd hemmed and hawed over every detail. He could've left work early and gone to Kyle's game with them, but instead he'd stayed late doing crisis control for his clients. He could have driven them all home, but instead she'd driven home alone. He could have done so many things to change the course of the events, but in the end, he'd had no control over any of it.

He turned when he heard the slam of a car door in the driveway. He watched as Meredith's sister closed the car door. Then the two sisters put sunglasses on and walked down the dirt path toward Jacob's barn and the Queen Bees.

He watched as they got out and walked through the blueberry fields, Meredith didn't look back at the view behind her, which made his anxiety grow. If one of the most beautiful places on earth wasn't enough to make her hesitate to sell, he was convinced no one would change her mind.

And he had no control over what Jacob's daughter would do. The best thing to do would be to let it go.

CHAPTER 18

*I*f Meredith hadn't felt completely defeated by life at that moment, she would have never let Remy take control of the situation. But there she was, letting Remy take charge.

"Let's introduce ourselves before going to the barn," Remy suggested as they walked outside. She walked to her black luxury car and took out a pair of Chanel sunglasses, instantly looking like Audrey Hepburn. She walked a bit ahead of Meredith, following the dirt and gravel road. "Did you know E. B. White wrote *Charlotte's Web* around here on the coast of Maine?"

Meredith hadn't known, but she also didn't know what that had to do with what they were about to discover.

Were there more portraits of her mother? More paintings of Jacob's madness? She wasn't sure she wanted to find out.

At the end of the road, she noticed a gray shingled barn as the backdrop to the fields. If she weren't so stuck in her misery, she may have been as mesmerized by the scenery as Remy, who gasped at the sight, but Meredith couldn't take it in. She felt outside herself, like walking through the motions but not being in her body.

"Oh, Mer, it's beautiful!" Remy went on and on.

This strange new world felt so very foreign that Meredith didn't even feel present next to her sister.

Remy began waving at the women. The one named Ginny, who stood in a beekeeper outfit, puffing smoke out of a tin can, stopped what she was doing when she saw Remy waving and put the can down. Meredith could see her say something to the other beekeepers, then she walked down through the bushes to meet them on the path.

"Good morning," Ginny said, removing her veil.

"Good morning," Meredith said back.

"I wanted to thank you again for letting us continue caring for Jacob's property," Ginny said, just before Meredith could say anything to the contrary.

Maybe Remy was right. What harm were they causing by taking care of some blueberry fields?

"Hi, I'm Remy." Remy held out her hand to Ginny. "I'm Meredith's sister."

"Pleased to meet you," Ginny said. "Heard a lot about you."

"Really?" Meredith said.

Ginny gave a nod. "Jacqueline told me all about you girls."

Meredith pointed back and forth to her and Remy. "She told you about us?"

This made Ginny laugh. "She never stopped talking about you two." She turned to Meredith. "I heard you were a pianist."

She smiled at the recognition. "Yes. I played for the BSO."

Meredith had landed her dream job at the Boston Symphany Orchestra as second chair pianist, but she'd gotten a big break when the first chair had broken his hand and couldn't play. *The Boston Globe* happened to have a writer there the night she'd played, who had written a stellar review.

Then just a few months later, she'd gotten pregnant, and it was just expected she would stay home.

"Do you still play?" Ginny asked.

Meredith shook her head. "No. Retired."

Meredith noticed Remy roll her eyes at that. But Remy was in her forties, childless, with no job and living off her husband.

Meredith had dreamt of when she and Phillip would retire down to Florida. They had already found areas they liked. Maybe the sale of this estate could fund her retirement?

"Have you thought about performing again?" Ginny said.

Meredith shook her head. The last time she played was for her mother as she'd lain dying. Her mother had been in hospice by that time. They had moved Jacqueline downstairs into what had been Meredith's piano room. Her solace as a child. Her mother would ask her to play something, usually a hymn or familiar tune.

After her mother's death, Meredith couldn't even stand listening to the sound of a piano. During her lessons, she'd cringe as the keys hit. She dreaded hearing the sounds.

Remy looked at Meredith. "Are you still teaching piano lessons?"

Meredith almost lied so she wouldn't have to explain but then shook her head. "No, I recently stopped."

Remy's mouth opened to speak, but Ginny started first.

"You shouldn't keep that talent hidden away," Ginny said. "Look what that did for Jacob. That man had so much talent, yet he never shared his work. Think of how many people suffered because of it."

Remy looked at Meredith right as Ginny said it. She was obviously checking Meredith's reaction. If anyone else had brought up Jacob, Meredith would have quickly nipped the conversation in the bud. However, it being Ginny felt different.

And Remy didn't keep it going, pushing Meredith to talk about stuff she wasn't ready to talk about. Instead, she stayed silent and let Ginny continue the conversation naturally.

"Have you seen inside his barn?" Ginny asked.

"We were on our way now," Meredith said.

Ginny smiled. "That's a special spot as well." She held her hat as a strong wind blew. "Make sure you take the path through the perennial gardens."

Meredith looked over to the group of women now closing all the hives. "Do you have a queen?"

"Sure do." Ginny removed her hat. Strands of silver hair fell around her face where it came out of her bun. She held out her hat at the other five women and said, "We're all Queens here in Blueberry Bay."

The women suddenly made their way toward Meredith and Remy.

"You must be Jacob's daughter," a woman with long, flowing gray hair said. She took Meredith's hand into both of hers. Meredith noticed an amethyst jewel hanging from a leather string around her neck.

"Jacob was a special soul," she said.

"Pamela grew up with Jacob as well," Ginny said. "Pretty much the whole town knows your father."

Meredith almost went for the usual correction, but she stopped herself when all the women circled her and Remy.

"Such a gentle man," one of them said.

"Never hurt a fly," another said.

One woman came right over to Meredith and hugged her. "We simply loved your mother and father."

Meredith looked to Remy, and realized she had tears in her eyes as the woman hugged her. And it struck her that she had been so stuck in her own pain and grief, Meredith had forgotten Remy's own pain of losing their mother.

Right after Jacqueline had died, that's when Phillip announced he was unhappy with their marriage so Meredith didn't even think about Remy. She was in crisis mode. She never even checked in with Remy to see how she was dealing with the loss of their mother.

"If you need help with anything at all, don't hesitate to ask," Ginny said, placing her hand on Meredith's arm.

Meredith stiffened at the touch, but then Ginny's gentle hand felt nice, comforting.

"Do you know anything about his art?" Meredith asked.

Ginny's eyes perked. "Yes. I do."

"If you have any free time, my sister and I were about to start going through some of his stuff," Meredith said.

"It would be our pleasure to help," Hazel said, as her smile grew. "Come on, Queens!"

Just as they all walked toward the barn, coming over along a path, Quinn met them with a leather bag strapped against his chest. "We started making an inventory before Jacob died."

Meredith followed behind the group to the barn. Quinn pulled open the massive barn doors as sunlight poured through the windows from outside. Dust sparkled in the air, making the whole space feel magical and mysterious. Just like the house, paintings leaned against every surface, each wooden beam, and stacked against each other.

"Wow," Remy said, slowly walking inside. "There must be hundreds of paintings."

"These are mostly of his own collection of art he painted throughout the years," Quinn said.

"Look." Remy pointed to a painting.

"It's Mom."

Another portrait hung in the center of the barn—a woman holding a child's hand on a rocky beach as she looked out at sailboats floating in a harbor.

"It's you," Remy said to Meredith.

Meredith studied the painting. She calculated her age by the height and the clothing she wore. She must've been young, four or five.

"It's right around the time she met Dad," Remy said, looking at Quinn's open computer screen.

Meredith looked over at what they were looking at. There on his screen were organized images of Jacob's paintings. Under the painting, a caption listed the information.

Mother and daughter
Jacob O'Neill
1978
Oil canvas

She'd been five years old. It must have been just before Jacqueline had married Gordon. Had Jacqueline still loved Jacob at that point?

Meredith looked out at the water, glistening in the sun. The bay appeared calm and peaceful. A white steeple marked the center of the tiny village of Blueberry Bay. Off in the distance, dotted along the coast, were white houses punctuated by their chimneys.

"After the boat accident, everything changed. Jacob changed," Ginny said. "He was never really the same. Your mother found out she was pregnant shortly thereafter, and well…"

Meredith waited for the sinking agitation that came when her biological story came up. But it didn't. A new feeling came instead, one she hadn't felt about Jacob…Curiosity.

"He never forgave himself for being the only survivor," Ginny explained. "That's when the drinking started, and he stopped communicating."

"But he obviously could through art." Remy looked at Meredith. "Maybe that's why he painted. He could communicate through his art."

"Yes, exactly," Ginny said.

Meredith looked deeper into the barn and noticed other paintings hanging—one of a porch with an old man rocking in a chair, another one with a set of women working in the blueberry fields, and another of what looked like a young Jacqueline walking along the sand.

Meredith walked up to the painting of the mother and daughter, her fingers reaching out for that little girl. She so badly wished she could have her mother by her side at that moment.

"Look, Mer!" Remy held up a portrait of a young family. "It's us!"

Meredith covered her mouth with her hand. In the painting, Gordon stood behind Jacqueline with Remy and Meredith standing on either side. Her mother beamed in the painting.

Ginny clapped her hands together. "You found it!"

Meredith looked at Ginny, whose smile grew. "Let's go through everything."

CHAPTER 19

"It was as if Jacob wanted you to find the painting," Ginny said to Remy as they went through Jacob's paintings with Meredith and her sister.

Remy smiled at this, and Quinn could see the resemblance between the sisters, if only slightly.

They had spent the whole morning showing Meredith and her sister Jacob's paintings in the barn. The barn held most of his work. Over the years, Jacob had sold some for thousands of dollars. The ones of Jacqueline he had heard would go for more. But the ones he painted after the accident, those were the most valuable of all.

They waded slowly through Jacob's inventory as his mother told stories about Jacob growing up and his family.

"How did the Queen Bees begin using Jacob's land?" Remy asked.

Meredith pretended to be looking at a painting, but Quinn could tell she was listening to the conversation.

"Most of the men in town were lobstermen," Ginny explained as they went through some of Jacob's early work—paintings of calm oceans and perfect sunsets. "But after the storm and so many of the men died, the women had to feed their families and that's when Jacob let us use the land."

"So, you harvested the blueberries," Remy said, totally captivated by the women who called themselves the Queen Bees. She held onto another painting from before the accident. They had started organizing them by year.

"That's right," Hazel said as Ginny nodded. "In return, we took care of Jacob, and Jacob let us use the fields to harvest the blueberries. Then came the honey. Then the tourists."

"If it weren't for Jacob and this land"—Hazel looked out at the fields—"I don't know what we would've done back then."

Meredith walked over to a standing easel with a half-finished painting, likely Jacob's last painting, and picked up a brush from the side table.

"I think I'm going to call it for now," Meredith said, looking down at her watch. "I'm getting hungry and should probably eat something."

"We should find a place to grab some lunch and eat by the water," Remy said.

Quinn felt his own stomach growl. "You should go down to the Blueberry Bay Café. They have a great menu. I'll let Jane know you're coming."

"You don't have to do that," Meredith said, still not warming up to Quinn, no matter how much he laid on the charm.

He didn't want to be that guy, but he usually didn't have to work this hard around a woman. What was her story anyway?

"You'll love the café," Ginny said to the women.

Remy smiled at Ginny as Meredith picked through more of the paintings.

"How much did you say these could go for?" she asked, pulling out another larger landscape and studying it.

Quinn shrugged. "I'm not sure, but the selectmen would be willing to put them on display in town hall."

"You could have an art auction," Remy said. "Here. Set it all up in the barn."

Quinn looked around. "You could..."

"You could market an oceanside estate sale and fine art auction during the Blueberry Festival. You'd get tons of eyes on this property," Remy said. "You could fix the old place up and sell it for a killing."

Quinn froze as Meredith seemed to be thinking the idea over. "I don't know the first thing about renovating a house."

"You don't necessarily have to renovate it, just reorganize and stage it," Remy said. "I could totally help."

Ginny shot Quinn a look. All afternoon, she had thought she was getting to the women, but who were they kidding? Why would Meredith want Jacob's run-down cottage and blueberry farm? He wasn't even sure if it was worth it for him at this point.

Meredith pulled out another landscape and studied it as Quinn waited for her response.

"Let's talk about all this later," Meredith said to Remy, but she clearly didn't want to speak in front of everyone.

"Nice meeting you girls," Hazel said, waving as she picked up her things before leaving the barn. "Make sure you stop by the library before you leave."

"We will," Remy said in delight. "Everyone here is so wonderful."

Quinn watched as Meredith collected a few of the paintings and held them in her hands. "Thanks for everything today."

"Want some help with those?" Quinn asked, reaching out as the paintings started to slip out of her hands.

"Um..." Meredith glanced down at two others and, with some reluctance, she said, "Sure."

Quinn grabbed the two on the floor. "Would you like any others?"

"Just the ones of my mom or painted by my mom." She nodded at a few more stacked against each other. "Thanks."

He nodded as he picked up the rest and followed her out of the barn, hooking the paintings under his arms. The frames wobbled as the assorted sizes hung by his sides awkwardly while they walked back to the house.

"How long do you think you'll stay?" Remy asked, carrying her own stack of paintings. They were small frames with different Blueberry Bay scenes—one of a beach rose, another of a sailboat in the harbor, and one of a dog resting on the porch.

Meredith shrugged. "I have no idea. Like you said, I have nowhere to go or no one to go home to."

Even he could hear the tone change in Meredith's voice with the last part of her sentence. Remy gave a little groan.

"I didn't mean to say it like that, Mer," Remy said. "I just meant, don't rush to get rid of this place. Take your time was all I meant to say."

Meredith sighed. "Well, I heard you and..." She suddenly stopped in her tracks. She looked at Quinn, then put the paintings down carefully, resting them against her legs, and said, "I need to take a rest."

She put her hands on her hips and looked out at the water, gathering her breath.

"I can take it all from here," Quinn said, reaching over to pick up the paintings. "Go ahead and I'll come back if I need to."

Meredith immediately grabbed them away. "I'm fine."

Then she picked them up and walked straight to the house without stopping. He looked at Remy, who rolled her eyes.

"She's a bit stubborn, that one," Remy said, following her sister toward the house. "But usually not so much."

He gave a smile, but immediately frowned as she walked ahead. There was no way they would convince her to keep the cottage. He might as well just call the real estate agent for her.

When they got to Jacob's cottage, he saw Meredith talking to someone on the front porch, but he couldn't make out who it was until he turned the corner.

Kyle stood holding the paintings in his hand as Meredith opened the house. The lawnmower sat in the middle of the unfinished lawn, and he silently thanked the heavens above that

Kyle had been on his best behavior since the arrival of Jacob's family.

"This is really nice of you, but not necessary," Meredith said as he reached the porch. "You don't have to mow the lawn for us." This gave her pause, and then she said, "Will I have to pay you?"

Quinn rushed to Kyle's side and shook his hands out. "No, no, no. Kyle's responsibility around here is to mow the lawns."

She looked at Quinn and then back to Kyle. "I guess I don't even have the equipment up here to mow myself."

He could almost see the things coming to mind in her head, things she would have to do with owning a second unfamiliar house.

It was a lot of work.

"Whatever we can do to help, we'll do it for you," Quinn said to her. He had promised Jacob he could have the house taken care of for at least a year.

She narrowed her eyes to him. "Why are you doing all this for me?"

"It's not just for you." He held out his hand at his mother and her friends walking back from the blueberry fields. "To be honest, we're all kind of freaking out that you're going to sell."

This seemed to surprise her. "Didn't you expect that?"

"We didn't, no," he said. "And none of us would blame you if you did, but this is all we know."

He held out his arms at the fields rolling slowly toward the end of the earth.

"My mother's whole life." He huffed out a laugh at the blunder and corrected himself. "All our lives. This is where we were born and raised our families. This is where our community comes together and celebrates. This is our home just as much as it was Jacob's."

This made Meredith frown. "Mr. Michaud."

"Quinn," he interrupted.

"Quinn," she said and let out a long sigh. "To be honest, this is the last thing I want to deal with right now."

His heart sank.

"I have a family and a house of my own," she said, and that's when her eyes moistened.

"I'm sorry. I didn't mean to make you upset," he said, guilt washing over him. What was

he thinking? Was he trying to guilt her into keeping it?

"Stop, Meredith," Remy said.

Meredith swung her head at her sister, who had set down the paintings among the others in the front hall.

"You are not in a rush to decide anything," Remy said, shaking her head. "Your children are all grown. They're fine without you. Your house is fine without you. Take the summer to really think things through."

This sounded like an excellent plan to Quinn, but the look on Meredith's face didn't seem like she agreed.

Meredith set the paintings on the porch floor a little harder than he expected and turned to her sister. "Mr. Michaud, do you mind giving me and my sister some time?"

He nodded, seeing her sister's smile turn. "Call or text if you need anything."

He didn't wait any longer, stepping off the porch just as Kyle was about to pull the cord to the lawnmower.

"Thanks, Kyle," he said as he reached his son. "I really appreciate you doing this for me."

"This is my house, too," Kyle said. "I don't want some lady ruining everything."

Kyle pulled the string hard and continued mowing where he left off. Quinn looked back at Jacob's cottage. At this point, he had no responsibility to Jacob's daughter. Meredith could do whatever she pleased with the property and house.

And when she did sell, what would happen after that?

CHAPTER 20

*M*eredith seethed inside. How could Remy just speak about her like that?

"You know I do have a life," Meredith snapped. "I can't just pack up and stay in Maine anytime I want. I have things to do."

Remy slanted her head like Meredith was making things up. "Come on, Mer. You have time to figure this out without rushing to sell."

"I don't just sit around eating Bonbons all day." Meredith didn't want to admit that she *would* be sitting around since she didn't have the kids at home and most of her friends were spending time with their own families. Even Gordon was too busy in retirement to hang out by the pool. Besides, he didn't go in the sun anymore.

"I know that," Remy said, too calmly, which irritated Meredith even more.

"Just because I'm not married and don't have a husband to take care of doesn't mean I have nothing to do." Meredith could feel her blood begin to boil. Just looking at Remy's lackadaisical smile made her even more upset.

"I didn't mean to hurt your feelings, but this could be good for you," Remy said, but she was still so completely unaware, like always.

"How?"

"Well, you haven't talked about Phillip and the new baby," Remy said.

And like a wave sweeping her off her feet, Meredith felt her blood turn cold by Remy's comment. "Wow, Remy, I can't believe you."

Remy's face went from a stupid smile to horrified. "I didn't mean to be mean, but you have a really big opportunity here and you're pushing to go back to being miserable."

"What's that supposed to mean?" Meredith's voice was starting to rise. She didn't want to get into it with Remy. She really didn't. But her sister had crossed the line by bringing Phillip into the conversation. "You don't even know what you're talking about."

"You let Phillip hang on to you, and I just don't understand why." Remy shook her head. "He was a cheater and a liar, and he ruined your family. Why do you still allow him in your life?"

"He was my husband for over twenty-five years. The father of my children," Meredith said. "I can't just pretend he doesn't exist. I can't just stop loving someone."

Remy shook her head. "You used to be so…"

"So what, Remy?" Meredith knew she was picking a fight. Egging Remy on to shut her down. She had no right to talk about Meredith's relationship, or to pass judgment. "At least Phillip will answer my phone calls."

She could almost see her words hit Remy.

"You're right," Remy said, looking straight at Meredith, going toe to toe with her older sister. "I would ignore your calls sometimes."

There it was. Her sister was ignoring her.

"You knew I was hurting." Meredith wanted to scream it.

"Yes, but you never even bothered to look outside your own

pain to see that other people were hurting, too," Remy said. "I lost Mom, too."

Meredith couldn't believe Remy right now. "I lost my mother *and* my husband."

"Have you ever thought maybe other people were going through stuff, too?" Remy crossed her arms against her stomach. "But you didn't even bother to know what was going on with me. You don't bother to know about anyone else."

"What's that supposed to mean?" Meredith said.

"You had a lifetime to ask about your father," Remy said, pointing her hand at the paintings Meredith had taken from the barn. "You never even bothered to ask about him. Ever."

Meredith stood there. "Why should I bother to ask about him?"

"Because you would've found out that he clearly couldn't be a fit father or husband, and that by letting you and Mom go, he gave you the greatest father instead." Remy shook her head. "And now you're fighting with me instead of asking about my own problems."

"Okay," Meredith said, crossing her arms against her chest, playing along with Remy's game. "Tell me then. What's going on with you?"

Meredith immediately felt ashamed of herself when she saw her sister's tears. What was she doing fighting with Remy? Why did she want everyone to be as miserable as her?

"Joe no longer wants to keep trying to have a baby. It's been too hard for him," Remy said. "Now he just wants to focus on work."

Meredith could feel Remy's pain as her sister wrapped her arms around her stomach.

Remy laughed cynically. "I didn't even get a say."

"Why not adopt?" Meredith had heard of many families who went different routes to start a family. "You could foster children."

"Joe doesn't want to foster or adopt." Remy's eyes filled with more tears. "He says he's fine with the way things are."

The tears clung, but as soon as Remy blinked, they poured down. Her hands covered her face, and immediately, Meredith pulled her in, wrapping her arms around her sister.

"I'm so sorry, Remy," Meredith said. "I know how much you looked forward to being a mom."

Remy had been the perfect aunt to her three kids. Just young enough to be hip in the eyes of the kids but old enough to be taken seriously, Remy spoiled her nieces and nephew to extreme levels at times, especially after she had married Joe.

Remy began to sob—hard, wrenching sobs. The kind of grief Meredith hadn't felt in a long time, she realized. Fresh grief.

"Why do you really want me to stay here this summer?" Meredith thought about all the things Remy had brought with her to Maine. The way her sister had continued to push back on moving quickly and to take her time. How she had offered to stay if Meredith needed her.

Remy heaved in short breaths. "Because I'm leaving Joe."

"What?" Meredith couldn't believe what she was hearing. "You're leaving him?"

"Oh, Meredith!" Remy's sobs were so heavy, it sounded like something was dying inside her. "I can't go back home. I just can't."

"Okay, okay," Meredith said. "You can stay with me as long as you need to."

Meredith led Remy around the porch to the daybed she had slept on the night before as Remy's shoulders heaved. She rubbed Remy's back as she leaned into Meredith's chest.

"I haven't told him I'm leaving him," Remy said, hiccupping. "I have no idea what I'm going to do. He's going to hire all these expensive lawyers, and I won't have anything, Meredith. He's going to say I've lived off his hard work. He'll win, too. Massachusetts isn't a fifty-fifty state."

Meredith had no idea their marriage was on the rocks.

"Talk to me," Meredith said, holding Remy's hand. "Tell me what happened."

"I didn't tell anyone about the first miscarriage because it had happened right after Mom died." Remy's eyes filled with tears again.

The first miscarriage, Meredith thought to herself.

"The doctor even blamed it on the stress from Mom's death. But then I got pregnant again." Remy paused, taking a deep breath. "I was just starting to show. So, we told Dad, and that night I started having contractions."

Meredith's heart broke as she calculated the weeks by memory of her own time frame for showing. Not long enough for a baby to be born healthy.

"He was perfect," Remy whispered out. "Ten perfect little fingers and ten perfect little toes." She exhaled.

"Why didn't you tell me?" Meredith didn't understand.

"You were so fragile at the time." Remy shrugged. "Phillip had just left you, and I didn't see the point in burdening you with more grief."

Meredith's stomach sank. "I wish I could've been there for you."

Remy sat back up and looked at Meredith. "You've been so stuck in Phillip's betrayal that it's clouding your view of everything else."

"How's it clouding my view?" Meredith felt as though she was clear about things. That life wasn't always sweet like honey, but salty and dangerous like the sea.

Remy started to laugh as though she had heard a joke. "Meredith, you were given a piece of paradise, and you can't even see it."

Remy threw her arms out at the ocean. "Literally, right before your eyes."

Meredith looked out. White caps foamed on the water's surface as the wind blew. Seagulls glided in the wind above the water. Feathery clouds spread across the sky like white ribbons against a silk blue fabric. The scene from that porch matched every painting stuffed inside the cottage.

"You're so focused on the fact that Jacob wasn't a good father that you're missing what he tried to do to make up for that." Remy shook her head.

"This place is a whole new burden I didn't ask for," Meredith said.

"Sell it to me." Remy leaned back, crossing her arms against her chest. "I'll buy it."

"What?" Meredith couldn't believe Remy would want it. "What are you going to do with this place? You already have a summer house on the Cape."

Remy shrugged. "I need a fresh start."

Meredith wished more than anything for her mother to be there. Jacqueline would know what to do. She'd figure everything out for both her girls. She always had.

If Meredith came home with a bad grade, Jacqueline would help her study. If Meredith bombed an audition, Jacqueline would sit next to her and listen to her play. If Meredith's heart was broken, Jacqueline would be waiting in the wings ready to mend her back up again by showing her the beauty she already had inside her. Jacqueline always helped.

What would Jacqueline do now?

"Let's start by cleaning this place," Meredith said, squeezing Remy's hand. "Jacob may have been an amazing artist, but he was not very clean or tidy."

"What?" Remy asked, confused.

"If we're going to figure things out here"—Meredith looked around the back porch—"we'll want to at least sleep inside." Meredith gave Remy a reassuring smile. "Let's go to the market and get everything we need."

CHAPTER 21

Quinn called Megan when he got home. The local real estate agent would be the best person to sell Jacob's property. She would do what was best for everyone.

"She wants to sell?" Megan sounded as surprised as everyone else. "Wow, Quinn. I'm sorry for you, but thanks for the referral."

This would be big for Megan, whose primary business was managing the many rental beach cottages along the shore.

"I can't believe the old place is going to be sold," she said. "I hope I can find a family who wants to keep it as a farm."

"Would you be able to give me a ballpark price for my parents' place?" he asked.

"Don't tell me you're thinking of selling, too?" Megan asked.

Quinn tapped his thumb against the kitchen counter as he looked out the window to the back yard.

"No, just curious, you know?" he said. But the truth was, he didn't know what they should do. Should they stick around just for nostalgia's sake? Or should he sell while he still had an unobstructed view of the Atlantic Ocean? Should he stay in Blueberry Bay and make pennies, or go back to the city where he could make a decent living and get paid with actual currency, not by bartering goods and trades?

But where would he go if he could?

And how could he leave Lisa? Or his dad. And Ginny was never going to leave, which meant Kyle would never leave.

He looked at Jacob's cottage. He hadn't seen Meredith or her sister leave since he'd left them that afternoon. He could feel the argument brewing between the sisters as they were going through the paintings. Quinn had thought Jacob had been a touchy subject with Meredith because she didn't trust him, but after a day with the two women, it was clear Meredith had more than just trust issues.

Remy, however, didn't seem to mind pushing the boundaries. She kept asking Ginny the questions while they went through the paintings. And, of course, Ginny loved to tell the stories to the women, which even got Meredith listening intently.

At first, Meredith had reminded Quinn of a porcelain doll—beautiful on the outside, yet empty and hollow on the inside.

How could she not be moved by a man who had struggled his whole life with being unable to be her father? The proof was painted all around her.

But then he'd seen her pick up one of the landscapes, one of his favorite vista views from Jacob's back porch, and trace her fingertips against a tiny figure with pigtails running on the beach. And that was when he'd seen the change in her eyes. She wasn't hollow and empty but filled with pain.

"I'll give her your number right now," he said when he saw the front door to Jacob's cottage swing open and Meredith come outside.

"Let her know she can call day or night!" Megan said on the phone.

"I will, Megan. Thanks again," he said as he hung up.

With a deep breath, he set his coffee down and headed out of the house, walking over to Jacob's like he was walking the plank. This was it. The life he had known for fifty years was about to change.

"Meredith!" he shouted out as she walked to her car.

She looked up, and he couldn't believe it, but she smiled. "Hello, Quinn."

"Sorry to bother you again, but I got that number for you," he said, passing Megan's card to her. "She's from the area and knows the value of the property. She'll get you what you deserve."

"I don't really deserve any of it," Meredith said, holding onto the card. "But thank you."

She gave him a nod, and he returned the gesture. But she didn't move. She tapped the card against her leg. Then suddenly blurted out, "I apologize for being so difficult."

He jerked his head back, but then shook his head. "No, I get it. This all must be difficult for you."

"Well, I appreciate your help," she said, holding up the card. "I realize this all must be difficult for you, too."

Quinn appreciated the recognition.

"I think I'm going to take some time going through his stuff," she said, looking back at the house. "My sister and I plan to go through everything this summer."

Quinn's heart started pumping hope.

"Really?" He stuffed his hands into his pockets. "That's good to hear."

She looked down at the card and then back at him. And that was when he saw the change in her. Her pained eyes appeared brighter, bluer. She looked lighter. Her shoulders were pulled back comfortably, not ready for confrontation.

She looked...happy. Well, not happy, he corrected himself. But no longer as troubled or as angry as she had been just a few hours ago.

"I know you're not technically my lawyer, but I wondered if I needed help with all of this, if I could—"

"I want to help. No need to hire anyone," he said, jumping in before she could finish. He wanted nothing more than to help and convince her to stay. "I want to do this for you and your family."

She smiled again, then looked out at the water. "I appreciate what you're doing for me."

He nodded, not sure why his collar was heating up while he looked at her. Was it because things might work out with the property? Or was it because he couldn't keep his eyes off her?

"Let me know if there's anything I can help you with," he said, darting his eyes away before she caught him staring.

She crossed her hands together, holding them in front of her. "I will."

And with that, he gave a wave goodbye and walked back to the house.

"Tell the Bee Queens or whatever…" she stumbled with their title.

"The Queen Bees," he said, his heart pumping more.

"Yes," she said, but she stopped as she headed back toward Jacob's cottage. "Tell them they can continue working the fields."

"Will do," he said, standing in place, tongue tied by his shock.

That's when Remy came out of the house, smiling at Quinn.

"Good morning!" she said, with sunglasses on.

As the two got into the car, they both rolled down the windows, and waved at Quinn as he stood shell-shocked by the sudden transformation.

What happened between the sisters?

CHAPTER 22

$\mathcal{M}$eredith and Remy decided to divide and conquer. Remy started in the kitchen. First, she focused on the appliances, cleaning out the fridge, then the stove and oven.

Meredith deep cleaned the two spare rooms. They decided to leave Jacob's room for Ginny who knew him best.

Meredith first pulled all the bedding off and dragged it to the basement and started a load of laundry in the thirty-year old washer and dryer. In one room, she named the yellow room for its yellow wallpaper. She opened the closet and found boxes of sewing materials, a sewing machine, and lots of different fabrics. If she had to guess, it must have been someone's sewing room at one point. She noticed how there were no paintings, except for one, in the whole room. Not even on the walls or stuffed somewhere. The painting had been of a field of yellow and white daffodils.

Going through the dresser drawers, she found more material —folded yards of calicos and cotton knit and velvet were all inside. She took everything out and set it on top of the dresser. In the corner of the room sat an antique sewing table with a wooden cover.

"Don't even tell me…" Meredith pulled off the cover. Inside, to her amazement, sat a Singer sewing machine. Her fingers went straight to the machine. She tried to pick it up, but the heavy machine's metal body wouldn't budge from the table. She looked down and noticed the drawer on the side and opened it. There was a piece of paper folded and stuffed in the back. She slowly opened it up, feeling strange doing so. Was she snooping by going through these things? Reading notes written by a man she'd never met?

The writing looked like a child's penmanship, and the date was from twenty years ago.

Meredith Miller O'Neill died peacefully with her son on Sunday, November twenty-seventh. She is survived by her son, Jacob.

The letters were crooked and big. The lines were hard and scratchy.

She thought to where she had been twenty years ago. She had the three kids underfoot.

A pang of sadness plucked at her heart. Jacob lost his mother, and he was all alone. How lucky was she that she had Gordon and Remy and Phillip at the time when she lost her mother. She had her kids who had been a great support as well. She had never thought of herself as lucky, but as she held Jacob's obituary for his mother, she could feel his loneliness.

She thought about how Ginny told her to look up the accident. Grabbing her phone, she started typing in Jacob's name and the word *storm*, and tons of phrases popped up.

Fifty Years Since The Storm Of The Century That Claimed Nine— Only One Survived was the title that appeared first, but as she scrolled through, there were dozens more stories of fisherman deaths. News outlets from all over Maine and the surrounding states had covered different stories. She clicked on a link to a news channel memorializing the news.

"There was only one survivor," the male news anchor said into the camera with a grave face. "Nine men died that fateful day."

Meredith thought about her pregnant mother going through such a tragedy.

She grabbed Jacob's paper and brought it downstairs, going into the kitchen.

"I'm almost done with the fridge," Remy said as soon as Meredith walked in. "I was thinking I'd go to the grocery store and grab us some essentials and something for dinner."

"Look what I found." Meredith handed Remy the paper. "I think Jacob wrote it."

Remy took it and read the two sentences that said so much. "You were named after your grandmother?"

Meredith nodded, thinking that Remy would've known that.

"I looked up the boating accident," Meredith said. Remy didn't flinch like Meredith at the idea of looking Jacob's accident up.

"He got really hurt," Remy said. "Mentally and physically."

Meredith nodded. "I guess so."

"Mom said he had a lot of guilt about being the only survivor," Remy said.

Meredith glanced at one of his paintings of a dark sea.

She kept rereading the obituary. It was strange how just two lines told her so much about her life. Meredith Miller O'Neill was her grandmother. And Jacob had been more unwell than she'd had any idea.

"Why don't we get containers to keep things like this?" Remy said, about the note. "Then you can go through everything later with it all together and decide whether it's junk or not."

Meredith looked around the kitchen. The space was already starting to look better. "Okay, that sounds like a good idea."

Remy left after that to go to the store, and Meredith stayed downstairs, cleaning out the bathroom on the first floor. She would tackle the upstairs bathroom later. She washed down every surface from floor to ceiling, wiped down the drawer and shelf and every nook and cranny.

By the time Remy returned, the kitchen looked pretty good. The pine floors from the kitchen continued throughout the house, even in the bathroom. The white tile backsplash was worn and used but looked clean and attractive against the wooden butcher block countertops. She could envision the cabinets looking darling with a clean coat of a creamy white paint. The more they decluttered, the bigger the space felt. Meredith had to admit, it really was very quaint with the woodstove in the corner.

"I know we just had lobster last night, but I found this fantastic little farmer's market and the guy gave me free steamers and clams and adorable little potatoes."

Meredith laughed. "That's crazy. Why would he do that?"

Remy dropped the burlap bags onto the island counter. "Because you're Jacob's daughter."

Meredith sat with the information as Remy continued to unpack the groceries.

"I got a great bottle of chardonnay," Remy said, pulling out a bottle opener. "Oh!"

She put the opener on the counter, then ran out of the kitchen, into the breezeway, and out the door. Meredith could hear her open a car door and then close it again. Through the window, she saw Remy carrying a big plastic tub. Meredith raced to the door before Remy reached it to help her.

"What is in there?" she asked. Remy's trunk was like Mary Poppins' carpet bag.

"I brought bedding," Remy said. "Nice Egyptian cotton bedding."

"That sounds magical," Meredith said.

And Meredith couldn't believe it, but Remy had brought more than just bedding. She brought fairy lights and lamps and candles. Lots and lots of candles. She brought bath salts and fragrant oil sticks and cooking books and novels.

"Were you planning on moving here?" Meredith asked.

Remy shook her head. "No, Dad's place."

Meredith thought of when Gordon had asked her if she wanted to move back home. Had he asked Remy or had he even known?

"What does he think about you leaving Joe?" Meredith asked.

Remy shrugged. "I haven't told anyone."

And Meredith's heart broke once again. Her sister was just as alone as she was.

"Well, you can stay here until you figure things out, okay?" Meredith said.

"Thank you, Meredith," Remy said. "I don't know what I would do if I didn't have you."

Meredith didn't have a timetable, but she knew she couldn't afford two houses.

"We'll figure this all out together," Meredith said.

We're all we have, she thought to herself.

"Let me make dinner," Remy said. "And you should take this glass of wine and call it for the day."

"I forgot the laundry." Meredith noticed the sun setting behind the barn and the sky glowing oranges and reds and pinks against the ocean water.

"Wow!" Remy said, pointing out the window. "Let's go take a baseline selfie."

"A what?" Meredith said.

Remy grabbed her phone from the kitchen table and ran out the back door to the porch. "Come on!" Remy stood, arm stretched out with her camera, ushering Meredith into the frame.

"What's a baseline selfie?" Meredith asked.

"Smile!" Remy said, rushing the photograph. She held her smile as she explained through gritted teeth. "It's the point where you start. We need to remember where we started to see how much we've grown."

CHAPTER 23

*M*eredith slept with the windows open. The yellow room had given her a magical night of sleep. When she awoke, the sun glistened off the water, shining into her eyes. The cries of seagulls echoed into the room, and the quiet, steady rhythm of waves lapping against the granite shore calmed her already buzzing mind.

What was she going to do?

She could keep the property up until fall, and then she *had* to return to Andover. She had exactly two months to get whatever plan she had together, and then she either had to pay Phillip for his half of the house or sell it.

Remy talked all night about what she thought Meredith should do with Jacob's house and property, but nothing about her and Joe.

Meredith hadn't pushed it. Remy had confessed a big truth, and that's all she could probably handle for now. But the fact was, Meredith never saw the end of her sister's marriage coming. Remy had enjoyed posting about their fabulous life on all the social media sites. Remy and Joe were always all smiles while doing regular life things, like going out to dinner and hanging out at their house with friends. They shared their spectacular weekends at their Cape house and took luxurious trips together. Never in a million years had Meredith thought there was trouble in their marriage. But then again, did she let people know about hers?

Meredith swung her legs out of bed, when the thought occurred to her.

She *hadn't* been thinking about Phillip. She hadn't fallen asleep wishing he was lying by her side. She hadn't woken to an empty, cold bed.

Meredith walked to the windows and opened them as high as they would go, looking out at the water, forgetting Phillip again and taking in the view.

The whole world *was* at her fingertips.

She thought back to the past year. So much had changed around her, but she hadn't evolved at all. She was still behaving exactly the same as if she had a husband and children at home. For goodness' sake! She cleaned a pool she hadn't been in for years. She had a five-bedroom home large enough for an army, not a single woman at fifty.

What was she doing hanging on to that Meredith?

She wasn't even that happy when she was that Meredith.

She'd been stressed most of the time, racing from here to there, trying to be the perfect mother, the perfect wife, the perfect piano teacher. She'd felt like a taxi service and an ATM. She'd felt like a therapist for everyone's bad days, and a servant on most.

Then her parents flashed through her mind. Gordon had loved Jacqueline, and from Meredith's point of view, Jacqueline had adored Gordon all the way up until the end. Her parents' love had been something she'd admired her whole life. She looked at the painting she'd taken from the barn and set it on top of the dresser facing the bed. The painting was of the little girl on the beach. Could Jacqueline have loved both lives? The one she and Gordon had, and the one she'd left with Jacob?

The smell of bacon floated through the window, and she

could hear someone in the kitchen below. Remy must already be up.

Meredith didn't know if it was the sheets or the pillow or the bed itself, but she would thank Remy for the good night's sleep.

"Good morning!" Remy said from the stove as Meredith walked into the kitchen. The burners were filled with what their father dubbed a Midwestern breakfast. Two eggs over easy, white toast with jelly, shredded hash browns, and two slices of bacon.

"I couldn't resist," Remy said as she set a jar of blueberry jam onto the table. "The Queens dropped the jam off this morning."

Meredith looked at the time—it was only a bit past seven. "They've already stopped by with jam?"

"They must've seen me go for a walk, because it was on the porch when I got back, and they were already out in the fields." Remy pointed toward the screen door. "They were there when the sun rose."

Meredith looked out to see the women. "What are they doing?"

"Checking on things," Remy said. "Ginny said they make sure everything's growing the way it should."

"Do you think they come every day?" Meredith wondered if farming blueberries was that difficult. Weren't they mostly wild in Maine?

"The lawyer's son is coming to the house," Remy said as the teenager walked up the seashell gravel of the stone path that led to the front door. "Do you want me to answer it?"

Meredith waved at Remy, who stood in a running outfit, cooking, happy as a clam.

"I got it." Meredith shook her head at Remy's perky attitude at eight AM. It was way too early to be that chipper. But was the hyper-smile and the *up and at 'em* behavior just a cover? Remy never admitted to being anything but perfect, and now, Meredith started seeing the cracks. She hadn't mentioned Joe. Or called him to let him know she was in Maine or to let him know she was staying indefinitely.

How did Meredith miss these cracks?

She needed to call her children. She needed to make sure she hadn't missed any cracks with them.

"Good morning, Kyle," she greeted him as she opened the door just as he was about to knock.

"Mrs. Johnson," he said. "Sorry to bother you, but I wondered if you knew what you were going to do with Jacob's boat."

She didn't wince at the *Mrs.* part. Most of her students continued to use the *Mrs.* She had used her married name when she'd introduced herself to the parents that year, even after the divorce. Did she really want to take five minutes to explain her divorce at little Betty Sue's piano lessons?

"You know, I haven't even seen it." Meredith had forgotten about the boat. "I should probably go and check that out today."

She knew she would be selling it.

"I was hoping you'd give me first right of refusal," he said.

"Sure," she said. She had no idea what the boat was worth, but she certainly had no use for a lobster boat. "Are you planning on catching lobsters with it?"

He smiled. "Lots of them."

Meredith suddenly noticed Kyle's clothes. He stood in a button-up and a pair of dress pants. He looked formal, like he was going to an office job. Not a teenage boy going to hang out for the summer.

"Don't you look nice," she said to the young man.

He put his hands in his pockets. "Thank you. I have a college interview this morning."

"That's great news!" The news seemed like something to celebrate, but Kyle didn't look happy.

He shrugged. "Yeah, I guess."

"Good school?" she said.

"Not my top pick, but I'll get a good amount of financial aid," he said. "But maybe if I had a boat, I could catch some lobsters and afford my dream school."

"You can earn that kind of money catching lobsters?" she asked.

Kyle nodded. "They don't call it the gold of the sea for nothing."

She smiled at that, but was hit by the thought of how Kyle's own great-grandfather had died in the boat accident and here he was offering to buy the boat from the only survivor. If he were her son, she'd have a hard time getting over their history and letting him go out in the waters.

"Do you know how much the boat is worth?" she asked him, having no clue. She had a feeling Quinn marked the estimated price somewhere in the portfolio he had created, but she still hadn't opened it to know.

Kyle nodded. "I have a rough estimate of the price."

She smiled at the confidence of the young man. She didn't know much about fishing boats, but she knew they'd be worth a lot more than just the price of a car. Did this kid have that kind of money? The kind of money that might save her from selling her children's home for a few months while she and Remy figured things out?

"Great, well, what are you doing in a half hour?" she asked.

"Excuse me?" he looked confused.

"I'm just about to have breakfast, then maybe you could show me Jacob's boat."

A wide grin expanded across his face. "I'll meet you here, and we can walk over."

"Perfect," she said. "Is it close by?"

She looked out at the water—the cliffs too high and rocky to dock a boat. The harbor in town had appeared to be full of lobster boats, and she'd assumed it would be docked there.

"It's behind the barn," Kyle said, then gave a wave and took off, running toward the house.

She laughed at his excitement and hoped she wouldn't have to burst his bubble if he couldn't afford it.

Coming into the kitchen, she asked Remy, "How much do you think a lobster boat is worth?"

Remy shrugged, plating the eggs with her spatula. "Depends."

Meredith grabbed her phone but realized she didn't even need to look it up. She had the portfolio. She looked in the corner of the room where she had dumped all the paperwork on top of Jacob's desk that Remy had cleaned off.

She walked over and grabbed the portfolio that listed all of Jacob's assets and market value at the time of the writing of the will.

She brought it to the table, where Remy placed down two plates beside a glass of orange juice and a steaming cup of coffee. She stared at the booklet before opening it. She read the detailed table of contents and found the tab where Jacob's boat was listed.

"It's worth twenty grand," Remy said, tapping on the price listed on the page.

That seemed like a lot of money for a boat that old.

"It's from 1972." The year before Meredith's birth. Goodness, she was old.

"Will you sell it?" Remy asked.

Meredith took a sip of her coffee. "What am I going to do with a lobster boat?"

Remy nodded. "Do you think you should talk to his father before selling an old boat to a teenager?"

"Right," Meredith said. She should most definitely talk to the boy's father before even entertaining the idea of selling it to him. "He probably doesn't have that kind of money."

That's when she thought about his bonfire with the young lady the other night.

"There's a small little cove," Meredith said to Remy. "I saw him having a bonfire."

"We should totally have a bonfire," Remy said, thinking the same thing as Meredith.

Meredith nodded. "We should totally have a bonfire."

"Let's make a list," Remy said. "For what we need to finish today."

Meredith could feel her shoulders suddenly relax. Today didn't need to be stressful. The situation didn't have to be negative. She could look at the gift Jacob had given her rather than the disaster she'd inherited.

Then she smiled at Remy as she worked on a list of what needed to be accomplished to get Jacob's art collection in order.

"I can call a friend who's a collector I know from the Museum of Fine Arts in Boston," Remy said. "He can help us figure out which of the pieces will be worth more than the others."

Meredith didn't know this world, the art world. Remy loved to live in it. Always attending posh art exhibits or openings, she had her own collection of fine art and a master's in art history. Remy's own art talent had been something Meredith had been a bit jealous of as a kid. And it was something that Remy and Jacqueline had in common.

Yet, when was the last time Remy had an art show or work on a piece?

More cracks.

Suddenly there was a thwacking on the door. Ginny stood in her straw hat and gardening gloves with a fanny pack.

"Whew, girls, it's getting hot," she said, opening the door. "Hope you don't mind me stepping in for a break."

Meredith sat there, shocked at the fact that this woman had just walked inside her home.

"Good morning," Meredith said, still in surprise.

Remy, however, seemed overly delighted to see the older woman.

"I used your jam!" Remy pointed to the jar on the table.

"Fantastic!" Ginny rubbed Remy's shoulder as she walked up to the table. "The Queens have one of our weekly summer meetings tomorrow evening if you care to join us."

"You meet once a week, too?" Meredith couldn't get over the commitment.

"The summer is our busiest time up until the festival," Ginny said.

"When's the festival?" Meredith asked.

"The last weekend in August," Ginny said. "Before school starts up again."

"Wow, that's dedication," Remy said.

"We've been caretakers of Jacob's property for fifty years," Ginny said, as though this should've been obvious.

But like the boat, Meredith was just starting to comprehend Jacob's situation for fifty years.

"You've been taking care of Jacob all this time?" she asked.

Ginny smiled as she nodded. "We sure have."

Remy was right. Meredith needed to think about the whole picture before selling. "We'll be there."

Remy smiled at that. "We look forward to meeting you all."

Ginny laughed at this. "That's just fantastic!"

"Is there anything we should bring?" Meredith asked.

"Just yourselves!" Ginny put her hand on Meredith's back, and the touch felt good, comforting. "All the girls will be tickled you came." Ginny waved goodbye and left.

Meredith turned to face Remy. "She's a lot, right?"

Maybe Meredith was a cranky old lady.

"I think she's fabulous," Remy said. "I bet Mom would've been a Queen."

That made Meredith smile. "She would." Meredith felt the ache she often did when thinking about her mom. The kind of ache one has for something in the past that can never be recreated again—her being in the safety of her mother's presence.

Her family unit had been the safest place she'd ever felt. It was why she lived down the road from them. It was why she had wanted to raise her children by them. It was why she had spent most of her free time, if she could, with her mother.

Would she have felt that safe with Jacob? After the accident?

"I think we should be Queens," Remy said to her.

Meredith shook her head at the idea. "We can't. We don't live here. This isn't our house."

"Meredith!" Remy slammed her hands on the island counter. "This is yours! This can be your home. This can be what you want it to be. All you have to do is to dream it."

CHAPTER 24

Quinn worked all day on a client's suit against his contractor. The whole thing would cost Quinn more in time and effort than the bill he would charge his client. But that was how small-town lawyers made their money. They stretched every ounce of their skills so they could represent family, friends, friends of friends, and daughters of dead people.

"That sister is going to change her mind about selling," Ginny said from her desk. "She's just like her mother."

"Make sure you don't get Kyle all amped up again," he warned his mother.

Ginny had a way of expanding the truth.

"I don't think we need to worry," Ginny said, filing papers as she whistled.

"Mom, I love you, but don't go and get your hopes up," he said. "She has no connection or ties to this community other than a statue in the middle of town."

Ginny frowned at him. "Well, we'll have to be her connection."

She shook her finger at him.

"Besides, those sisters need some quality time together," Ginny said, going back to her computer. "They need to put some work into their relationship."

"That's not any of our business," Quinn said, looking at the time. He slapped down his laptop and stuffed it into his bag. "I've got to run some paperwork down to the sheriff. Will you make sure Kyle does some of the chores on the list before he goes out with Brianna?"

"Will do," Ginny said. "And what chores should he be doing?"

"He should be doing the trash tonight, along with our own lawn." Quinn had fallen behind in everything lately, including reminding his son of what he was supposed to do. "When did I learn to do chores on my own?"

"You still don't," Ginny said. "You left the dishes in the sink this morning."

"I'll end up doing them," he said.

"Will you?" Ginny swiveled in her chair to get a look at him.

"Whatever, I try my best," he said.

"And I'm sure Kyle thinks he's trying his best," Ginny said, always the one with the last word.

Quinn mumbled something incoherent just as he went to peck his mother on the cheek. "I'll probably stop by Bruce's place on the way home."

"Do you want Kyle to meet you there?" Ginny asked. Kyle usually did.

Quinn shook his head. He was going to talk to Lisa's father about Kyle's college fund. Ginny may be optimistic for Meredith to change her mind about selling, but he was a realist. He knew dreams could be shattered as quickly as a drunk driver gets into a car.

"Nah," he said. "You know Kyle can barely stand Sundays with Bruce."

"God bless Lisa for dealing with that grouchy old man all her life." Ginny tsked her tongue as though Lisa deserved some sort of medal for dealing with her own father.

"He's lonely."

"He's an absolute nightmare," Ginny said, shutting down her

own computer. "Don't visit with Bruce too long, because I have a special dinner planned."

"Don't tell me you invited her and her sister to dinner," he said. He didn't want to deal with a night of entertaining people. He just wanted to go home and watch the game.

"Then I won't tell you."

"Mom, you're going to wear them out," he said, rubbing his forehead. "Not everyone can handle us all the time. We're a lot."

"I get it," Ginny said, nodding her head, but the dangling bee earrings told a different story.

"Don't overdo it," he warned her.

"When have I overdone things?" She laughed before he could respond with at least a hundred instances of her overdoing things.

"Seriously?" He couldn't believe her.

"They bought lobsters," Ginny said.

"And…" he waited for the punch line.

"And they asked for a big enough pot to cook the lobsters," she said. "So, I offered to cook for them. She and her sister are coming at six. So, dress appropriately."

He stared at his mother. "You're having them over tonight."

"Mm-hmm," she said, grabbing her purse out of the bottom drawer of her desk. Then she pointed to his hand with the papers. "You might want to hurry all that up."

He looked down at the paperwork. He wouldn't have enough time to run down to the sheriff, drive back to Blueberry Bay with the traffic, and get ready for dinner.

"Why are you being so pushy?" He worried this would only turn Meredith and her sister off.

"They're Jacob's family," she said.

Even Quinn could see the stretch in that statement. These women knew Jacob less than the rest of the town. And they only knew of Jacob as the recluse in the cottage by the sea.

" Le gîte en bord de Mer." Quinn didn't mean to say it aloud, but there it was. "Sounds like a cute name for a hotel."

"Stop that," Ginny said, not wanting to hear the truth. "She's not going to sell."

"The only person not willing to sell that land is dead." Quinn didn't mean to be harsh, but there the truth was. Jacob was dead. They had to face the facts that things could change.

Ginny didn't say anything, just gave him that look of slight disappointment and slight curiosity. "How'd you get so pessimistic?"

So many reasons, he thought to himself. He wanted to ask her why she buried her head in the sand all the time. Like when his father had died of a stroke, Ginny hadn't stopped to mourn. She just moved on like it was any other day. Even on the day of his father's funeral, Ginny was working the fields, organizing the dinner for after the funeral, and meeting with the Queens to take care of the bees.

"I'll see you later," he said, leaving before things became an argument.

"For dinner," Ginny said.

He shook his head. "I don't think I'm going to make it."

She let out a huff. "Don't be like this. Something changed from yesterday to today. She even offered to go down to the boat with Kyle."

"Kyle offered to take her to the boat?" He closed his eyes at what he imagined his son was trying to do. "Is he trying to buy that dang thing?"

"No." But Ginny's eyes couldn't hide the truth.

"Dang it, Mom, why are you encouraging him?" He stomped out of the office, slamming the door open.

Ginny followed him. "I'm not encouraging him. It's in his blood. He wants to fish. He wants to be out there with his cousins."

She pointed at the water. "This is his family, too. Not just yours."

"He's *my* son." He didn't mean to come off harsh, but Ginny had crossed a line. "And he's *all* I have."

"You don't think I love that child as my own?" Ginny's eyes flashed with hurt. "Quinn, you know the secret to raising bees? It's that you can't cage them. Your job is to protect them by giving them a safe space and room to grow. Otherwise, they won't stay."

He knew his mother was right. The right thing to do was acknowledge it and just let it go. Right now, he needed to just let it go. He looked down at the docks, then at the paperwork. His hands were shaking.

"I wish you would just stay out of it." The regret of saying it hit him as soon as the words left his mouth.

"Maybe you shouldn't join us for dinner." Ginny left after that, walking to her car parked right out front of his empty law office.

He smacked his hand on his forehead. His mother was right. She was always right about things. She was always right about raising Kyle. She had five children. She should know.

But Ginny often got people wrong. She saw a woman coming home to her roots, whereas he saw a woman being shoved by her past.

He got into his truck and drove to the sheriff's department, trying to think about anything other than the fact that his son was going to fish no matter what he did about it.

He just hoped he'd get Kyle to college.

Lisa would have killed him. Right?

He rubbed the back of his neck, thinking of Lisa's hopes for Kyle. She had wanted him to become a doctor. Not a lawyer like they were.

"It's all so sad," she'd often say about the criminal justice department. "There are so many sad stories."

Working for the justice department had been Lisa's dream job, but she'd always had a tough time separating work and home life.

Would she have wanted Kyle to follow his dreams? Even if that meant he put himself in danger?

It didn't take long to file the paperwork since he knew most of the officers at the police department.

When he reached Bruce's place, he pulled up to the opulent gates and pressed the call button. The gates opened slowly, dragging slightly and making a horrible cranking noise. One of the gates bounced and looked as though it might fall off at any moment. Bruce should just leave the gates open at that point.

He pulled in his normal spot at Lisa's childhood home and got out.

Windswept never disappointed. The early nineteen hundred colonial had been built to display wealth and power. Everything about the place was to show off. The six chimneys, the large wraparound porch. The sprawling manicured lawn and carefully trimmed landscaping. Quinn always wondered how much it cost just to live day to day there.

But Quinn had never had the nerve to ask such a personal question for fear someone might interpret Quinn wanting to know about Lisa's family's money. Because a poor fisherman's son was only curious about money if he wanted to steal it from them. There would be no other reason for him to wonder about their trust funds and properties along the coast of Maine and their strange connections to powerful people.

Quinn walked to the back door, where he'd find Bruce's caretaker.

"How's it going, Eileen?" he asked as she opened the door for him.

She was eating something at the kitchen counter while watching a soap opera.

"Who's sleeping with whose husband?" he asked.

"Looks like Nicolas's new wife kissed his brother, Adam," she said, shaking her head.

"That Adam Newman is never going to change," he said, making Eileen smile.

"It's good to see you, Mr. Michaud," she said cheerily. "He's in his study this afternoon."

Quinn nodded and walked through the kitchen to the main part of the house. The place felt like a grand hotel, not someone's home, as he heard his footsteps echo throughout the large dining room. He walked through the front hall, past the curved staircase, and down another hall to the end, where Bruce sat in a leather recliner.

He knocked on the door.

"Good to see you, Bruce." Quinn had never gotten used to calling his father-in-law by his first name. The owner of the law firm where he had started his career would always be senior partner Bruce Gerard.

"Quinn," he said. "Kyle didn't make it?"

"He had football," Quinn said.

This satisfied Bruce for now.

"What couldn't wait until Sunday?" His voice came out short and hard, as though Quinn's visit was an inconvenience. He'd never liked the fact that his daughter had married Quinn, the nameless associate that he liked to boss around.

"Isn't Kyle starting his senior year?" Bruce asked, not understanding the reason for Quinn's visit.

"Yes, he has one more year." Quinn took a deep breath. "And I'll need to start paying for college."

He hoped Bruce would pay for college like he had promised Lisa.

"Seems to me families go to the government for that kind of thing," Bruce said gruffly. "Not a grandfather he can't bother to stop by and see."

Quinn gritted his teeth. "I'll come back to work for you."

Bruce's mouth had opened to say something, but this stopped him. "Really? You'd come back to the firm?"

Quinn wanted nothing more than to tell this man where to shove it, but instead he nodded. "Yes, I'll come back to Portland."

"Well, I thought you were too good for *our* kind." Bruce fixed his cuff links. He still wouldn't let it all go.

"Lisa wanted Kyle to go to college," he reminded Bruce. What was he doing here? He should just take off and figure things out another way, but he knew Bruce would be on Quinn's side about fishing for lobsters. He didn't want his grandson to captain some fishing boat where he could lose his life. Quinn wasn't going to lose any more of his family if he could prevent it.

"If I come back to work," he said, "I want you to promise to pay for Kyle's college."

"Then what?" Bruce huffed. "You want me to pay for his apartment and wife next?"

Quinn squeezed his fists. He didn't need Bruce. He could go to another law firm that would pay enough so he could afford college and the house and all the expenses. It may be Ginny's house by right, but it had been his measly earnings that paid for it all. The electricity, the heat, the bills, the food, the taxes, the third mortgage his parents had decided to take out for an addition.

"It was good seeing you, Bruce," Quinn said, giving a small wave.

"You've become more sensitive than I remember," Bruce said. "If you come back, you'll need to promise me that you'll give me time. Not some four-year stint and leave when you get Kyle through college."

What was he doing? He should just leave, keep Bruce out of his life.

But Lisa loved that man.

"I'll come back to the firm," he said, but not committing. He wasn't that crazy. "But you have to get him to go."

Quinn hated to admit it, but Bruce would be the one who got Kyle to go to college. "He's interested in buying a boat with his college money."

He saw the anger seep into the hard creases of Bruce's face. He made a snarky comment that Quinn couldn't decipher into real words.

"He wants to fish?" Bruce looked disgusted. "Doesn't he know where he came from?"

That's the problem, thought Quinn. "I'll need to finish a few things before I can start."

"No grandson of mine is going to be slopping through

lobsters." Bruce looked like he smelled rotten fish. "Why is he wasting his life?"

Even after twenty years, Quinn still couldn't shake his inadequacies in front of this man. Where he had come from. Who his father was. What he'd grown up in. But he wasn't going to play into the shame he still harbored for growing up in the small nothing town around Bruce Gerard.

"I should go," Quinn said, jabbing his thumb behind him. "I have to meet up with clients for dinner."

Bruce got up from his chair. "I expect good work from you."

"I think I'll be ready to return to the firm as soon as the fall," Quinn said. "But only if you can secure Kyle's funding."

"Are you really that broke that you can't even afford college for your kid?" Bruce grumbled.

Quinn could feel his face heat up, and a quick slight sat on the tip of his tongue. There was so much he had stored in his mind to say to Bruce on his dying bed. Not when he was begging for college money.

"Bruce, I appreciate you keeping your promise to Lisa." Quinn watched Bruce's eyes shoot over at him at the mention of her name. "I know you want what's best for Kyle."

"I do," Bruce gruffed back.

Quinn nodded. "It's good to see you, Bruce. I'll talk to Kyle about coming by and seeing you on Sunday."

He would leave the rest up to him.

The drive home took a lot longer than he wanted it to. The heavy traffic crawled along 95. Once he took Blueberry Bay's exit, his nerves became more jittery the closer he got to home. A different kind of energy than with Bruce.

What was it about Meredith that got him all rattled? She was stunning. Like Cindy Crawford stunning. The kind of woman that woke up gorgeous without even putting on make-up. She also had a presence that he enjoyed in confident women—the way she didn't care how she behaved or what she said. So many women played nice.

Lisa had been the hardest bull attorney Quinn had ever worked with. It was why she'd been so good. No one had seen it coming from the five-foot-two petite woman.

She had also been the only one that wasn't afraid of Bruce. In fact, she could make him turn to mush by just giving him a look. His only daughter, his pride and joy, his only family besides the law firm.

Quinn thought about how that might be the last time he saw Bruce because he wasn't going back unless Kyle was going to college. He wanted his son to be able to play some football and be a kid. He could go somewhere close. Maine had great state schools, and New England had some of the best schools in the world. But he could go anywhere with Bruce's kind of money. The kid deserved more than just fishing.

CHAPTER 25

*M*eredith would never be able to describe it, but when she saw the boat, she almost cried.

She had never experienced a spiritual moment, never had that sense of something beyond her, but when Kyle walked them to the spot and showed her Jacqueline, a feeling of peace blanketed over her as she stood there staring at the boat sitting in the field behind the barn.

"He named it after Mom," Remy said. Her sister had fallen completely in love with the romance of their mother's first marriage, the whole story of Jacqueline and Jacob romanticized in her mind.

"Are you comfortable climbing up?" Kyle asked politely, but she couldn't help but laugh at how old he must think she was.

"I'm good," she said, holding onto the ladder and climbing her way up.

As they climbed aboard, she looked out at the boat's bow, which viewed the Atlantic. The water shimmered under the blazing sun. Behind her, a field of blueberry bushes climbed up the hill.

"You can sleep in it?" she asked, peeking inside the cabin and seeing a bed underneath.

Kyle's face blushed. "I must've forgotten to clean up."

This made her do a double take. "You slept in here?"

He nodded his head. "It's sort of like my treehouse. It's how Jacob figured out I wanted to learn to fish. I'd be up here pretending to be out on the water while he painted inside the barn. My dad would be at work, and Gram couldn't contain me."

She looked back and could see blankets and tossed pieces of clothes and books from years of use. "That must be fun."

"It was the best," Kyle said. "Jacob even let my dad put up a rope swing in the barn."

Meredith snuck a glance at the barn, imagining being a kid on this piece of land. And all the resentment that usually would anger her about Jacob didn't rise to the surface. A different, more curious feeling came. "That sounds incredible. Did Jacob ever take you out on the water?"

Kyle grinned wide. "All the time...once he got clean."

Kyle wiped off a bench along the side of the boat, and they all sat down in the sun.

"So, he went back out on the water?" Meredith had heard he never went back out.

"Only with me," Kyle said. "He taught me how to drive a boat and fish."

"You and Jacob fished together?" The thought of an old selective mute and a young boy amused her. "I think he felt like he had to help me."

"Jacob felt like he had to help you?" Meredith couldn't believe the relationship.

"I didn't talk either back then," Kyle said, and he paused for a moment. Then he dropped the bomb Meredith hadn't expected. "Not after my mom died."

Her heart immediately crushed at the thought of a silent little Kyle grieving his mother.

"It must've been wonderful to play on this farm," she said, holding back her own emotions.

"It was the best," he said again. "At first, my dad didn't like me playing on the boat and being with Jacob all the time, but then Gram got Jacob to stop drinking if he wanted to be around me." Kyle shrugged. "Gram can be very convincing."

Meredith laughed. "Yes, she seems like it."

"My whole life, I had heard about the storm of the century and the boat accident," he said, and like Ginny, Kyle had the gift of storytelling. He told the women about his first time fishing out on the water and how scared he was going out there after hearing stories about his great-grandfather. "But Jacob wasn't afraid. He felt most comfortable out on the water. I think he was afraid of being stuck on land like this boat."

"Why didn't he just go out then?" she asked, surprised that she even wanted to know more.

Remy took a double look at her.

"He couldn't drive it anymore." Kyle shrugged. "Gram says that part of him never left the ocean that day."

Kyle told more stories about going on the water. How he had learned to set traps and collect them days later. How the lobster will move with the seasons. How lobstermen are protective of their territories. And how he had inherited the whole cove from Jacob.

"Hardly anyone fishes anymore," Kyle said. "They're mostly paper pushers like my dad."

"Being a lawyer isn't being a paper pusher," Meredith argued. Then she thought of Phillip. She hadn't thought of Phillip in…a while. She smiled at herself. "Well, I guess, maybe a little."

Remy smiled at this, as though she was waiting for Meredith to have a breakdown at the mere mention of law or lawyers, which would surely lead her to think about Phillip.

They left the boat and returned to the barn to sift through Jacob's paintings, but the idea that part of Jacob had been left in the sea stuck with her. As she tagged and organized them the way Remy's friend had told them to, she couldn't help but notice how many paintings there were of the ocean.

As the day wore on, she could tell Kyle had better things to do than help her. He continuously checked his phone.

"You don't have to stay here and help," Meredith said, impressed that he had even offered. Would Ryan help a stranger sift through his neighbor's stuff?

"I'm happy to help," he said, stuffing the phone back into his pocket.

Ryan didn't even know about his grandfather's death or the house or anything that had to do with her.

In fact, what did her children know about her? They would call and check in, but her daughters lived their own lives. They were self-sufficient. And Ryan, well, he was still in his early twenties and in his own world.

But did she tell them things? Did she just hide her feelings like Remy? Or did they not bother to ask because they knew she would be bitter and angry toward their father?

She needed to call them.

Kyle took off at lunchtime, and Ginny came over midafternoon and began telling more stories about Jacob, about living in Blueberry Bay, and living on Jacob's "little slice of heaven," as Ginny referred to it.

"We started the Queen Bees so that we could feed the families who had lost their husbands and fathers in the storm," Ginny said. "For Jacqueline, for you, my mother, and all the others."

"For me?" she asked.

"Well, your mom was pregnant with you," Ginny said.

"The farm took care of my mother and me?" Meredith hadn't put that piece of the puzzle together.

"After the storm, well, we had to take care of each other," Ginny said. She pulled out another painting of Jacob's. "Now look at this one."

It was of a dark sky and stormy sea, but deep in the corner, along the horizon, was a soft light glowing in the distance, as if leading the ship to safety.

How could someone survive mentally after being the only survivor of such a horrific accident?

"Did he remember what happened?" Meredith asked.

"Jacob stopped talking after that," Ginny said, her eyes down at her fingers. "Your mother tried her very best, but Jacob was never the same." Ginny's face lit up as she remembered something. "That was when your dad came to Blueberry Bay."

"What do you mean?" Meredith took in Ginny's words. "Jacob?"

Ginny now appeared surprised. "No, your father, Gordon."

Meredith blinked a few times, processing what Ginny had said but not comprehending a single word.

"Gordon was in Blueberry Bay at the time of the accident?" Meredith said out loud. She whipped her head at Remy. "Did you know this?"

Remy frowned and nodded. "That's how he and Mom met."

"I'm the worst human being," Meredith said. "I let Jacob live all alone all this time because I didn't get birthday cards." Her throat closed at the thought of him dying alone in this house full of paintings, his mind going crazy. "He couldn't even write the cards."

Ginny gently placed her hand on Meredith's shoulder. "He wasn't well, dear. He got angry sometimes. He never hurt your mother but had become a bit violent. He drank, which exacerbated the whole situation. He was haunted a lot of other times. We know now it was PTSD, but back then, your mother didn't have the support. She had to stay with us some nights when things got real bad."

"But you all make him out to be this saint." Tears sprung to Meredith's eyes. "He took Kyle out on the water in the boat."

"He was complicated." Ginny sat down, sighing as she adjusted her position. "By the time Kyle came around, he was fully medicated. But back when you were a baby, he was very sick."

Meredith looked at the painting, and a memory so bright came flashing through her head.

It was of her mother and her on the beach, standing next to a man who was holding out his hand, showing off a piece of dazzling blue sea glass. Meredith's little fingers had reached out for it right away, and the man had given it to her, laughing. She'd held the azure glass up to the sun and looked through it.

"This is a mermaid tear," he had said to Meredith, squeezing her hands between his own. "You take the mermaid tear and make a wish, then throw it back to the sea as far as you can."

She hadn't waited a moment to make a wish, though she couldn't remember what she had wished for. She knew it was something frivolous, like a new bike or to have some new toy her friends had, because Meredith had been a very happy child. She had a wonderful childhood with a great family.

It had been Jacob who'd been abandoned.

Meredith wiped a fallen tear with the back of her hand. "Did he die alone?"

Ginny shook her head. "Don't you see?"

Meredith grabbed for a tissue and blew her nose. "See what?"

"We took care of him." Ginny smiled. "We all took care of him. He wasn't alone."

Ginny leaned over, patting Meredith on the knee. "And neither are you. We've got you, too."

And it was as if Ginny's words hit a release button, and Meredith's emotions flooded out.

Ginny leaned over, pulling Meredith into her arms. "Don't you think you're alone. This is your family now."

Meredith's head came up with the rational argument. They weren't her family. They were people who, through happenstance, lived next door to a father she never knew. But that was when she felt Remy's hand on her back.

"This is his gift to you," Remy said. "He gave you this as a gift, not for you to be burdened."

Meredith nodded, wiping her eyes with another tissue. "You're right."

She blew her nose again, feeling stupid and emotional and sensitive—as Phillip would say—and waited for the usual weight of anxiety and irrational stress to drape over her, but it peeled away as she exhaled out.

Her shaky hands began to calm down as she sat with Ginny and Remy, listening to the waves come in from the open windows. She steadied her breath, noticing a seagull crying out in the sky. A light breeze blew through the kitchen, lifting the to-do list off the table. Meredith reached out, slapping her hand down on it and holding it to the table. She looked at the list.

Call the real estate agent had been her next thing to do.

"When should we start dinner?" she asked, smiling at Remy, then Ginny.

CHAPTER 26

*W*hen Quinn reached the house, he pulled into the drive just as he saw Meredith step out onto the front porch. The evening sun still hung high. She held up her hand to cover her eyes.

She looked stunning in a blue linen dress, which flowed behind her in the wind. Suddenly, he saw the similarity between her and the bronze mermaid statue.

He waved, wishing he had driven faster down the highway. She waved back, and a smile grew across her face. And that was when he felt his heart skip a beat.

"Good evening," he said.

"Good evening." Meredith held a plate with a tin foil cover in her hands. "I brought my famous chocolate chip cookies."

"Kyle's going to be in heaven," Quinn said. "He's always loved homemade chocolate chip cookies."

She handed over the plate.

"Sorry if my mom pushed this dinner on you," he said, taking the plate in his hands, hoping that Ginny hadn't bothered them all day.

She shook her head. "Ginny's a pleasure."

This made him smile. "Glad to hear it. She can be pushy when she wants to be."

He held out his free hand to let her go first toward the house, but she hesitated and smiled at him. And that was when he felt that crazy knee-buckling thing he'd done when he'd seen Lisa that very first time.

He was in trouble whether Meredith sold the house or stayed.

"Meredith!" Kyle called out from their porch.

Her smile grew when she saw Kyle waving at her. "Kyle! Guess what?"

"What's that?" Kyle asked, stepping over to Quinn. "Are these the chocolate chip cookies?"

"The same ones we were telling you about," Meredith said, walking away from Quinn to Kyle.

Quinn couldn't pinpoint what had transpired since he'd left after breakfast that morning besides the fact that Kyle hadn't mowed the lawn, but things had changed.

"Kyle showed me everything about the boat," Meredith said, not realizing the fuse she'd set off.

He shot Kyle a look, and the relief he had been feeling sunk like an anchor. "Right, the boat."

"Gram already has the lobsters stuffed," Kyle said to Meredith and took the plate from Quinn's hands.

"Great," Quinn said as Kyle led Meredith to the house.

"Hi, Quinn," Remy said from behind, holding a large bouquet of flowers in her hands. She passed a bottle he immediately recognized as a very expensive Michelin chardonnay. "Thank you for inviting us."

"Well, I'm glad Ginny hasn't scared you all out of town," he joked, wondering if this change of heart was actually true.

Remy smiled and said, "Kyle helped us all afternoon moving the paintings around so we could put them in categories. I have a friend coming up from Boston in a couple of weeks."

"That's great," he said, watching Kyle through the window as he talked to Meredith and Ginny. "I'm glad he's been helpful."

"He's been great," Remy said. "He's also been a big help moving furniture around, helping us tidy up the place. It's amazing how much better it looks just after a little bit of cleaning."

He looked up at the house and saw Meredith laugh with Kyle as Ginny opened the door for them to come inside. Meredith's eyes closed, her head thrown back, her hair falling just perfectly from her face.

Man, he was in so much trouble.

Because he couldn't afford to fall for a woman who clearly wasn't over her ex-husband, who had issues with her recently deceased father, and who wasn't likely sticking around.

Why did he always find the one woman who would give him the most trouble?

Dating Lisa should have taught him not to mix his business life with his personal life, especially when it came to dating his boss's daughter.

What was he doing checking out Jacob's daughter?

Inside, Ginny had music playing.

"Is this Carol King?" Meredith asked.

Ginny smiled at the recognition, and that was when he saw the same love in her eyes. She had fallen for this woman as well.

It had been Remy who started clapping as the lobsters came out, but Kyle joined with Meredith, so he started clapping too. Kyle poured everyone water, while Quinn gave the adults a glass of wine. Ginny had the kitchen set up with real dinner plates and napkins, along with the proper silverware, though it was mismatched.

Everyone talked throughout their meal. First came the compliments to the chef, then stories about Blueberry Bay. Kyle told them about school and football and his girlfriend.

"What was it like playing for the Boston Symphony Orchestra?" he asked, amazed at the level she must have been to be in such a profession. "It must be even harder to be a professional musician than a professional athlete."

Meredith nodded. "As a woman, it's a hundred times harder."

"Meredith was one of the only female pianists ever to play piano for the orchestra," Remy said, clearly proud of her older sister's accomplishments.

"Do you teach?" Ginny asked.

"I have students, but they usually take the summers off," she said.

"What about performing again?" Ginny asked. "We have music at the park on Tuesday nights."

She shook her head. "I'm afraid I don't have the time to be as good as I used to be."

Quinn felt that one. He had loved so many things before Lisa died and now he rarely did anything other than work or drive Kyle around or watch television. When was the last time he had a project or went biking or hiking? He used to love working outside and building things with his hands. Now he hardly left the couch.

"Should we have those cookies?" Kyle asked at the perfect time, shifting the moment back to the present, and it struck Quinn at how mature his son was becoming.

The women stayed for a cup of coffee and a few cookies each. By the time they left, Kyle had taken off with his girlfriend.

"Thank you for such a nice night," Meredith said. "And everything else. Really, thank you for everything."

Ginny hugged Meredith like she was a long-lost daughter, swaying her back and forth. Quinn knew Ginny was squeezing the air out of her, but Meredith didn't seem to mind. She held onto Ginny like one would when they didn't want to be let go of.

After the sisters left, Ginny went to take her nightly bath while Quinn cleaned up the kitchen. A rule enforced since he was a kid—the cook never cleaned. And since he never had the time to cook, he spent his nights cleaning up. He didn't mind tonight. He had quite a bit to think about, and his hands needed to do something when he had a lot to think about.

It was a couple of hours later when he finally decided to go to bed. When he climbed the staircase, he couldn't help but notice all the lights were off in Jacob's cottage. When he reached the top of the landing, he saw the flicker of a fire on the beach.

Kyle. What was his son doing at this time of night having a bonfire on someone else's property? Did the kid not think?

He rolled his eyes as he looked at the time. It was midnight for goodness' sake. He had wanted to get up early and finish some things at the house before heading to the office and dealing with Kyle's football schedule. He could give Kyle the truck and walk to work or at least get Ginny to drive them both. It was silly how they drove from the same house to the same place of work.

Though, Ginny never came on time or stayed the full day. She had too much to do for the Queen Bees and the other town activities to devote a hundred percent, which meant he would end up walking anyway.

He dragged himself back down the stairs, put on his shoes, and left the house with his flashlight. With the moon as full as it was, Quinn didn't need the flashlight. Not like he would've really needed it even without the moon. He knew the trail to the beach as well as the back of his hand. Apparently, so did Kyle. That could become a real problem, with Meredith being the new owner.

He kept his eyes on his footing as he stepped around the granite boulders and thorns of the beach roses on the sandy path. When he glanced over at the bonfire, he realized it wasn't Kyle but Meredith sitting alone and facing the water.

He stopped in his tracks, the sand shifting under his shoes, wondering if he should continue. The fire glowed against the silhouette of her face, and she looked content, at peace watching the waves lap up against the shore.

When he turned around to leave, he slipped on a rock and the sand underneath his shoe's sole, and she turned just as he caught himself.

"I'm sorry to startle you," he said as she stood right up, her eyes wide with fright. "I thought you were Kyle and his girlfriend."

She put her hand on her chest. "You scared the living daylights out of me."

He held out his hands, steadying himself and wishing he had never bothered to come in the first place. "I'm so sorry."

She sat down, back on a piece of driftwood, and began to laugh. "That totally freaked me out."

"I know," he said, not sure what to do at this point. "I'm really sorry."

She shook her head. "I actually saw a bonfire the other night with Kyle and his girlfriend."

He groaned silently to himself.

"So, it makes sense." She pointed up to the sky. "My son used to sneak out at night and meet his girlfriend at his grandfather's house." She shook her head. "My dad never heard a thing."

Quinn laughed. "They think they're being so sneaky."

She smiled at that. "I didn't mean to wake you."

He shook his head. "I was awake. I just saw the fire. I should've figured it wasn't any of my business. I apologize."

"Would you like to join me?"

He hesitated but recognized the gesture. She hadn't offered for him to come into her space like she had with Ginny and Kyle. She had been polite, but this felt different. Her energy felt different. Calm.

"Sure," he said, walking down toward the fire. The night had a chill from the breeze coming off the water. He sat down in the sand to her right, his focus toward the house. He hadn't told anyone where he was going, and he hadn't thought to bring his phone. "Is Remy back at the house?"

Meredith nodded. "She went to bed just a bit ago."

"Ah," he said. He wasn't sure where to take the conversation. Did he bring up business as usual? Talk about Jacob's assets? But instead, he asked, "Do you still play?"

She looked at him as though she didn't know what he was talking about.

"The piano?" he said, wondering if he got it wrong. "You played the piano, right?"

She nodded and looked out at the water. "No. I stopped playing after my mother died."

That was when he saw the familiar grief wash over her.

"When I lost my wife, I stopped everything that didn't involve Kyle," he said, wanting her to not feel so alone about it all. "So, I stopped going to my poker night, my racquetball group, my career, dating…"

Meredith thought about her own grief. "I thought I was fooling everyone, but it was only myself."

She leaned her head on her arms, looking into the fire.

"I've taught piano lessons for years," she said. "I loved it." Her eyes danced back and forth as she watched the flames. "When my mother was sick, I stopped most of my lessons to take care of her, but after she died, the kids I had taught had moved on."

He thought how she must have felt. How alone she must have felt. He knew that loneliness. "I'm so sorry."

"My children had left the house by then," she said, shrugging. "I had been so wrapped up in my own grief that I never saw my marriage falling apart around me."

"That's a big blow."

"So is losing your wife."

He nodded. "I'm sorry you lost your father before you knew what a good man he was."

Tears sprung to her eyes as she smiled. "Thank you for that."

She looked back at the water, exhaling out a long breath.

He looked out to the moon. Its light drew a line across the ocean, splitting the Atlantic in two. Looking down, he saw a piece of sea glass and picked it up.

"Make a wish," he said to her, holding out the blue piece.

"What did you say?" she asked, her eyes widening. She held out her hand to the piece of sea glass.

"Make a wish?" He placed the small piece in her palm when he looked up and focused on her lips. "It's a mermaid kiss."

"I thought it was a mermaid tear," she said, looking at him questioningly, but with a smile across her face.

"Oh, right!" He laughed at his fumble, embarrassed of his Freudian slip. "A mermaid tear."

"I think I'm going to hold on to this one," she said, keeping it in her palm. "I need to save my wishes these days."

He needed all the wishes he could get as well.

"Thanks for coming for dinner," he said. "I can't remember the last time the house was that boisterous."

It had been well before his Pops had died. Maybe even since Lisa had passed.

"How long has it been without your wife?" she asked.

He could feel her reluctance to ask the question. Funny thing was, he wanted to talk about Lisa, but everyone tiptoed around her death, even him.

"She died about ten years ago." Ten years and twenty-two days, to be exact.

"I'm so sorry," she said. Her eyes met his with a sadness that pulled at his heart. "I can't imagine losing my spouse when my children were practically babies. It must've been so hard for both you and Kyle."

Quinn didn't like thinking about the little boy who had lost his mother. "People kept telling me time would heal all, but with a kid, I feel like it's harder now that he's getting older, becoming an adult himself."

Meredith rested her head on her knees. "No one told me that parenting gets more complicated the older they get."

Quinn laughed out at that one. That was exactly how he felt. "I just wish I had someone to run things by. Remind me I'm doing okay as a dad. You know? I'm the good parent and the bad parent."

"My children are grown and out of the house, but I still live like a housewife with three little ones at home," she said. "I get up at the same time and do the same things. Go to the grocery store, clean the house, run errands, do laundry. I'm still making dinner every night as if someone will stop in. Not even my dad, who lives down the street, stops by that much. I don't even eat half the time. Then I watch television and go to bed."

"I still sleep on one side of the bed," Quinn confessed. The feelings of losing Lisa came and went like the waves. "Sometimes I feel like I just lost her yesterday, and other times it was a whole other lifetime." He couldn't explain his crazy thoughts or why he was even sharing them in the first place with this beautiful woman, but somehow Meredith felt…safe.

"I think about how much things have changed since my husband and I divorced and if I'm this whole new person," she said, staring back at him. "I'm probably a whole new person since last week!"

She laughed as she looked out at the water. The fire danced across her face and Quinn couldn't take his eyes off her. Meredith had never looked more at peace and more beautiful than she did at that moment.

"This has been the most bizarre week of my life," she said. She wiped sand away from the cuff of her pants.

"I understand if you want to sell," he said, wanting the elephant sitting between them out in the open.

She focused on the water. "I don't think I do want to sell. Not right now at least. Not after learning so much, while also not knowing enough."

Something about the way she didn't look at him made Quinn hold his breath for the bad news.

"But…" He waited for it.

"I can't afford two houses, that's for sure," she said, sticking her finger in the sand. She paused and he could feel her about to release a bomb.

"Kyle asked me to sell the boat to him," she said.

He closed his eyes.

"I wasn't sure if you told him I was thinking of selling, but I thought I'd come to you before I do sell it," she said.

He appreciated that she did. "Thank you."

"So?" she said. "What does a seventeen-year-old want a boat like that for?"

"He wants to catch lobsters," he said. How could he break his son's dreams by telling him to use his hard-earned money for a degree he doesn't want?

She picked up a handful of sand and let it softly fall back onto the ground. "You don't sound like you like that idea."

"I would rather he go to college than fish for lobsters," he said. "It's dangerous."

He could see the twitch of recognition in her eyes. "I won't sell it to him."

He didn't want her to sell it to him, but he also couldn't tell her what to do. It was her boat now. "I can't force you to sell or not sell."

"You aren't forcing me to do anything," Meredith said, drawing a circle in the sand.

"How much did he offer?" He didn't know if this was being too nosy or not.

Meredith looked up from her circles. "Twenty thousand dollars."

Quinn choked at the amount. Kyle had that kind of cash? How much did fishermen make these days?

"That's money that could go to college, I'm guessing," she said. Her face twisted as she waited for his response.

"It sure is," Quinn said, feeling totally defeated as a parent. He had no idea Kyle had saved up that much. He knew he had been hauling lobsters since he could get out on a boat, but twenty grand? "I promised my wife that I would make sure he went to college." He sighed. "I can't even do that."

"Is it safe?" she asked. "Have you ever taken Jacob's boat out before?"

He hesitated, hoping she wouldn't be upset by this. "Sure, I have."

"Is it inspected and registered?" she asked.

He nodded.

"And what about selling it?" she asked. "Is twenty thousand dollars the right price?"

Kyle giving cash would make the deal easy and fair. Quinn hated being so honest. "It is."

She looked at him. "Well, I've never been on a boat before, so I'd really like to see what it's like before I even think about selling it."

"Okay," Quinn said.

"But, in the meantime, I think I'm going to start selling his art," she said. "There's no way I can display all of it for my own use. Remy thinks I should have an auction. I would rather people enjoy his work than have it hidden away and slowly destroyed by mildew in an old barn."

He sat up at the prospect of her selling the art and holding onto the boat for now. "That sounds like a great idea."

"Remy keeps telling me to look at Jacob's cottage as a gift." Meredith turned to Quinn, her gaze set on his, and fire danced in her eyes as she said, "I think she may be right."

CHAPTER 27

*M*eredith woke to another night of great sleep and could feel something *had* changed with her. She could feel a shift. She didn't have that stab of pain at waking up alone. She didn't grab her phone to see if Phillip had called, even though she knew he wouldn't. She didn't dread the day that lay ahead of her but looked forward to it. And she looked forward to seeing someone.

The thought of Quinn walking her home made her smile. When was the last time a handsome man had walked her home? Had Phillip even?

She loved her husband...ex-husband, but he wasn't one for opening doors and making sure she made it home. He never checked to see if she was okay or brought home chicken noodle soup when she was sick. Besides money, Phillip never really took care of Meredith at all.

And now, with the divorce, he didn't even offer her share of their money but, instead, he legally took it from her.

Maybe she did need a lawyer—not some negotiator like Phillip had suggested at the beginning of his mess.

She could feel the usual anxiety start to make her restless. She threw back the blankets and went straight to the window and threw

175

it open. She stuck her head out, closed her eyes, and inhaled. Two seagulls swooped by feet away from her head, and it made her jump, which made her hit her head, and she opened her eyes to see Remy on a yoga mat on the back porch, stretching her arms up to the sky.

"You okay?" Remy asked in her sun salutation.

Meredith grabbed her head. "I'm good. Just clumsy."

The sun just peaked above the line on the horizon, and Meredith froze at the sight of it all. Pinks, lavenders, fuchsias all spread across the whole span of the sky. The world looked as though it had been set ablaze.

When Meredith went downstairs, Remy came inside with a towel wrapped around her neck.

"Let's go swimming," Remy said.

Meredith's first instinct was to say no, but she stopped herself. Why was she saying no first?

"Let me make a cup of coffee," she said.

Remy beamed as she said this. The two sisters made hot drinks and took them as they walked along the sandy path through purple lupines and pink beach plum roses, giggling like two schoolgirls on an adventure.

"I bet Mom's watching us right now," Remy said.

"I bet she is," she said to Remy.

To get to the beach, Meredith learned from Quinn to follow the smaller path along the rocky side of the cliff, not the grassy path around, even though it looked safer. Like a mirage, the grassy path looked like it led to the beach, but it only led the traveler to a high vista and a dead end.

Carefully, they climbed through the granite rocks, holding the cold stone with one hand, and their drink in the other until they reached the beach.

"Do you know what this beach is called?" Remy asked.

"No." Meredith shook her head. Out on the horizon, a lobster boat sped along the water. Its engine quietly roared from a distance.

"You ready?" Remy asked, pulling off her sweatshirt.

Meredith dipped her toe in. The cold shot right up her leg. "We should have run here to warm up first."

"Once we get in, it'll be fine," Remy said. "We just have to do it."

"It's Maine."

"So?" Remy didn't understand the reference.

"It's known for its freezing waters." Meredith looked at the water, the boat gone, and all she could hear was her breath and the waves rolling to shore.

"Lame." Remy pulled down her pants and stood in her bathing suit. "Chicken."

"Okay." Meredith pulled down her leggings. "Let's not stand around if we're going to do this."

On a count of three, the sisters ran forward, jumping over the waves and falling into the water. The whole thing must have looked uncoordinated and blundering. Meredith came to the surface, floating in the Atlantic, and wiped the salt water away from her eyes. All she could see was water all around her. She had never felt so alive.

"This is amazing!" she yelled out, floating up and down with the waves coming to shore.

Remy laughed, diving into a wave. "We need to do this every morning!"

And Meredith realized she could do this every morning.

The sisters floated for a long time, just listening to the waves. Their bodies adjusting to the cool Atlantic water.

"I need to call the kids and let them know what's going on," Meredith said, breaking the silence between them.

Remy nodded as she floated on her back. Meredith waited for her to stick her advice in somehow, but Remy stayed quiet.

"But I think I will stay until the fall at least," Meredith said. She didn't know what was holding her back from calling them. She knew she had to do it. Was she afraid they wouldn't care? Or was she afraid they'd be upset with her for not talking to them about their grandfather?

Remy's arms moved back and forth, keeping her afloat. "I think that's a great idea."

Meredith nodded, looking up at the sky. "I mean, the festival is at the end of August. We should at least stay for that."

"What about home?" Remy asked. "What about Ryan?"

Meredith floated over a wave. "He'll be okay on his own this summer."

Remy stopped floating and stood. The water line hit her neck. Meredith knew her sister wanted to stay, too.

"You need to call your husband," Meredith said.

Remy nodded. "I know I need to talk to him. I just don't know what to say."

"Maybe you should just start by talking about what we've been up to." The past few days, she hadn't seen Remy talk on the phone or text him or even mention Joe. "It's none of my business, but shouldn't he know what's going on with you?"

Remy smiled and it was the saddest smile Meredith had ever seen. "That's the thing. He does know. He just doesn't care."

"What?" Meredith didn't understand. "He knows you're this upset?"

Remy shook her head. "It's complicated."

Meredith knew complicated. "If there's one thing I have learned from my own divorce, it's that not talking about things is what lead to our problems."

Remy shrugged. "I'm pretty sure Joe's done talking at this point."

Meredith wouldn't push it. Remy didn't need a mother hen. Remy needed a friend. She needed her sister.

"Let's skip the list today," Meredith said. "Let's lay out all day and go out to that restaurant tonight."

Remy's eyes sparkled, even if they were flooded with tears. "That sounds fabulous."

The two sisters got out of the water, collected their things from the beach, and rushed back to the cottage, talking the whole way about their new plans.

When they arrived back, they saw a few women in their straw hats floating among the blueberry bushes. The sight of them brought comfort to Meredith for some reason, as if the day would be just fine because they were working the fields.

As Meredith opened the door to the kitchen, an older woman stood in the kitchen with the refrigerator door wide open.

Meredith dropped her drink and Remy screamed out. "Ah!"

"Oh, hello!" the woman said as Meredith held onto the door.

"Hello?" Meredith asked, wondering how this stranger had gotten in. Did she need to start locking all the doors?

"I'm sorry I startled you," the woman said, either completely unaware she was trespassing, or she didn't care. "I'm Carolyn, Ginny's sister."

"Can I help you, Carolyn?" Meredith asked, wondering why she was standing in the kitchen.

Remy appeared amused by the woman's presence inside the cottage.

"I'm just dropping off my blueberry coffee cake for you girls," Carolyn said. She slowly closed the refrigerator door and held onto her cane. "It looks good in here. You ladies did a nice job picking up Jacob's mess."

Meredith eased as the woman looked around the room giving her approval. She felt a sudden pride. The place did look good. Really good. Meredith, Remy, and Kyle had worked until the whole kitchen was sparkling and shining. Remy removed the clutter from all the shelves and most of the random furniture stuffed with more junk. In its place, Remy found two wingback chairs and sat them in front of the woodstove.

Before, a big, bulky China hutch stood in front of a set of pocket doors that led to the dining room. It took all three of them to move the hutch out of the kitchen and open the doors. Kyle and Remy moved the oversized table and desk out of the kitchen, which opened the space even more.

Jacob must have used the dining room for his "entertainment" room, but he had no television, only a radio, a record and tape player, and an old Boston upright piano. They removed the recliner and all the paintings except a few chosen by Remy, kept the piano, and brought the table in.

"Gosh, I haven't seen it look this good since your grandmother was alive," Carolyn said.

Meredith's interest was hooked. "My grandmother?"

Carolyn nodded. "She was so good at taking care of a home."

The elderly woman looked at Meredith. "You look a lot like her."

In all of Meredith's life, she never reminded anyone of her family. Not Jacqueline, or Gordon. She and Remy looked nothing alike. She had never met Jaqueline's family, but her mother never said she looked like anyone. She wanted to know even more. "Would you like to sit down and have some coffee cake with us?"

Remy took the hint. "We were just about to make some coffee and have something to eat."

Carolyn seemed pleased at the idea. "I'd love to join you ladies."

Meredith ushered Carolyn to the dining room.

"Your grandmother only had Jacob," Carolyn explained as she shuffled along. "When the boys didn't come back after the storm, the whole town went out looking for survivors for days. Your grandmother, Meredith, was beside herself. Then came the miracle that Jacob had survived."

"Did you know our mother?" Remy asked.

Carolyn nodded. "Sure did. Jacqueline was lovely. I'm sorry to hear she passed away."

Remy grinned at the stranger.

"Then your grandmother got sick," Carolyn said, looking around the room. "Which is how your parents met."

"What? I thought my parents met during the summers here," Meredith said, setting a napkin down on a decorative placemat Remy had found.

"Your father is Dr. Johnson, isn't he?" Carolyn said. "Nice fellow. He was your grandmother's doctor when she fell ill. He was all our doctors. The only town doctor at the time. When your grandmother got sick, your mom took care of her. You were just a kid back then."

"Gordon was the town doctor," Remy said, sitting down next to Carolyn.

Meredith looked down at the table, trying to focus. Then like a bubble bursting, she suddenly remembered that exact room and the fabric of the placemat before. "I was around four."

"Yes, that's right," Carolyn said, pointing to her.

Meredith had a quick memory of a fireplace and paintings. "It was during the winter." She tried sifting through the rabbit holes of her memories, but she didn't remember Jacob. "Was Jacob there?"

Carolyn shook her head. "At that point, Jacob's drinking was out of control. He was barely around." Carolyn shook her head as she wrapped her hands around the mug. Meredith handed her a napkin as Remy set down a small plate of blueberry coffee cake with a silver fork. "Your mother tried to make it work, but how much can you have your daughter exposed to before you need to make a better choice?"

Her mother had to leave.

Carolyn sunk her fork into the coffee cake. "And look at how wonderful you turned out to be!"

Meredith smiled at the elderly woman.

"But he sobered up," Meredith said, but it was more of a question.

"There were times he could stay away from drinking," Carolyn said after she finished chewing. "But he was a very private man. Hardly left the house. Ever."

Remy bit into the coffee cake. "Oh my goodness! This is good, Carolyn."

The older woman didn't look surprised by her reaction. "It's your blueberries."

The pronoun made Meredith take her own bite. The sweetness of the blueberries and the sugary crumble mixed in with the light and fluffy cake was heavenly.

"This is amazing," Meredith mumbled. She had never tasted anything like it—just like with the scones and the blueberry muffins before that. "There really is something about the blueberries around here."

"They're one of a kind," Carolyn said. "Very few places in Maine grow this kind of wild blueberry."

Meredith took another bite and thought about that winter with her mother and Gordon. It held some of her first memories. She didn't remember a dying grandmother or an alcoholic father, only a mother who had taken her to the beach in her snowsuit and a man who had dinner with them, who was Gordon.

"You girls really did a nice job in here," Carolyn said again, looking around the room.

Meredith hadn't noticed all the changes Remy had made just this morning. Purple, pink, and white lupine sat in a vase on a buffet. A large painting of the vista, which Meredith referred to as the beach plum trail, hung above it. The windows shined as light streamed in from outside. Instead of paintings stuffed and piled everywhere, a cute fireplace now became a focal point with built-in shelves surrounding it.

And like finding that last piece of a puzzle, Meredith could see the whole picture.

"My parents didn't start dating until she moved to Boston that following spring," Meredith said. She scratched her forehead, trying to focus a foggy memory. "Did you visit us in Boston?"

Carolyn nodded. "That's right. We helped you and your mother move into your apartment down there."

Meredith suddenly remembered women helping her mother with boxes and a van. That memory now vivid and alive in her mind.

Carolyn stayed for over an hour talking about everything, including the local theater group. "I heard you play the piano."

Meredith didn't know what to say because she wasn't sure where this might be going.

"We're looking for a pianist at the local theater," Carolyn said. "I've been all they've had for years, but I'm afraid these old girls aren't as they used to be."

Carolyn held up her arthritic hands, and Meredith flinched at the sight.

"It's why I can't work in the fields with the Queens," she said, looking down at her fingers, then waving them. "But I can still bake some blueberry coffee cake."

"Thank goodness for that," Remy said, taking her finger and picking up the last few crumbles on the plate.

When Carolyn left, Meredith grabbed a few things and took out a wicker picnic basket she'd found in the garage. She stuffed it with the beach essentials, sunscreen, a few books from the bookshelf, jugs of water, snack foods that had either salt or chocolate in them, and more of Carolyn's coffee cake.

She changed into a bathing suit she had picked up at the beginning of summer that she had never worn. The one she forced herself to buy with her friend but would never be brave enough to wear in public.

"I think I'm going to call the kids today," she said. She thought about the Fourth and if she would go back to the house in Andover, just in case Ryan decides to come back.

"You should invite them up here," Remy said. "We could get the other rooms ready. How great would it be to have everyone here?"

"We should include Dad," Meredith said.

Remy smiled. "I bet he'd love that."

Meredith nodded, closing the picnic basket. "Why don't I meet you on the beach in a little bit."

Remy took the basket and popped her earbuds in. "I have a great new audiobook I need to finish anyway."

Meredith appreciated Remy giving her space.

She picked up her cell phone and dialed her eldest daughter

first. Cora had been living in South Boston for a few years working as a waitress. From a mother's perspective, Cora had been an amazing first child—easy as a baby. So easy, she had gotten pregnant right away with Muriel, who had been anything but easy. When the girls were both in school, Ryan came along.

"Hey, Mom," Cora said into the phone. Meredith could hear someone talking in the background.

"Did I catch you at a bad time?" Meredith asked, looking at the clock.

"Well, it's ten o'clock on a weekday," she said, almost exasperated.

"Right. Well, I just wanted to invite you to a cottage on the beach up in Maine," Meredith said.

"When?" she said.

"Whenever, really." Meredith didn't know how she could explain everything in the brief time period Cora usually gave her on the phone. "But there's a blueberry festival at the end of August. It should be really fun."

"Um, sure. Where is this place?" Cora asked.

"It's on the beach in Maine. Right on the beach, actually," Meredith said. "I'll send you pictures of it, because it's mine."

She couldn't believe it. The cottage by the sea was hers. *Le gîte en bord de Mer.* That's what it's called. The cottage by the Sea. I inherited my father's cottage—my birth father."

Cora didn't say anything for a while. "Are you okay?"

"Yes, why?" Meredith could hear the concern in her daughter's voice.

"Well, if you've inherited a cottage, doesn't that mean your birth father died?" Cora asked.

"Yes, he did," Meredith said. She thought of the dozens of little reasons why she shouldn't have told the kids. Phillip and his wife just had the baby. She hardly ever mentioned Jacob being her father, so his death meant even less than it had to her.

She stopped the excuses, but the truth was, his death *had* meant something to her.

"Yes, he passed away at the beginning of the summer," Meredith said. "I just recently found out myself."

"How long have you been in Maine?" Cora asked.

"Only a little while," Meredith said. "I'll send you the address. It's beautiful."

"Are you going to stay there?" Cora asked, surprised.

"For the summer, yes." She was a little more confident with her answer this time. Then before she knew what she was saying, she said, "I'm thinking of selling the house."

"Really?" Cora sounded as shocked as Meredith felt.

"Yes, I think it's time to downsize." It was the truth, but she hadn't ever cared about the size before. "I wish you kids wanted it."

It had been a wonderful house to raise a family in.

"Maybe Muriel and her boyfriend will leave the woods of New Hampshire," Cora said.

Meredith knew how Cora disapproved of her sister's choices.

"I don't think a teacher's salary can cover it," Meredith said. Only a lawyer's salary could keep up with the costs of living in Andover. "The property taxes alone are outrageous."

Cora sighed into the phone. "I guess I could try to make it up there."

"That sounds great," Meredith said. "Aunt Remy is here with me."

"You're with Aunt Remy?" Cora didn't hide her disbelief. "Since when did you two start hanging out?"

"Well, I called her about Jacob," Meredith said.

"Who?"

The question hung in the air, and Meredith looked at the painting Remy had hung up in the living room, the one of Jacqueline holding Meredith's hand along the beach. She did remember, and now she was starting to remember the man following behind her.

"My father," Meredith said.

CHAPTER 28

Quinn watched as Meredith walked into the second floor of the town hall, where the meeting of the Queen Bees officially took place. It was also where the sock hop and community basketball league were held.

"Quinn," she said, surprised to see him in the crowd of women wearing their bee pins proudly on their chests. Quinn did not wear one. "Are you a Bee, too?"

A smirk grew as Meredith watched his reaction.

"I can't officially become a Queen," he said.

"Really?" Meredith seemed surprised by this. "Because they're female?"

He shook his head. "I'm allergic to bees."

"That's why I haven't seen you in the fields," she said. "That's too bad."

He stuffed his hands in his pockets. "I'm here to explain about Jacob and the property."

"Right," she said. "They invited me and Remy to meet everyone."

"Good luck getting home," he whispered. "Pauline tends to be long-winded."

"Who's Pauline?" Meredith whispered back.

He gestured his head at the badly dyed blonde who came marching her way over to Meredith.

"You must be Jacob's daughter!" Pauline said, sticking her hand out at Meredith before she even reached her.

"Oh," Meredith said as Pauline took her hand into hers. "Good to meet you."

"Ginny's told us all about you girls," Pauline said. "Quinn! So glad you finally made it."

He almost objected by countering that he had attended their emergency meeting just a couple weeks ago when he'd given the news of Jacob's passing, but he didn't want to look like a jerk in front of Meredith.

"I want to support any way I can," Quinn said.

Sue smiled, patting him on the arm as she walked away. "Don't forget to grab something to eat over on the table."

He noticed Remy already standing over there, checking out what they had.

"They have the scones!" Remy said, holding one up.

Meredith leaned over. "Is everything made with blueberries?"

"Your blueberries," Pauline said from across the room, as she hit a small gavel on the makeshift podium. "Let's get to it, shall we?" Pauline said to the group of women who stood around the baked goods.

And that's how the meeting began. Pauline banged the gavel, Ginny took her spot as secretary, and Mary Ellen gave the treasury report. From the beginning of the meeting, things were more serious than usual. For one, Carolyn didn't talk throughout the meeting. No one had to take a bathroom break, and everyone seemed to have come. They haven't had full attendance in years.

"We want to start off the meeting by saying a small prayer, followed by a moment of silence for our brother Jacob O'Neill," Pauline said. She began the Lord's Prayer, and then she looked at Meredith. "There were a lot of stories shared about Jacob O'Neill over the years, mostly legends at this point."

The crowd murmured in agreement.

"But I will never forget, after I lost Michael that day, how scared I was," Pauline said. "Scared about paying my bills, scared about raising two children, scared I wouldn't be able to even shovel my driveway. Michael had done everything."

Quinn saw Remy pull out a tissue as she sat beside him. When he saw tears in Meredith's eyes as she listened to Pauline, he couldn't help but be more enamored with her. Here was a woman who had been beaten down by life, yet she was empathetic as she sat there among the Queen Bees.

"Then winter came," Pauline said, looking directly at the sisters with tears in her eyes. They were the only ones who hadn't heard the story.

The other women hummed out different sounds in agreement, nodding and waiting for Pauline to continue.

"That's when we got hit by the nor'easter, and the whole town lost power." She looked out at the crowd and smiled. "And who was out there plowing before anyone woke up?"

The ladies all said his name in unison. "Jacob."

"And who put money in our mailboxes that winter to feed our children?" Pauline said.

"Jacob," the women said.

Pauline nodded at the small crowd. "So ladies, tonight let's dedicate this meeting to our dear friend Jacob. May he finally rest in peace."

And Meredith closed her eyes and quietly said, "May he rest in peace."

After Pauline passed the floor to Ginny, she sat down in the seats with the other ladies as Ginny introduced Meredith.

"This is Meredith Johnson," she said correctly. "She's Jacob's daughter. She's now the owner of the estate. She's agreed to allow us to continue with our season as usual."

All the ladies smiled at this.

"How wonderful," Hazel said, clapping her hands together.

"However, we cannot continue on as normal." Ginny narrowed her eyes at Carolyn. "We must respect the new owner and not treat the property like we have with Jacob over the years. We can't go inside without permission."

Carolyn made a face. "Sorry, girls."

Meredith waved her hand at Carolyn. "It's fine. Just make sure we're home before going in?"

Quinn couldn't help but laugh at Meredith's polite response. He leaned forward in his seat. "Ladies, you should only be using the fields and the barn. If you need to use a restroom, Ginny and I have always been happy to provide that for you."

"Oh, if you need a restroom—" Meredith began to say, but Quinn held out his hand.

"If they need a restroom, use Ginny's place for now," he said, shaking his head at her. "Our house is closer anyway."

"We're not saying you've been impolite," Remy threw out. "We have been completely welcomed into the community. My sister and I are just in awe at all you've done to take care of one another over the years."

"We didn't have a choice," Ginny said. "We needed one another."

Quinn looked out at the women. All of them were later in age. How long could they continue working as Queen Bees before they all couldn't do it anymore? Most of them had passed away.

"Now we'll want to start thinking about this year's yield and next years," Barbara Roberts said.

"Now that she's moving the paintings out of the barn, maybe we can use it," Hazel said. "Set up in there for the festival like the old days. That way we can keep the equipment for the spring right on the property."

"Well, I, um—" Meredith began to say.

"And we could store the trimmers there for the winter," Carolyn said, leaning over to Remy. "We got a heck of a deal about five years ago."

"Has it already been five years?" Ginny asked, and every one of the women began calculating the time by events in their lives.

"It was when I had my glaucoma surgery," Hazel said. "Remember?"

"Um, well, I might not be here," Meredith said. It was spoken so quietly that the women arguing about when they'd bought a power trimmer for the bushes couldn't hear the bomb Meredith had just dropped on them.

"Ladies," Quinn said, using his deep voice to power over their volume.

All the women turned in his direction.

He cleared his throat, a tad nervous with everyone waiting for him to talk.

"Meredith is allowing you use of the land *this* season," he said, emphasizing the use of this.

"Oh," Hazel said.

The chatter around the room stopped.

"You're selling the farm?" Barbara asked accusatory.

"I don't know what I'm doing," Meredith said and added, "Yet."

Quinn held up his hand when Linda began to ask another question. "Look, ladies, we all knew at some point this would happen. Fortunately for us, Meredith has kindly agreed for the Queen Bees to continue to farm the blueberries for the festival this year."

"I'm sorry to disappoint you all," Meredith said. "But I can't afford two homes. And my children's home is in Massachusetts."

Ginny smiled among the rest of the sad faces. "We know you need to do what's best for you and your family."

"I will try to figure things out," Meredith said.

"You've been more than kind," Quinn said, looking at the long faces. "Thank you for allowing the Queen Bees to continue through this season."

"Of course. I want to help," she said.

"Well, I guess making her the Blueberry Queen seems a bit silly," Carolyn said loudly.

"Wear your ears next time," Ginny said to her sister.

"Bring beer next time?" Carolyn looked confused.

Quinn waited for his aunt to stop talking and then said, "You may want, as a collective group, to consider how you will get other blueberries if the property becomes unavailable to you."

"Why would we need other blueberries?" Hazel asked, not understanding the situation—or maybe she hadn't heard the whole conversation.

"Because Ms. Johnson may not keep the property or run it like Jacob has over the years," Quinn said as clearly as possible. He closed his eyes and then looked at Ginny.

"Mom, did you tell them something different?" He hoped Ginny hadn't gotten their hopes up that things would continue as usual.

Ginny made a face. "Well…"

"If we don't have a field of blueberries for the festival…" Linda said, letting her voice trail off.

"Then we don't have a festival," Pauline finished for her.

Linda finally looked as though she understood what was at stake. "The town needs to do something to prepare for that. It's been a tourist attraction for fifty years. People come up here for it. We need to provide something to continue the business, or we need to ask the town to buy the property."

Quinn had been telling her selectman husband that for weeks now.

"Maybe we can work something out with other farms around the area." Pauline looked doubtful as she said it. "I'm sure of it."

"I'm really sorry," Meredith said, but Ginny shook her head.

"No need," Ginny said. "We'll be fine."

But the faces in the room told another story. They knew what Quinn knew—there wasn't another farm that would give them the blueberries they needed, nor for free. The money they earned from the festival gave the town enough to spend on beautiful landscaping for the main street and the harbor park and kept walkways and common areas maintained. But the majority went to the local food pantry for local families in need. It went to help with heating costs for those who couldn't keep up in winter. It went to help with services for the elderly, like taxi services and food deliveries. How would the town earn that kind of money?

"Did she say we could use the barn?" Hazel asked.

CHAPTER 29

*T*hings went by in a blur for Meredith after that. Her days were spent with Remy fixing up the house, spending time at the beach, and getting to know her neighbors. Quinn, Kyle, or Ginny would stop by almost daily, offering help around the house and farm, and one family would eventually invite the other over for dinner.

Each night, she and Remy would sit out on the porch and watch the stars and listen to the waves, planning for the next day.

With the festival just a week away, she needed to do all she could to have the house ready for her children who would arrive that weekend.

All three reacted differently about coming up. Cora had been the most excited, whereas Ryan had seemed indifferent. And Muriel seemed busy.

Remy worked on decorating, and Meredith spent her time fixing things up with Kyle or Quinn—both would offer their help for projects around the house.

At first, she and Remy would go through a room to clean and remove all the clutter. They'd go through the artwork, tag everything, then comb through all the other items stuffed into shelves and drawers.

Then Remy would use her magic to rearrange all the things and place it all into new spots. And voilà! She'd make the room look like something straight out of a magazine.

Each day, Meredith would pick another room to go through. She'd find neat trinkets to place somewhere whimsical in the room. A collection of wooden pears that had been hand carved. A glass bottle with a ship inside. Candles were placed around the rooms. Throughout the barn, she found different kinds of pottery and antique tools and old mirrors with cool frames. Lots of lanterns. And books—books were everywhere.

Each day, the sisters would drive to the hardware store, or the fabric store, or the grocery store. One of the Queens would bring a blueberry dish, and Meredith and Remy would meet the women out in the fields at some point during the day.

Remy started asking for recipes and keeping them in a journal.

Some days, when the sky beckoned them, they'd spend the day at the beach. Most days, they spent together.

"I can't believe this is the same place," Quinn said, helping Meredith move a bookshelf from the bedroom downstairs to the living room. "It looks great in here. Like a whole new house."

"It still needs a lot of work," she said. "Like the plumbing and the electric, and probably the floors and the foundation. A fresh coat of paint." She shrugged, looking around the room, thinking of what to do next. "But for now, it's really turning out to be a perfect little spot to spend the summer."

"If you can stick around, the fall is when Maine is really magical," he said. "Going up the coast and seeing the colors."

She imagined what it might be like. "I've always wanted to go out on a boat and see the coast that way."

"Have you been on a boat?" he asked.

She shook her head. "No, not really."

"Well, now you own one," he said.

"I'll have to ask someone to take us out for a ride," she said, smiling.

"But it's not really the kind of boat you cruise around and look at leaves in," he said.

"Ah," she said. "More like dropping some pots kind of boat."

"Look at you," he said. "You sound like a true Mainiac."

She laughed and noticed Quinn looking at her. "What is it?"

He shook his head. "You have a really nice laugh."

She could feel her cheeks immediately blush. "Thanks."

"How much time do you have until everyone arrives?" he asked, shifting the conversation suddenly.

"They're coming for the festival." She was worried it wasn't enough time.

When they got the bookshelf where she wanted, he looked down at his phone. "Shoot, I better get going. Let me know if you need help with anything else. Kyle's home today until football practice."

"Does he need a ride?" she asked. "I'm happy to take him again."

He shook his head. "He'll be okay."

The other day, she had seen Kyle walking with all his football gear and had picked him up.

"It's really no trouble," she said. She enjoyed the teenager's company. It felt good to be needed in some weird neighborly way. She liked being useful.

"You know what? I'll ask him if he would like one," Quinn said. He walked out of the living room and to the kitchen. He glanced into the dining room and pointed at the piano.

"Have you played it yet?" he asked.

She glanced over at the upright. She hadn't even opened the cover. She shook her head. "I'm afraid I'm a bit too rusty at this point."

"Do you miss playing?" he asked.

She wished it were that simple. "All the time."

He nodded as if he understood, his eyes warm and comforting.

Quinn made it easy for Meredith to keep talking. "It just brings memories of my mom."

She laughed at herself, feeling completely vulnerable at that moment. The truth was, she felt like she fell apart because she didn't have her music.

"I should let you be," he said, rubbing his hands together, and heading toward the door.

"You don't have to rush out," she said. "We have blueberries."

He looked right at her. It was the kind of look he had been giving her that made her wonder if she could have another chance. Another chance to be happy with someone again.

"*Your* blueberries," he said.

She smiled back at him using the newest catchphrase from the Queens. "*My* blueberries."

But *her* blueberries and *her* cottage and *her* beach and *her* view still didn't seem like hers at all.

"So? Want something?" she asked.

He tilted his head, keeping his eyes on her. "That sounds great."

He walked back into the kitchen where she pulled out a bowl of fresh blueberries. "Ginny brought some of the ripe ones."

She set it down on the counter as he sat down on the stool placed on the other side.

"So, what else needs to be moved around?" he asked, plucking a blueberry up with his fingers and popping it into his mouth.

"I'd like that table in the barn moved to the porch," she said. "We're going to start tackling cleaning out the barn next."

"You and Remy are doing a great job," he said. "This place has never looked better."

Even if this hadn't been her and her sister's work, she would agree. The small beach cottage now looked like a sophisticated home with boutique French country style.

"Meredith!" Remy called out from the bathroom from the top floor. "Look out the window!"

Meredith walked up to the window to see a whale breach out

of the water. "It's a whale!" She pointed to the water splashing into the air.

"You're kidding." Quinn rushed to look out and stood right next to her.

Meredith could feel him next to her, sending an electric wave throughout her body. The smell of his aftershave made her forget about the whale and notice how handsome Quinn Michaud was.

"Would you look at that," he said, gazing at the water shooting up into the air. "You never get used to seeing that."

He smiled at her as she realized she had been staring at him and not the whale. "I bet not."

Quinn stayed next to her, looking at her a second longer than expected, but then he gave her a nod and backed away, returning to his stool.

"I'll let you know if Kyle needs a ride," he said, grabbing another blueberry.

Meredith stared at his lips as he chewed. That's when she remembered to take a breath. "Yes, let me know."

He put his hands on the counter and stood back up. "Right, well, I should go."

And with that, he walked out the door, leaving her standing by the sink, having a hot flash, wondering what the heck just happened.

"Hey," Remy said, coming into the kitchen. "What's up with you?"

Meredith didn't even know how to answer. "What do you mean?"

"Why are you all sweaty?" Remy's face twisted in disgust. "Why don't you open a window?"

Meredith walked to the back door and flung it open, letting the cool breeze from the ocean come into the house. She inhaled the sweet scent and gathered herself.

As Meredith stood there, she saw Kyle walking through the beach plum path headed toward the water, holding his girlfriend's hand. Technically, it was her path, her piece of land, but the name on the deed didn't matter. She watched as he expertly navigated through the bushes and rocks, stepping on the edges of the granite boulders like a tight rope and gracefully climbing over.

His girlfriend took hold of his hand, using her other hand to help her balance. She wasn't as coordinated but still easily climbed with Kyle down to the beach.

"Should we just let them swim?" Meredith asked. She enjoyed having the beach to herself but also knew how much the place must mean to Kyle.

Remy shrugged. "Why not?"

"I don't know, legalities?"

"You think Quinn will sue you?" Remy didn't seem to be concerned.

"No, but you never know what could happen," Meredith said.

Remy sighed. "I think it's safe to say Quinn is someone you can trust."

Meredith thought about it. She did trust Quinn. Everything he said and did was trustworthy. He did what was best for Jacob and her, not for him and his family. Would Phillip have been the same to his client? Or to her?

After a little bit, Remy said, "I'm going to call Joe tonight."

This made Meredith do a double take. Remy was wearing her wedding ring again.

"That's good," Meredith said encouragingly. "You should talk."

Remy bit her bottom lip before saying, "I just hope he will."

"You need to be honest about your feelings." Meredith thought back to when Phillip told her he wanted a divorce.

He had told her over dinner. She should've known something was up. He had never arranged to go out to dinner. They had usually just decided to go out without a plan. But this time had been different. This time, he'd arranged to meet at a restaurant.

Now, she understood he hadn't wanted to leave the restaurant with her, but at the time, she had been so fixated on how ridiculous it all was that she had called to cancel.

"Let's just have dinner at home," she'd said, annoyed he had wanted her to drive into the city.

"I want to check this restaurant out with you."

"Can't we do it on a weekend?"

"What do you have to do?" he had snapped at her.

The bite in his voice had made her pause, and then she'd answered, "Sure, okay."

And like walking into a haunted house, not knowing danger had lurked in the shadows, she'd met Phillip at the new restaurant.

"But first." Remy pulled out the blender and said, "How about a blueberry margarita?"

"Or we could open that bottle of wine?" Meredith pointed to the newest and most curious blueberry item of all—blueberry wine.

"Let's do it," Remy said, putting the blender back.

She went to the cabinet and grabbed two mason jars they had been using as their wineglasses, threw in some frozen blueberries from the freezer, and passed the glass to Remy.

"Oh, that's a good idea!" Remy said as she poured the wine into the glasses.

Remy picked up the first glass and held it up to Meredith. "To second chances."

Meredith held up her glass, and an idea popped into her mind. "Invite him here."

"What?" Remy said, holding her glass steady.

"Invite Joe up here," Meredith said. "Have him see the cottage and spend time together. Just the two of you."

"Where are you going to be?" Remy asked, surprised.

"I should go back to Andover for a bit," Meredith said. "See how my pool's doing. Check in with Dad. I haven't been there in weeks."

Remy thought about it for a second and then tapped Meredith's glass again. "Alright, I will."

Meredith tapped her glass against Remy's, hoping she'd take

her advice. Maybe they just needed a new place to figure things out.

Remy picked up her phone. "Would you mind if I called him?"

Meredith shook her head. "Of course not. Go." She gestured toward the porch.

"I can work on things upstairs," she said.

Remy started dialing but then stopped. "Thank you, Mer."

Meredith waved off her thanks. "No need. You would've done the same for me."

Remy shrugged. "I didn't though. I should have come to you and helped you through your divorce. I'm sorry about that."

"You had enough going on," Meredith said. "Let's not worry about all that happened. Let's figure out what's going to happen next instead."

Remy took a long breath, her chest expanding. "You're right."

Remy opened the screen door and went out on the porch. Meredith shut the door behind her to give her some privacy.

As Meredith cut through the dining room, she stopped in front of the piano, right in center position. She used her thumb to slowly lift the fallboard, letting the white keys peek out. Gently, she folded the cover over, exposing the bottoms of the eighty-eight keys. With a soft tap of her right thumb, she pressed down center C. The key's pitch was perfect.

She glanced back into the kitchen, looking out the window and seeing Remy's head walking back and forth.

She opened the fallboard fully and placed her hands into position above the keys, memories of her dying mother flooding her head. She closed her eyes, and that's when she remembered her first recital, or at least one of the very first. She wore a daisy-yellow sundress, just like the fabric that sat in the sewing room, with her hair done in pigtails. She dressed the part to perform "You Are My Sunshine" as her song.

Her mother's favorite.

She hit the low G, holding it, then center C, and quickly to D, then two long Es.

"You are my sunshine," she whispered out, her throat catching. She stopped playing, removing her fingers from the keys.

She stared at the piano as a light breeze billowed out the curtains. She could hear laughter coming from outside.

She grabbed the lid to close the piano back up again, but something stopped her. A need to finish the song. To hear her mother's favorite song again.

Pulling out the wooden bench, she sat down and placed the top part of her right foot on the pedal. She shook out her hands, stretching out her fingers, and then held them in place above the keys as if they might get burned if they touched.

With one long inhale, she closed her eyes, placed her fingers down on the keys, and began to play. She used just her right hand at first, but then her left naturally found its position, and the song played without her even thinking about it.

"Are you playing the piano?" Remy asked, coming into the house.

Meredith quickly dropped the wooden cover. "Just playing around. How'd it go?"

Remy shook her head. "He doesn't have time to come up."

Meredith jerked her head back. "But I thought I heard laughing."

"We had a nice talk." Remy shrugged. "But he can't make it up right now."

"Oh, Remy, I'm sorry."

"Yeah, me too," she said. She set her wine down on the counter. "I think I'm going to lie down."

"Did you tell him it was important for you?" Meredith asked, wishing she could knock some sense into that man. "Does he know?"

"Meredith, do you think I'm just hoping he can read my mind?" Remy huffed. "I have told him flat out that I want to leave him if he doesn't try. And he doesn't want to. He just doesn't want to."

At this point, Remy no longer talked but cried. She cried so hard her whole body shook and she held onto the counter's edge for support. Meredith rushed up to her, and Remy fell into her arms.

"It's going to be okay," Meredith said. "I promise you're going to be okay."

CHAPTER 30

*J*acqueline hadn't been the kind of mother who had packed a lunch and sent her kids with a kiss to school. She was messy, disorganized, and scatter-brained half the time.

But there was no question that Jacqueline loved her kids. She devoted all her passion to her daughters. She gave everything she had to give them the best childhood possible, even if that meant leaving the love of her life for a better father for her child.

"Do you think she loved Gordon and Jacob the same?" Meredith asked while she and Remy went through the last of the paintings in the living room. Remy's friend from Boston was on his way to check out Jacob's collection.

"I think you have different kinds of love," Remy said, flipping through the stacked pile of Jacob's landscapes. "I just feel like she never got closure with Jacob. Like the one who got away, but she had to let it go, which I think brought a lot of conflicting feelings for her. I think she loved Gordon, but she also always loved Jacob."

Meredith thought about the mermaid statue and how at peace her mother looked. If she had come up to model for it at that time period, she would have already been going through chemotherapy. Her body had already been failing and deteriorating by that point. Had Jacob only seen her beauty, even up until the end?

"I think a true love story is about second chances," Meredith said. "I think the true story is how they found their way back to one another."

Remy picked up a smaller painting. It was of a pink beach rose with its yellow center. She placed the painting against the others of the same time period. The last paintings they believed Jacob had painted, based on the similarities to the few he had signed and dated.

"I guess she loved both of them," Remy said.

Meredith nodded at that. Would she ever fall in love again?

She thought about the way her stomach had that fluttering feeling when she stood next to Quinn, and she couldn't help but blush at her sudden crush on the neighbor.

A ding went off from Remy's phone. "He's almost here."

"What's this man's name?" she asked.

"Greg," Remy said. "He's fabulous at what he does. I use him all the time."

Meredith didn't understand one thing about the art world.

"He's an appraiser and an art dealer," Remy said. "He can find the people who will want to buy Jacob's work."

"And you think he'll get a lot of money for Jacob's pieces?" Meredith felt doubtful that Remy's art friend could get the prices estimated for Jacob's art.

Remy nodded. "Yes. I think you could get a good amount for the sheer volume of work he had that hasn't been shown to the public."

Meredith crossed her arms against her stomach, wondering what the best thing to do was. Did she keep the art for her children? Did she keep it for her?

She stood in front of a painting with a sea dark as night, the sky even darker, and a wooden dinghy heading out to sea. A shadowed figure huddled at the bow. Off in the distance, along the cliff's edge, stood one purple lupine lit up by a single ray of sun.

"Do you think I was cruel for never wanting to meet him?" Meredith asked.

"You have never been cruel in your life," Remy said, shutting the portfolio they had created for Greg. "You have always been the best, most protective big sister a girl could ask for."

Meredith smiled, but Remy hadn't answered the question. "But with Jacob, I never listened to Mom and reached out to him. And now I'm selling his life's work."

Remy scoffed at that. "So?"

"She wanted me to meet him and I didn't." It had been one of Jacqueline's wishes at the end of her life.

"Mom had her own reasons." Remy sighed at this. "But you had no reason to go and hunt down a man, who clearly could reach out himself." Remy shook her head. "Look, I understand all the stories and how he offered the land and took Kyle out fishing and helped all the widows, but you owe this man nothing. He had fifty years to sober up and do the right thing, but he didn't, so don't blame yourself for his mistakes. Just like Phillip. You were the best wife. You didn't do anything wrong to make him leave you. It was Phillip who made the mistake."

Meredith studied the painting in front of her. The rocky cliffside had pines on top of the earth, and the dark sea hung below, churning on the edges of the world. Madness came to her head as she continued to examine the oil painting. The strokes of color were thick and heavy clumps of paint. It felt messy, rushed, and darker than his others. They estimated that the painting had been Jacob's last finished piece.

Had he known his body was dying? Had he ever experienced more than this isolated madness?

"We should have a public viewing of his art," Remy said. "Invite the Queens and stuff. We could display all his work. I bet no one around here saw much of it besides Ginny."

Meredith made a face at first, but then she thought about it.

"I think that's a great idea," Meredith said.

Remy beamed. "I can plan everything. All you need to do is show up."

Meredith shook her head. "No, I want to help. I think it's a great idea."

"We could have something here," Remy said. "Let people see the farm and display his work in the barn. Let the Queens show off their hard work over the years."

Meredith sat up thinking about the Queens. "Maybe more people will want to join."

Remy looked at Meredith. "Then maybe we shouldn't."

"What do mean?" Meredith said.

"Well, if you're going to sell this place, the whole thing is over anyway," Remy said. "There will be no Queens."

Meredith didn't want to end the gardening club but could she really keep this place?

Car tires pulled up into the drive, and the conversation stopped, but Meredith couldn't stop thinking about the idea of the Queens ending if she sold the property.

But she simply couldn't keep up with two houses. She didn't even want to think about what the lawn looked like in Andover. She would have to sell it—she knew that. But would she sell the cottage?

A month ago, she wouldn't have hesitated.

But now...

"Thank you so much for coming," Remy said, walking a middle-aged man into the living room.

Meredith stuck out her hand. "Hi, I'm Meredith."

"Greg," he said, holding out his hand to meet hers.

"Let me take you to his studio," Remy said, and then walked Greg through the house.

Remy let Greg walk in first, and he walked deeper into the room before saying anything. "This is the collection?"

Meredith couldn't read if he was disappointed or not. They had spent the night putting some of Jacob's best pieces around the studio on easels and against the walls in order from oldest to most recent.

"This is just part of it," Remy said, her fingers clasped together. Remy's confidence was unshaken. "There's more throughout the house and the barn. We organized it like you suggested."

"And this is just some of the collection?" he asked again.

Meredith questioned his credentials for repeating basically the same question.

But Remy smiled at this. "Yup."

Greg started laughing. "And no one else has seen this?"

Remy shook her head. "Not that we're aware of."

Greg's mouth widened into a large grin. He looked like he had just found buried treasure. "Wow. Okay. I promise you, that if I run this auction, I can bring in the top buyers that will pay exorbitantly for his work."

"Seriously?" Meredith saw the beauty in Jacob's work, but a landscape was a landscape.

"I'll need to go through all of it," Greg said to Remy, who pulled out a small notebook. He laughed again. "But this…" Greg turned in a circle as he said, "This is an extraordinary collection."

Remy took over from there, and Meredith was happy to let her sister do so. Remy knew more about art than she did.

"Love that piano." Greg pointed at the upright as they passed through the dining room.

As Remy and Greg went to the living room, Meredith fell behind and stopped at the piano. She lifted the cover. Then with her index finger, she hit F sharp and listened to the sound until it faded to silence. And she hit it again, listening until it faded.

"Mer!" Remy called from upstairs. "You coming?"

They showed Greg around the whole house before taking him out to the barn, passing two of the Queen Bees that Meredith had recently met.

"This an incredible collection of your father's life's work," Greg said, taking photos with his phone and typing something afterward. "I mean, I've never seen someone's full collection like this."

"So, you think they could sell?" Remy asked.

"I think you have something very, very special on your hands," he said, his eyes gleaming with excitement. "We need to tell people about this collection. Call some museums around New England and New York," he said. "Seriously, this might be museum-worthy. Maybe even set up a traveling art exhibit. Let me call a few friends. We can have an invite-only viewing with some of the most prestigious dealers and collectors on the East Coast. Have an auction either in the city or even have it here."

"Wow, you think people will travel all the way up here to buy his pieces?" Meredith couldn't believe this.

He nodded his head, walking into the barn. His mouth opened in awe. "I mean, when Remy showed me the chaos at first, I thought it would never be put together."

Remy flashed a look at Meredith, and something happened between them right then. A mutual acknowledgement of what they had accomplished together. A renewed bond. A promise to take care of each other without even having to say a thing. The two sisters had gone through a lot as they'd unpacked Jacob's art collection from a disorderly mess into an amazing collection.

"Like how much are we talking here?" Meredith asked, but she watched Remy's face when Greg started calculating numbers out loud.

"Let's not get too ahead of ourselves" Remy said, holding out her hands. "You haven't gone through the whole collection."

Meredith realized she trusted no one more than her sister right then, and she felt confident Remy felt the same. She would do anything for her sister and her family. They had each other's backs. Their sisterhood was stronger than marriages and friendships. It was Meredith's strongest relationship.

When they finished showing most of Jacob's work, Remy took Greg on a walk to show him the property.

"This place is unbelievable," he said when they returned to the cottage. "You should Airbnb it."

"We're going to go down to the village to grab something to eat for lunch," Remy said, grabbing her purse. "Want to join us?"

Meredith shook her head. "I think I'll stay and finish up a few things here."

She wanted to go through some more of the basement.

"We'll be back," Remy said as she closed the door behind her.

Meredith walked into the kitchen and poured herself a glass of water. With her water, she meandered into the dining room and stood next to the piano. She opened the cover, hitting F sharp, and listened to its magical sound fill the room and slowly disappear.

She set her water down on the table's placemat and turned to the piano. She listened to the empty house. Then, carefully, she pulled out the wooden bench and sat down at its keyboard. With her heel anchored on the floor and the ball of her foot on the pedal, she closed her eyes and began to play.

The song had been one of her mother's favorites from her days of being a little girl playing for her own mother. "Till We Meet Again" was the title, but Meredith had never seen the sheet music for it. She had only memorized it by heart from hearing it over and over throughout the years. Once, as a little girl, she had played it one day for her mother, and it had made her cry.

After that, Meredith loved seeing people's reaction to her performing music. She enjoyed seeing the emotions it brought out in her and others. The days of performing at school, then college, and finally her dream job at the Boston Symphony Orchestra, had been her whole world.

And when she'd had Cora, she hadn't wanted to give up her career, because stepping down from the orchestra to take care of her children would end it. And she'd known that. The last concert she had performed in Boston, she'd cried. She had blamed it on the pregnancy, but she hadn't stopped crying until she had fallen asleep that night. Phillip had never even acknowledged her sacrifice. Why only now did she see the problem with that?

Meredith finished the song and let the quiet settle around her, listening to the soft crashing of the waves from outside.

She got up, walked to the back porch, and stepped outside, looking out at the foaming whitecaps on the waves' crests. The endless blue sky didn't have a cloud in it, just a flock of birds floating above the water's surface.

Her phone vibrated in her pocket. She picked it up, hoping it would be one of the kids, when she saw it was Phillip.

She tried to calculate the age of the baby and couldn't. How old was she now?

A month? Six weeks?

She silenced it and stared at his name. Months ago, she would have been relieved to see that he was still calling, and she would have taken the call immediately. She'd have listened to his complaints, like always, and would have eased his worries about everything. Then she would have hoped and prayed he'd changed his mind and come back to her.

She pulled open the screen door and walked inside, back to the piano, and sat down in front of it.

She turned on the screen of her phone and called Gordon.

"Hey, sugarplum," he answered.

"Hey, Daddy," she said, tears immediately stinging her eyes.

"What are you all up to today?" he asked.

She took a second, collecting herself before answering, and said, "I wanted to check in. See how you're doing."

"I'm doing great," he said. "Just waiting for my buddy Bill to come and pick me up for a round of golf."

"That sounds nice," she said.

"Yes, it does," he said. "How's it going up there?"

"Remy has her art collector friend here today," Meredith said.

"Is he there to help with Jacob's paintings?"

"Yeah, he suggested we have an auction and invite collectors to come here and see his collection," she said, wishing she could just get to the point.

Her whole life, she had tiptoed around Gordon when it came to Jacob and his paternity. Never once had she ever asked Gordon his feelings about her real father or his wife's first husband, because she had thought Gordon wouldn't want to talk about it, but it had been her who hadn't wanted to talk. Gordon had always talked about things.

"What was he like?" she finally asked.

"Who? Bill?" he asked, confused.

"No." She tapped her index finger on the middle C lightly so it wouldn't make a sound. "Jacob."

"I didn't know him that well," Gordon started. "Not like your mother, obviously, but I did help after the accident."

"Is that when you met mom?" she asked.

"It's how I met the whole town," he said. "I went to Blueberry Bay to help with the search. I had just graduated from medical school and worked in Portland. They had asked for volunteers to help. I wanted to help, so I went up there. That was when I first met your mother, when she was pregnant with you."

"How long were you in Maine?" she asked. Had her parents had an affair? Is that how Jacqueline had left Jacob?

"I ended up working through a local hospital, but I did house calls around the more rural areas, like Blueberry Bay."

"And when did you leave to work in Boston?" Meredith asked, trying to piece the story together from the details she had heard from the Queens.

"I stayed in Maine for a few years," he said.

"How did you and Mom…" She didn't have a lot of time before his friend would come and interrupt. "Get together?"

She could hear him exhale. "She tried working things out with Jacob, tried to make the marriage work, but he was a very sick man. He drank. He became belligerent at times. He'd leave for days. And when he did come back, he wouldn't leave the house. He stopped talking."

He stopped for a moment.

"Dad?" she asked, wondering if she had lost him.

"I'm here," he said. "Look, Meredith, your mother always felt guilty about leaving him. She always felt like she could've done more, helped more, but she wanted the best for you."

Meredith thought back to the cottage when she had arrived—Jacob's madness displayed in the chaos of his art and the hoarding of it.

"I had been a good friend to her during those years, but nothing else," he said. "Then I moved to Boston and one day, I walked into the office and saw you and your mother in the waiting room. She needed a family physician and looked me up. And, well, you know the rest."

Meredith did. As the story goes, when they went into his office, Meredith had given Gordon a hug, and he had fallen in love with the little girl in pigtails. Then just as quickly, he'd fallen in love with her beautiful mother, who he had helped in Maine.

"I asked her to marry me six weeks later," he said.

Meredith smiled at the idea of Gordon falling deeply in love with Jacqueline.

And that was when Meredith felt the jolt of her mother's absence again. She wouldn't ever really know the answers to her questions.

"They worked through things," Gordon said. "Jacob and your mother."

"What do you mean?" She wondered if he knew about her statue.

"Your mother connected with him before she died and made amends," Gordon said. "And she wanted you to do that, too. Not for Jacob, but for you."

She felt the sting again. She pressed the piano key, and it made a soft noise.

"Are you playing the piano?" Gordon asked.

"Yeah," she said, wishing she hadn't made the sound.

"She loved hearing you play."

212

"I just played her favorite."

"'Till We Meet Again!'" he said loudly, happily remembering her favorite song to play. "She said you brought angels to tears."

Meredith wiped away a tear that had fallen. "I miss her so much."

"Oh, sugarplum, she's there. Just play for her," he said.

Bill came and picked Gordon up, but not before he told her he loved her.

"Are you coming up with the kids?" she asked. "Cora will pick you up if you want."

"That's a good idea," he said. "I'll think about it."

When she set the phone down, she saw a notification of a voicemail. She picked up her phone and hesitated for a moment. Should she listen to what Phillip had to say—same thing but different day? Did she want to feel worse? Because she always did after she listened to his excuses. Her thumb hovered over the button to listen, then with a swipe, she deleted it.

Meredith set down her phone, put her fingers in the proper position on the piano, and played.

She played song after song, anything she could remember. She replayed "Till We Meet Again" and played some of Gordon's favorites as well. She hadn't played that much in years. And it felt good. Really good.

When she finished the last song, she heard soft clapping coming from outside. She looked to see where it came from and saw Quinn standing there on the back porch looking in through the screen door.

"Meredith," he said, "that was unbelievable."

Her face instantly heated. "Thank you." She looked at her fingers at the keys. "I'm a little rusty."

"I haven't heard that played...ever," he said. "I didn't even know Jacob had it before you all came."

She pulled down the wooden cover and pushed away from the piano. "What's up? Did you need something?"

He smiled but stayed on the porch. "I didn't want to bother you."

"You can come in," she said, walking through the kitchen and opening the door.

"I couldn't help but stop by and see who was playing that beautiful music," he said, staring at her.

"Oh, no," Meredith said. "You could hear it all the way to your house?"

She looked across the yard, hoping she didn't appear ridiculous. She could really fall into her music, and like dancing, she moved to the rhythm.

"This is so exciting. A real musician right next door!" Ginny clapped her hands appearing out of nowhere by the front door.

"Ginny?" Her blushing turned to mortification. How many more people in Blueberry Bay had heard her play? "I haven't played in years."

"You-hoo," a woman's voice said from another open window from the back breezeway.

"Pauline?" Meredith swung around to see the town councilwoman holding a casserole dish. "When did you show up?"

"I was stopping in with some of my blueberry crisp." Pauline pulled back a blue-and-white-checkered cloth with what appeared to be a crisp underneath.

"Pauline won first place with that crisp in the baking contest last year," Hazel said, now standing next to Ginny.

"Seriously?" Meredith swung her head to Quinn, who gave her a smile.

"You play beautifully," Carolyn said, now with Pauline.

"The sound travels to the fields?" Meredith looked out at the bay. The cliffs and hillside did create a natural amplifier with the cottage smack dab in the middle of it.

"Gorgeous music," Quinn said, his eyes right on her, making butterflies flutter in her belly.

Whoa. What was that?

"Thanks," she said again.

"You're coming to the meeting tomorrow, right?" Ginny asked.

When Meredith realized Ginny was talking to her, she broke Quinn's stare and tried to remember the question.

"Yes, Remy and I will be there," she said.

"Is that Remy's husband?" Carolyn asked about Greg.

Meredith shook her head. "No, it's an art appraiser. He's going through all of Jacob's things."

The women all started swapping glances, and their smiles disappeared.

"You're selling his stuff?" Carolyn looked concerned.

"Yes, we're selling some of his paintings and some of the extra furniture we don't want," she said. They had almost all the furniture they wanted to sell out in the garage. Half of the stuff was junk, but the other half were antiques and could sell for something.

"Are you selling the cottage?" Linda asked.

All the women and Quinn looked at Meredith, waiting for her to answer.

She shrugged. "I don't know, to be honest."

She could see their disappointment right away, and Meredith could feel her own.

"I'm sorry, I just don't know what I'm going to do with the cottage and other things." Meredith didn't want to say *blueberry fields*, because she knew she would be the villain in this story if she were to sell.

"Ladies, it's not fair to bombard Meredith with questions she's not ready to answer," Quinn said, giving Meredith a nod.

"Let's leave the crisp and get out of her hair," Ginny said to the women.

Ginny was clearly the Queen Bee among the group.

Everyone cleared away from the house, except Quinn.

"Do you plan on playing again?" he asked.

She laughed. "Right now?"

He shook his head. "No, professionally."

That made her giggle. She wasn't a professional of anything.

"You looked really happy to just play for yourself," he said. "But you had the rest of the bay stopped in their tracks with the sounds."

She smiled at the recognition as her phone started vibrating on top of the piano's lid. She went to grab it and saw Phillip's name across the screen. She picked it up, silenced it, and stuffed it into her back pocket.

"What are you doing right now?" Quinn asked, leaning against the doorframe between the kitchen and the dining room.

Meredith's heart skipped a beat. "Nothing."

"Want to take the boat out?"

In the pit of Meredith's stomach, fear mixed with excitement and pure adrenaline.

"Absolutely."

CHAPTER 31

$\mathcal{E}$arlier that day, Quinn had watched as Kyle walked through the fields to the back of the barn with a bucket and cleaning supplies. He knew exactly where he was going.

Jacob's boat.

He decided to leave him alone. Meredith hadn't mentioned anything about selling the boat since that night of the fire, which he'd taken as a good sign considering she was starting to sell Jacob's things. She'd had an art appraiser at the house that morning all the way up from Boston.

As he watched his son sneak through the fields, his phone dinged from the kitchen table where he worked that morning.

Meredith's name lit up the screen, and his heart skipped a beat. He wanted to ignore the feeling he got every time he thought of Meredith, but the feeling started happening more and more.

He opened the text.

Remy and I want you, Ginny, and Kyle to have these.

She had texted him photos of Jacob's paintings—flowers, birds, different parts of his garden, and then some of Blueberry Bay's landscapes, the water and ocean scenes.

He looked out the window of the kitchen at the cottage. The visitor's car with Massachusetts plates had left.

He looked back at the pictures. The gesture had been so unexpected and so kind, he left the house at once and knew exactly what he needed to do.

He found Kyle on the boat with all his cleaning supplies and buckets of water and his earbuds blasting.

"Looks good!" Quinn yelled at Kyle, who froze the minute he heard his voice.

Kyle then let out a breath. "You scared me. Let someone know you're coming."

Quinn rolled his eyes at his son. "When was the last time you took this out?"

Before Jacob's death, Kyle had been taking out the boat—a contentious point between his client and him. Jacob had wanted to give Kyle the boat. A man whose whole life had been damaged and haunted because of a boating accident had wanted to give a teenage boy a boat.

The whole thing drove Quinn insane.

He remembered why he came.

"Do you really want to buy this boat?" Quinn asked.

Kyle sat down, dropping the sponge in his hand into a bucket of sudsy water. "Yeah."

"What if you buy it but go to college, too," Quinn said. "You can play football and go somewhere local."

Kyle shrugged. "I just don't belong in school. I belong out there." He pointed to the water.

"Just get a degree first, then you can do whatever you want."

"Like you?" Kyle laughed. "What did your degree get you? You hate your job."

Here we go, Quinn thought to himself. The never-ending argument.

"Your mother wanted you to go to college."

"You don't get to use her to make your point."

That one stung. "I just want to make sure you use all your potential."

"Well, all she ever told me was she wanted me to be happy," Kyle said. "And fishing makes me happy."

Quinn put his hands on his waist, holding back his irritation. "Just get a degree and you can fish all you want."

"Why is that piece of paper so important to you?" Kyle asked.

He didn't want to bite the hand that had fed his family for decades, but the truth was, history wasn't a liar. "Because living in a bubble, being ignorant to everything out there, you'll end up like the rest of us."

"And how's that?" Kyle asked.

"Miserable." Quinn didn't know if Kyle just didn't see the misery in the faces that went out every day on the water or if he just didn't want to see it.

Kyle's shoulders collapsed. "I just want to fish. Nothing else. Why is that so bad?"

There were a million different reasons why fishing was bad in Quinn's mind, but as he looked at his son, he had to realize this wasn't his life. Or Lisa's. It was Kyle's.

"I heard you offered to buy it with your college fund."

"Yeah. It's my money."

"When you go to college," Quinn said, though the twenty grand would only get him a semester or two *maybe* at a local state school nowadays.

Kyle's eyes flashed with anger. "You can't tell me how to spend my own money."

"You know she wanted you to go."

Kyle growled. "Stop doing that with my mother!"

Quinn froze. Kyle had never yelled at him like that before, especially when it came to Lisa. They both knew their sensitivities when it came to his wife and Kyle's mother.

"She was my mother, and I don't want you to weaponize her anymore, okay?" Kyle's eyes were wide and wild.

"That's a really harsh thing to say. I'm trying to make you see how important it was for her."

"There you go again." Kyle shook his head. "You just can't help yourself."

"What about football?" Quinn said. Kyle had already racked up some offers to local schools. "You could play football in school. Why do you want to give that up?"

Kyle had a gift that many didn't, plus the drive. He loved playing the game. Why did he want to stop playing a game he loved to work an eighteen-hour day of hard labor?

"Let me show you," Kyle said. "Let me show you that I can handle this boat."

Quinn recognized the request and saw its significance. This could be a changing moment in their relationship. Quinn could do what Kyle wanted or say no and keep badgering him about school, but he was tired of it all.

"Alright," Quinn said. "But we have to include Meredith. It's her boat."

"Really?" Kyle's eyes widened with shock. "You're going to go out on Jacob's boat with me?"

Quinn nodded. "But we're staying close. In the bay."

Kyle jumped up from the bench and climbed over the railing and down the ladder set up against the boat. Then he went back to the buckets, dumping the dirty water over the side. He dropped the supplies on the ground, then climbed down.

"Let me get ready," Kyle said, running toward the house.

"I'll go to see Meredith and ask about it all," Quinn said as Kyle took off.

He walked down the dirt path from the barn to the cottage. The winding road hardly had travelers these days.

Quinn's mind went back to Meredith's text and the photos of the paintings. How much could they be worth? She could easily sell the pieces. They had to be a lot considering how many people kept hounding him about Jacob's art. Even the governor of Maine had his assistant call for a painting in the Governor's mansion.

He would tell Meredith that the gift was unnecessary. Keep it for her own children, Jacob's grandchildren. They deserved it more than the people leaching off him for decades.

Before he reached the house, he heard the music playing.

At first, it blended in with the waves, drifting with the wind but becoming louder the closer he got to the cottage. He thought maybe it had been Jacob's records playing. When he reached the back porch, he saw Meredith sitting at the piano and playing. Her eyes were closed and her whole being played the keys. She hit the notes hard, pounding the pedal with the keys, and the sounds echoed throughout his chest.

He was mesmerized.

He had never seen or heard such a beautiful sight in all his life.

And it struck him that he wasn't falling for Meredith, he had already fallen. Hard.

When he asked her to come on the boat, her eyes brightened at the idea. "Absolutely."

And he could feel his heart skip again.

"Kyle and I got it hitched up and ready to go," he said.

"That's so nice," she said.

"We just need to stay in the bay," he said.

"Can Remy and Greg come?" she asked.

"Sure," he said, glad to see her so excited.

Kyle had mentioned how happy Meredith seemed since she'd first come, and he could see the change too.

Quinn turned to her. "The paintings. That's so thoughtful, but we can't take them from you."

"You're not taking them," she said. "I'm giving them to you."

"But they can go to your family," he said.

She looked around the cottage. "He has plenty to give to his neighbors. The people who loved him most."

He wondered if that stung. Because the more he learned about Meredith, the more he understood her hurt about Jacob's absence and the need to understand why he had chosen the life he did.

"The thing I have learned through Jacob," she said, "is holding onto things doesn't do anyone any good. The things just pile up, causing nothing but chaos." She rubbed her hands together. "No one even got to see his art because it was hidden away. Maybe now those pieces will be appreciated."

Quinn let her words sink in, and that's when he said, "I hope you stay. Here in Blueberry Bay."

The energy shifted completely, and he wondered if he was an idiot for not keeping his little crush to himself. But her smile grew as she kept her focus on him.

"I think I might." Her eyes sparkled as she said it. "At least until after the fall."

His heart jumped inside his chest, and just as he took a step forward to get closer to her, a horn beeped from outside.

"Kyle's here," he said, not moving from where he stood.

"Right," she said, looking out the window, breaking the stare. "I should text Remy to meet us at the harbor, then."

"Is she down in the village?" he asked, wishing the moment wouldn't end, because he was certain he wasn't the only one who felt something.

She took a deep breath, her chest lifting as she nodded her head. "Yes, she's grabbing lunch."

Quinn stood frozen, not sure what his next move should be, when he heard Kyle get out of the truck.

"Do you need a few minutes to get ready?" he asked, as he heard the truck door slam closed.

She didn't move either. "Yes, I'll be quick."

They stared at each other, both recognizing the moment.

Kyle looked in the window, knocking on the glass once he saw them in the kitchen.

"I guess I need to teach Kyle a few manners."

She laughed, and an urge to hear it again came over him. He wanted to keep Meredith laughing.

"Can we take out the boat, Meredith?" Kyle asked, walking straight into the house without permission.

"Yeah," she said, her grin widening at the sight of him. "That sounds wonderful."

"Are you coming, too?" Kyle asked.

Quinn had thought Kyle had been excited about taking the boat out with him, but he could see he was also excited about taking Meredith out.

"Can I take a few minutes to get ready?" she asked Kyle.

"No problem," he said.

He and Kyle walked together back to the truck and waited. When Meredith came out, she jumped in the passenger's seat and leaned over to Kyle in the back.

"You going to be the captain today?" she asked.

And that was when he saw the relationship between Kyle and Meredith in a new way. She fit in that seat. He liked having her next to him, sharing this moment with her and Kyle. Their families may be neighbors, but their connection was clear, and he liked having her in his life.

And it was clear, so did Kyle.

CHAPTER 32

*E*verything became clear for Meredith that day on the boat.

She almost felt silly to compare Ariel's transformation in *The Little Mermaid* to her own, but she suddenly felt a connection to her favorite children's story. Ariel didn't belong in her life under the sea, whereas Meredith no longer belonged in the world of motherhood and being a wife. She needed to fight her demons to be happy with who she was all along.

Just Meredith.

And becoming Meredith meant she needed to be happy by herself.

She sat on what Kyle called the starboard side and looked out at the views. Everyone talked about the beauty of the Atlantic water, the shores of granite cliffs, and the sugary-soft sand. As they drove the boat through Blueberry Bay, Kyle and Quinn pointed out the landmarks.

"That's the Isabella Lighthouse," Kyle said, pointing out the white-and-red lighthouse that sat alone on an island of pines and granite.

"Does anyone live there?" Remy asked.

Quinn shook his head. "It's run on its own generator. No need for a lighthouse keeper nowadays."

The view felt completely foreign to Meredith as they glided up the coast, looking from the water back at the little village and ocean shore. From the harbor, she couldn't find the little cottage at first, but then she finally made it out.

" Le gîte *en bord de Mer.*" A feeling of warmth filled her chest as they floated past the little gray clapboard cottage.

In that moment, everything changed. Everything.

And Meredith knew what she needed to do.

CHAPTER 33

*Q*uinn drove to work thinking about the few projects he had to do that day. He had to run to town hall, then drop off the bin full of food to the pantry at the local Congregational Church that had been collected at the last fundraiser, and after, he had to stop by the high school and give them Kyle's physical form. If he worked for Bruce, he wouldn't be able to go to most of Kyle's games. He wouldn't have time.

Then he remembered the Queen Bees meeting he had said he would attend later that night. What else was there to say? *Jacob is dead. Talk to Meredith?*

He arrived at the office, and it took Ginny less than a half hour to show up and start in on the argument from last night.

Kyle, like he suspected, had been thrilled to take out the boat. He had talked with Ginny about it all night at dinner.

Ginny had assumed that the news of the boat trip meant Quinn had changed his mind about Kyle fishing, though he had quickly reminded her that he still wanted Kyle to go to college. That hadn't changed. And that had set Kyle off.

"I know you're worried about Kyle," she said.

"I'm his father, so it comes with the territory," he said, not wanting to get into this before the meeting.

"If you keep pushing school, he's just going to keep pushing back," she said, putting her purse in the drawer.

He took off his readers and looked at his seventy-three-year-old mother. She was tired. He couldn't continue to have his mother work. Another glaring reason why he needed to help his family by getting a job that actually paid the bills. "You know who was the hardest on me about going to school?"

She stared at him because Ginny knew dang well who. "You were the one who had the drive."

"And now I know I *am* lucky. I know what a college education can do for people around here."

It allows them to get out, he thought to himself.

So many of his friends and family had quit school. They hadn't even made it out of high school to start earning money. Lobstering was a very lucrative business if someone was willing to give up their whole life for it. Aside from the danger, catching lobsters, dragging the cages up from the water and betting on nature, sometimes making bank, other times scraping just to get by, would wear a person down. The physical endurance of pulling and dropping the pots into the water. The changes of New England weather on a good day. The catastrophes that could happen at any given moment. A leg getting caught on a line, a loss of a finger in the mechanical pulley, the endless amounts of ways one could injure themselves or worse.

Not to mention the storms.

How many funerals had he been to for fishing accidents? Everyone knew someone in Blueberry Bay who's loved one had died in some way out on the water.

It was the way of life. They were stuck together as a community through tragedy.

And he wanted more for Kyle.

He could send Kyle to a private school in Portland for his senior year. Get him out of here and forget the idea of fishing for a living.

"Some things you can't fight," Ginny said.

He laughed at that. "Like you forcing Meredith to stay."

Ginny looked offended. "I'm not forcing her to stay." She shook her head. "I'm showing her a second chance. A second chance at getting to know her roots. A second chance at community. A second chance with her sister. A second chance at a new way of life."

"Is that what you're calling it?" he said.

She walked to Quinn and squeezed his shoulder. "You are the best dad that boy could ever ask for. But being stressed and unhappy so he can go to some fancy school certainly isn't what Kyle would want. He wants a dad who wants to go and fish with him."

"It's not what people want all the time, isn't that your motto? It's about what we need." He stopped talking at that point, holding back so he wouldn't come out disrespectful toward his mother.

He shut the computer screen and moved his chair back, getting up. He reached out to hug his mother. He knew she could feel his anger, but it wasn't going to break their relationship. He still loved her whether they agreed about Kyle's next steps or not. But the fact was, he was Kyle's father, and he would do what he had to do for his son.

"Quinn, I didn't mean to upset you," she said. "You're doing the best you can."

"Yes, I am." He couldn't continue with the conversation. He had too much to do. Once Bruce talked to Kyle, Quinn wouldn't have any control in the matter.

"See you later tonight at the meeting," he said.

She raised her eyebrow. "You sure you're okay?"

"I'm fine," he said. He grabbed his stuff and threw it into the leather bag Lisa had bought him when he made partner. It was something casual and not too formal. It said that he was a partner at one of the biggest firms but had also shown that he was one of the youngest and most hip partners the firm had ever had.

When he turned the corner, he almost bumped into someone coming from the other direction.

"Quinn!" Meredith said, a smile across her face. "I was just about to see you."

He looked down at his watch. He barely had enough time to run to the pantry if he stopped and talked.

"Hi Meredith," he said, smiling. "What are you doing here?"

"Do you have a minute?" she asked.

Quinn didn't answer at first. Unable to slow down. The stress of everything had piled up as much as it could, and even though his problem with her seemed to have taken a pause and wasn't as dire as before, it still hadn't been solved. She was still probably going to sell the cottage. The Queens were hitting ages where many of them were no longer able to keep up with the property. Meredith couldn't keep up the work of the fields alone. The town hadn't done their share at recruiting new volunteers to take over.

They could raise taxes on some of the things, ask people to donate more. There had to be other ways Blueberry Bay could earn the money.

If Meredith decided to sell, maybe the town would benefit by having a new hotel or places for tourists who like to spend their money in Blueberry Bay. Take advantage of the vacation state and play in the ocean.

"How can I help you?" he asked.

She looked behind him from where he had come from. "Do you mind talking somewhere private?"

He nodded. "Of course. Let's go back to my office."

"Somewhere your mom might not be?" She looked a bit embarrassed by the request.

"Sure, no problem." He gestured toward the gardens by the pier. "Let's go for a walk."

As they walked down the road, she looked at him and smiled, making his heart skip a beat.

Her hair fell softly below her shoulders, tinted with the sun's highlights. She wore a sundress that showed off her tanned shoulders, and he couldn't help but notice her pink cheeks.

When they stopped at the crosswalk to wait for the traffic to clear, he asked, "Did you go to the beach today?"

She smiled wider, brighter. She looked lighter, freer. "Yes. Remy and I spent the whole afternoon there."

"Is she still there?" he asked.

She shook her head. "No, she's making dinner." She held her hands out before him. They looked cut up, almost like paper cuts. "We found clams! Some men came to the beach and pulled all these clams for us! They're sharper than I thought."

He couldn't help but laugh at her obvious excitement.

She laughed as well. "Ugh, I must look dreadful." She patted down her hair.

"You look incredible." He caught her eye and kept her stare. It would be so much easier to look away. Not put himself out there. What kind of regret would he feel if he didn't even try? So what if he hadn't felt this way about another woman since Lisa?

Maybe there would be another woman that would make his heart skip a beat seven years from now. Or maybe not.

"Should we cross?" she asked, gesturing toward the street. Her smile wider than before, like she knew what he thought about her.

Quinn smiled back at her, holding onto her eyes. "Let's go."

They walked in sync, crossing the main street that cuts through town. The brick sidewalk brought them through the public garden. A water fountain sat in the center, but it was dry. On the other side of the street, stores with gray clapboard storefronts showcased their goods in their windows. Some of the restaurants had outdoor seating. Antique stores were sprinkled among gift shops that displayed surf boards and T-shirts in the windows. A classic-style diner sat at the end of the road. On the pier, there was a candy shop and arcade.

He loved growing up here and was even glad that when he

had needed a refuge after losing Lisa, he could come back to this beautiful spot.

"I want to hire a lawyer," she said, getting right to business.

"Ah," he said, slightly disappointed this wasn't a social visit. "I see. What kind of lawyer are you looking for?"

"I'm looking for a good family lawyer," she said. "One who would be able to help me sell a house."

"You're selling?" What did that mean?

"Well, it's too big for little old me," she said. "And my ex will expect half of the sale of the house."

A melancholy grin graced her face, and she looked exactly like the mermaid statue behind her. The mythical goddess who had saved the sailor and got banished to the depths of the sea seemed to be watching over her.

"It's still in my husband's name, but he promised to split it fifty-fifty."

Now Quinn understood the situation. This was good news. She was selling her house in Massachusetts. "I'm happy to help, but you'll need an attorney who is licensed in Massachusetts."

She frowned at that. "Well, I also wanted to set up something for the Queen Bees to continue working on the property. Maybe make it all conservation land or something," she said, shrugging. "My sister said if you make the land conservation, then you don't have to pay a ton of taxes on it."

"I'm not a tax attorney, but I can definitely find out for you," he said, excited to hear she was thinking of preserving the land as conservation but impressed as well. She had been able to put aside her hurt for the greater good. "You definitely want to set up a conservation?"

"I don't know, maybe?" She shrugged. "I guess that's why I need an attorney. But someone who knows how I can keep this whole thing going."

"This whole thing going?" He didn't understand. "What thing?"

"The cycle of giving, you know?" she said. "The way everyone takes care of everyone around here. Give back what I can like everyone did for me and my mother." She paused, then said, "And my father."

He couldn't help but grin at that. "I think that's a great idea."

She looked at the statue, covering her eyes from the sun. "I think this place will be a good spot for me." She tilted her head, looking at the mermaid.

He wished more than anything he could've reached out and taken her in his arms. Tell her how happy he was that she decided to stay. Instead, his phone vibrated in his pocket, but he didn't have to look. He knew who it was.

Bruce.

If he closed his one-attorney family practice law firm and went to work for Bruce in Portland, he'd have to move. There was no way he could commute two hours from Blueberry Bay to the city each day. Some people rented a small apartment to make it through the week and came home on the weekends, but he couldn't imagine not seeing Kyle each day.

But he couldn't afford college otherwise. Not with the salary he gave himself. And could he really afford to keep paying Ginny for her work?

Jacob had promised to pay when everything had been cataloged and documented, but he had died before Quinn had had a chance to bill him. Now it looked like he was trying to take it from a dead man.

"It's Kyle's grandfather," he said, silencing it. "I'm happy to call him back later."

"Do you think you can maybe help me with the conservation?" she asked. "I'd like to present this idea to the ladies tonight at the meeting."

His heart raced at the idea of her staying in town just as a ding sounded out from his phone. Bruce had left a voicemail. Maybe Quinn didn't have to leave. Maybe he could stay another year and let Kyle figure things out on his own. Maybe he could find a community college to attend that had a football team. And maybe Quinn could see more of Meredith.

"Great. I'll see you tonight," he said, facing her, the water behind her and the blue of her eyes glowing in the sunlight. He had never wanted to kiss someone more than he did in that moment.

"I'll see you tonight," she said, holding his eyes with hers.

Just as she turned to go, he blurted out, "Would you like to join me for dinner tonight, before the meeting?"

She stopped, and a smile grew across her face. "I'd love that."

"Not with the Queens," he said, making sure she knew it was a date.

She laughed, and he wondered if he was too confident as she looked at him, not answering.

"I hope not," she said.

And that was when he felt the hook sink into his heart.

Quinn drove home after running by the food pantry. He blasted the radio, happier than he had been in years. He felt excited about the next moment, excited about going out with Meredith and having dinner, excited to have someone to do something with other than just driving them here to there.

"What's up?" Kyle asked as Quinn came in the house. "You're home early."

"I'm headed out actually," Quinn said.

"Where are you going?" Kyle asked.

"Out to dinner." He wondered now if he should even mention it to Kyle. What if things turned south?

"When?" Kyle asked, but like a typical teenager, he didn't really care about Quinn's plans or the fact that Quinn had never gone out to dinner alone before.

"In about an hour, why?" Quinn could tell his son was fishing for his own motive.

"I was hoping to talk to you about something," Kyle said.

"What's that?" Quinn could tell this was serious, and he waited for bad news. "What's wrong?"

"Nothing at all, actually," Kyle said. He started pacing the kitchen floor. "I just started thinking, and I talked to Brianna and Meredith about next year. Did you know that Meredith's son went to UNH? Anyways, I think I will try to go to a local college next year."

Quinn couldn't believe it. "Really?"

All Kyle had to do was talk to Brianna and Meredith and he changed his mind? After months of fighting, that's all it took?

"You sure I could play football, too?" Kyle asked.

"Of course," Quinn said. He kept his grin for his son, but the dark truth hit him. He would have to work for Bruce. "You can go wherever you want."

CHAPTER 34

"I'm going to have dinner with Quinn before the meeting tonight," Meredith said to Remy and Greg, who sat on the back porch planning out the art auction. She and Greg were scheduling vendors and were in the middle of creating a list of caterers.

"There's a meeting tonight?" Remy had clearly forgotten. "Oh, right. Do you think I need to go?"

Remy was so caught up in what she and Greg were doing she didn't seem to notice that Meredith didn't invite her like usual. And Meredith didn't want to bring attention to the fact she and Quinn were going out to dinner alone. What if things go badly? What if he doesn't think it's a date? Is it even a date?

Meredith started freaking herself out.

Remy's attention went back to Greg and Jacob's abundant art collection. Remy clearly liked having her longtime college friend and spending time together. And Meredith enjoyed seeing Remy so happy. Ever since her call with Joe she had been quieter than usual.

"You don't have to go to the meeting. I can go on my own," Meredith said. She had wanted the conservation land to be a surprise, but it was as good a time as any to tell her. "I decided to take your advice."

"What advice?" Remy wrinkled her forehead.

"About the land," Meredith said.

Remy smiled. "Really? You're going to keep the cottage?"

Meredith nodded. "I am." And she laughed at the idea. She would stay at the cottage. "At least through autumn."

When winter came, she wasn't sure. "But if the house sells in Andover, then I'll probably stay here until I figure things out."

Remy held up her glass at the news. "Congratulations! That's great, Meredith."

Greg nodded with Remy. "You've got a charming place here."

"I think you're going to be really happy here," Remy said.

Meredith looked around the cozy cottage. She imagined waking up to the orange glow of the sunrise reflecting off the waters of the Atlantic into her bedroom windows. She pictured herself walking along the beaches and greeting her neighbors. She could smell the sweetness of the blueberry treats she would learn to bake. She heard the crackle of a fire in the woodstove and the lull of the waves calming her to sleep at night.

"I think I will too," she said.

Remy and Greg moved inside as the afternoon sun cooled and Meredith got ready for dinner. With her sun-kissed cheeks, she didn't have to wear much make-up. She wore her favorite sundress and wore her hair down.

She met Quinn outside when she saw him cutting across the yard. Knots twisted in her stomach as he came closer.

She waved when he looked up at her, and he waved back, but the smile he wore earlier had vanished.

"Hey, Meredith," he said, his eyes just making contact, but something felt different. "You look beautiful."

"Thank you," she said, noticing the small bouquet in his hands. "They're beautiful."

He smiled, but it quickly faded, and she felt a different energy radiating out from him.

"Do you still want to go to dinner?" she asked, suddenly unsure.

He didn't answer right away, and her heart started beating faster. She hadn't expected him to have changed his mind about the night.

"I'm sorry, Meredith, but I don't think it's a good idea if we got involved," he looked away. "It's just that, Kyle's decided to go to college next year…which means, I'll need to take a new job. I'll probably be moving closer to the city and the hours will be demanding." His whole face fell as his eyebrows wrinkled down. "I just don't know how it could work. I'm so sorry."

"Sure, no problem." She pretended to smell the flowers. Then took a step back. "I get it."

"I have to think about Kyle right now," he said.

She waved him off. "It's totally fine."

He closed his eyes, but then he looked at her, his eyes sincere. "I really am sorry."

"It's not a problem," she said, stepping even further back.

Quinn just stood there with a look on his face she couldn't really read, because she realized she didn't really know this man.

"Thanks for the flowers." She held up the bouquet. "I should put these in some water."

She started to walk away when Quinn called out after her. "I'll write that conservation proposal up for you as soon as I can."

She stopped dead in her tracks. Was that what this was all about? He'd gotten what he wanted, and now he didn't need to pretend around her anymore? Quinn seemed sincere, but her history with men had her second-guessing everything.

"Sure, thanks." She turned back toward the house and went inside, shutting the door behind her. She leaned her back against the wood, holding her breath, then exhaling hard. Her heart was elevated, pounding in her ears. She pushed off the door. She wouldn't break down, not until she reached the bedroom.

Then she'd scream over the waves.

She dropped the flowers into the sink, put her purse onto the counter, and walked through the living room to her bedroom.

"Hey, I thought you were going to dinner?" Remy asked, sitting on the couch with Greg and a glass of wine.

Meredith wished Greg would get lost, because for the first time in her life, she was ready to open up about how she felt right now. But Remy looked happy, and Greg was helping them out, and it was the same old story. Meredith was a fool.

"I actually have a bit of a headache, so I think I'll just talk to Ginny tomorrow," she said, changing her mind again. She walked toward the staircase, and before she went up, she turned to Remy and said, "I think I might head to Andover tomorrow morning. Right away. Go through things there."

Remy looked surprised. "Really, why all of a sudden?"

"I just want to get it over with, you know?" Meredith shrugged. "Do you think you could continue going through everything without me?"

Since making up her mind, Meredith just wanted it all to be done. She didn't miss the Andover house as much as she thought she would, and no one in the neighborhood had started to complain about the lawn. She wondered how bad the pool looked by now.

"Of course." Remy raised her eyebrow, questioning Meredith. "Are you okay?"

"Yes, just a headache," Meredith said, going up the stairs before Remy asked more questions.

When she got to her room, she shut the door and opened all the windows, letting the ocean air swirl through the room. Why had she let her guard down? Why had she let a man inside her heart? She knew what would happen. She knew what men did.

They left.

CHAPTER 35

"*I* thought you wanted us to come to Maine?" Cora asked on the phone.

"You can. I mean, don't you want to come to the house in Andover?" Meredith said, hoping her children would make the decision for her. Should she just stay in Andover? Figure out how to sell the cottage in Maine while also leaving the land to the Queen Bees?

"Dad mentioned you were selling the house?" Cora said.

"No." Meredith hadn't told Phillip anything. "I never said I was selling. When did he say that?"

"A few months ago," Cora said. "He said you can't stay there."

"He said that *I* can't stay here?" The old feelings rushed back—the anger, the anxiety, the miscommunication, followed by the irritation.

"That you can't afford it teaching piano lessons," Cora said.

Meredith looked at the baby grand piano that sat in the front formal living room in her Andover home. A room for the piano and nothing else. She'd loved it when she'd first moved into the house. The two-story room carried the sound beautifully. Phillip had installed soundproofing when she had started teaching lessons as the kids got older. She had recitals each year and set up a party for the kids afterward.

Never once had Phillip told her to go back to her career so she could help earn. Never once had he made her feel she wasn't contributing by staying home. In fact, she had given up her career, her dreams, to stay home for them.

She clenched her jaw and held back from saying something rude about Phillip. The insult wasn't that she didn't make the kind of money he did to afford the house. The insult was that she didn't contribute to his wealth. If Meredith hadn't stayed home, Phillip's career would have looked very different at the law firm that prided their attorneys on working day and night for their clients, which Phillip did.

He became partner because she took care of everything at home. The house, the kids, all of it.

"Well, then you should come to the house anyway to pack your things. Maybe go through some stuff and take what you want."

"I don't think I have anything I want there anymore," Cora said. "I mean, where will I put it? My apartment's the size of a shoe box."

"What about your porcelain horses?" Meredith had driven all over the state, spending hundreds of dollars on them.

"And your yearbooks and all that stuff?" Meredith thought about Christmas. "I have all the ornaments for Christmas. Will you want some for your apartment?"

"I have no room, seriously," Cora said.

Where would Meredith put all her stuff? Where would she go if she sold the house? Would she stay in Andover? Go to Maine and live there by herself? Or sell the cottage and stay?

She could just stay. Live the way she always had and be fine.

Just fine.

But she sighed, feeling the old anger, anxiety, and irritation seep back in.

She hadn't been fine. But she wasn't fine now either. All she had done over the five-hour drive back to Andover from Blue-berry Bay was think about Quinn. Think about how happy she had been in Blueberry Bay. How much she had enjoyed her time with Remy. How excited she had been riding in the boat with Kyle.

And Quinn. She couldn't stop thinking about Quinn.

What had gone wrong?

Things had just ended so suddenly. One minute they were going to dinner, and the next it was over, just like that. He hadn't even called or texted after sending information about the conser-vation land laws in Maine.

"I think you should just sell the house," Cora said.

"Well, I'd like to talk to your sister and brother about that first," Meredith said.

"Do what makes you happy, Mom," Cora said. "You've always done what everyone else wants. Maybe it's time you think about you."

Meredith's breath was swept away by her daughter's thought-fulness. She choked up as she said, "I think I'm going to do just that."

"Good," Cora said. "That house is just a reminder of what used to be, and it's time to move on."

Meredith looked around the room, remembering the pitter-patter of little feet pounding the floors. The soft lights of the Christmas tree glowing in the room. The smell of the fireplace on a winter day. The splashing in the pool during the summer. Her mother dropping in to have coffee and a chat. None of that existed anymore.

"I'm going to have an auction for all my father's things," Meredith said. "I'd really like you to come."

"Okay," Cora agreed, and quickly. No arguments, no vague maybe.

"Great, and if you want to choose some of his paintings for yourself, you can just choose what you want," Meredith said.

Over the past weeks, she had studied the paintings, found her favorite, then changed her mind with the next painting she studied.

At first, she hadn't really seen what the hype of Jacob's work was all about. She even questioned the value of it. They looked like the typical landscapes that you find on calendars.

But as she'd gone through each one, examining the use of color, shadows, and texture, she had been drawn into his creative beauty.

Jacob could capture a moment, a feeling from the scene. Not one landscape was the same. Or of the same spot. There were hundreds of paintings, yet Jacob never repeated any of his images.

Except of Jacqueline.

He painted her all the time. Sketched her. Drew her.

"Your grandfather Jacob was an incredible artist," Meredith said.

"Really?" Cora asked. "Did he sell his work?"

That's when Meredith felt something she had never felt before when discussing Jacob—a little bit of pride.

And she began telling Cora everything that she and Remy had done over the past month at The Cottage by the Sea.

Suddenly, the doorbell rang. Meredith looked at the time and realized they had been talking on the phone for over an hour. When was the last time she'd had this long of a conversation with Cora?

She looked at the front door and saw Gordon standing in his golf clothes.

"Cora, I have to let you go," she said. "Grandpa's here."

"Okay, call me later?" Cora asked.

And the question made Meredith take pause. It had been the first time her adult daughter had asked her to call her back.

"I will," Meredith said. "I'll send you the dates of the auction."

"And I'll make a plan to come up and go through some stuff," Cora said.

Meredith smiled. "That sounds great."

She walked to the front door, opened it, and at once, hugged her father.

"Hi, Dad," she said, letting him into the house. "Golfing today?"

"I met a buddy for nine holes," he said. "I thought you were staying in Maine for the summer."

"I was, but now I need to do some things here," she said. "I was thinking about selling."

Gordon nodded. "You know, I'm thinking about that same thing."

"You are?"

That's when he pulled out the bag from behind his back. A pint of ice cream.

"Want to eat out by the pool?" she asked.

"Sounds great," he said.

They walked to the back yard. She had hoped Gordon would always stay in their house, for some reason. Her childhood home had been such an anchor of comfort for her. The one steady thing in her life. She wondered what Remy would think.

"I was thinking maybe I'd retire in Maine," he said, pulling out the ice cream from the bag and setting it down on the table.

"Really?"

"I was looking into it, just for fun, since you two girls are having such a good time up there," he said. "I always loved living there."

And it hit Meredith.

Gordon had been her constant. He had been there for her mother when she was pregnant. He had given them shelter when her mother had left an unfortunate situation. He had opened his heart to her daughter as his own. He had raised Meredith as a Johnson and had always put her and her sister first.

"I think you'll love it up there," she said, smiling, as she thought about how this would make her own decision so much easier. She placed two bowls on the table and handed him the scoop. "It's a beautiful place."

"I heard there's a great golf course up around there, right on the water." Gordon opened the pint, scooped out a perfect round bit of ice cream, and placed it into Meredith's bowl. "I thought maybe we could scatter your mom's ashes there as well. Maybe with Jacob's so she doesn't have to go on her last journey alone."

Tears sprung to her eyes, and she could see Gordon's eyes were watering as well.

"I think that's a really beautiful idea," she said, reaching out for his hand.

"I do, too." Gordon grabbed a tissue and handed one to her before blowing his nose. "Just what you want is an old emotional man following you to Maine."

"I would want nothing more," she said.

He squeezed her hand. "Thanks, sugarplum."

CHAPTER 36

*M*eredith waited for Gordon to finish packing his winter clothes. Maine wasn't like Massachusetts in the fall. Meredith had been told that it was cold. Really cold.

With her decision to sell the Andover house, she took Quinn's advice and hired a lawyer in Massachusetts that specialized in family law, specifically divorce law.

As it turned out, Meredith had more leverage than she had thought, even though the house was in Philip's name.

Phillip stopped calling her after that.

"Come on, Dad!" she called up the stairs.

Gordon decided to rent out his house for the time being. He would stay with the girls until he found his own perfect spot.

He wanted to be close to them but also somewhere in the village so he could walk to places.

Meredith's house sold within minutes of listing it. She didn't even have time to change her mind, it went so fast.

The couple who had bought it had three boys, saw the pool, and put down an offer higher than the asking price.

She got fifty percent of the sale of the house, which gave her enough to live comfortably in the cottage. She didn't have the luxurious retirement she and Phillip had planned—a house in

Florida while keeping the house in Massachusetts—but she didn't know if she even wanted that anymore.

"I'm ready!" Gordon said, coming down the stairs, wearing a coat and holding a bag.

"Dad, it's eighty degrees out," she said. "It's still August."

"I know, but I couldn't fit it in the bag." Gordon walked by her to the car.

He's adorable, she texted Remy with a picture of Gordon from behind.

Remy hearted her picture and sent, **We'll see you guys soon!**

Remy and Greg had done everything to get ready for the auction while Meredith stayed in Massachusetts to sell her house.

The drive took longer than expected because they stopped for Gordon a few times to get out and walk around. They also stopped for lunch, and as dinner approached, they pulled into the little village of Blueberry Bay.

"My goodness, it looks exactly the same!" Gordon said, looking out at the town.

Meredith enjoyed seeing the clapboard shingled buildings again. "Want to go see the statue?"

Gordon nodded. "But maybe see Remy first."

Her father always thought of everyone's feelings. Remy would want to be there too.

They drove up the hill, past the Congregational Church, then the fire station. When she took a left, following the shore, Gordon rolled down the window.

"This is what I remember." He inhaled a deep breath.

Meredith took in the familiar briny scent, and she suddenly couldn't wait to get back to the cottage.

They drove down Blueberry Bay Lane to the very end, where The Cottage by the Sea sat.

"She made a sign!" Meredith squealed out as she pulled up to the cottage.

Hanging above the door, a sign read, "*Le gîte en bord de Mer.*"

"It's perfect!" she said as she got out of the car, meeting Remy at the front door. "I love it!"

"I knew you would," Remy said. "Wait until you see what Greg and I did in the barn for the auction."

They brought Gordon around the cottage, showing him each of the rooms and explaining what they had done to clean it out and make it look the way it did.

"It was mostly Remy," Meredith said.

"You did all the planning and organizing," Remy said.

All three retreated to the back porch as Remy pulled dinner out of the oven.

"I made pulled pork with a blueberry chutney sauce." Remy closed her eyes and sniffed in the aroma. "It's absolutely delicious."

They ate at the table they had brought out to the porch and talked about the auction tomorrow.

"Quinn and Kyle have been a godsend," Remy said. "It's too bad about Quinn's new job being so far away."

"What?" Meredith said.

"Yeah, he moved to be closer to the firm in Portland. I thought you knew?" Remy looked confused.

Meredith put her fork down. "I knew he was going, but not so soon. What about Kyle?"

"I guess Quinn's going to come home on the weekends so Kyle can finish his senior year here with his friends." Remy shrugged. "I don't know the whole story because things have been just crazy, but he just moved out a few days ago."

Meredith couldn't believe it. Quinn had left Blueberry Bay?

When Meredith woke up the next morning, she felt a rejuvenation from a good night's sleep that she hadn't felt back at the house in Andover. She had missed waking up to the gentle lull of the waves and the soft rays lighting up her room.

As she got dressed, she unpacked some of her things from her luggage, putting her clothes into drawers and in the closet, and she started thinking about incorporating some of the things she had kept from the Andover house into the cottage and start making it *her cottage.*

She went downstairs, noticing Gordon and Remy were still asleep.

As she walked by the coffee maker, she turned it on and went to grab a glass of water. She stood at the sink, looking out the window at the water, wondering if the auction would go as Remy believed.

Something caught her eye off in the distance, and she saw Quinn walking the path to the beach. She almost went out the door to follow him, ask him about the move, but she stopped herself. He wasn't expecting her. He might not even know she was in town. He hadn't texted or called after she had left.

Why was she going to chase after him?

"Hey, sugarplum," Gordon said, walking into the kitchen.

"Hey, Dad." She walked to the coffee machine and pulled out a few mugs from the cabinet. "Do you want cream or milk?"

"Cream if you've got it," he said, walking to the door and looking out its window to the back porch. "I'm going to take it outside."

"It's pretty chilly out there," Meredith warned.

"That's why I brought my winter coat," he said.

She smiled at her father. Not once had he made any remarks about Jacob or the relationship between Jacqueline and him. He seemed pleased to see his daughters celebrating this man's life's work, and Meredith wished she could take some of his acceptance with her.

"Did you want to see the statue when Remy gets up?" Meredith asked as she poured Gordon his coffee.

"That would be nice," he said. "But I'm in no rush. I'm going to be here for a while."

She handed him his coffee, and he took it with both hands. She noticed he appeared a little bit more wrinkled than before, and grayer. If she had been married to Phillip, she would be leaving for Florida for the winter months and might not have noticed her father aging.

"I'm going to make some blueberry pancakes before setting up the sleeping arrangements for the kids," she said. She looked at the time. She had a few hours before the kids all started showing up.

She would put the girls in the bedroom next to Gordon. She and Remy would share the master, and she'd put Ryan on the pullout in the den downstairs. She had brought all her good linens and towels from Andover. Along with new pillows and throws to spruce the place up.

When Remy got up, Meredith started the pancakes just as Greg showed up from the city.

"This is going to be amazing," he said, dressed in a three-piece Italian suit. Greg was running the auction and being the auctioneer. "Have you seen the barn set up? Remy did a fabulous job."

"I can't wait to see everything," Meredith said, hoping they'd run into Ginny and the other Queens before things got crazy with the auction and the kids arriving.

The fields would soon be swarmed with tourists from the festival picking their own blueberries. This was the moment of the year for the Queens.

After they ate, they all got ready. Meredith wore a new dress she'd bought for the auction. She did her hair and put on more make-up than usual. Remy looked amazing in a fitted dress, and Gordon wore a button-up and a blazer.

She could feel her excitement grow as cars with out-of-state license plates started pulling up to the cottage and parking wherever they could find space.

They all walked together to the barn, where Greg met them outside.

Remy and Greg pulled the doors open for Meredith. What once had been a dusty old space full of junk now looked like a museum of art. Jacob's paintings hung on every wall, hung from the second-floor loft. Fairy lights draped across the ceiling and were wrapped around the rafters and beams. White folding chairs were set up facing the podium that stood in the center of the barn.

"It's gorgeous!" Meredith said, truly blown away by what Remy had done. "When can people start coming in?" she asked, noticing a crowd milling around outside.

"Now, if you're ready," Greg said.

"Wait," Meredith said. "Do you mind if I have a private word with my family?"

Remy tilted her head as she and Gordon waited for Meredith to speak.

"Thank you for everything," Meredith said to Remy first. "Thank you for helping me find my way. I appreciate it and I appreciate you." Then she turned to Gordon. "And thank you for always being my anchor."

Gordon smiled and hugged her.

Remy signaled to Greg to open it up to the public, and the barn was soon filled with art collectors and dealers and art enthusiasts coming to see Jacob O'Neill's work.

The Queens worked in the fields, as tourists came to pick their own blueberries, and even the local news station showed up to do a story about the event.

Meredith hadn't put up all of Jacob's work. She had saved plenty for the children and for herself. Then she thought about Kyle and texted him.

Maybe we could take the boat out for one last ride? she wrote.

Then she would give the boat to Kyle. He deserved it more than anyone here. The only person to have been with Jacob from what she had learned. The only person to have heard him talk, besides Ginny years ago. The only one who could get Jacob back out on the water. The person who Jacob had cleaned up for at the end of his life.

From around the corner, Quinn came walking into the barn. He wore the same suit he had on the day she'd met him, when he had seemed so uptight and out of touch. Now, he looked more handsome than ever before.

"Quinn," she said as he came closer.

"Wow, this place looks great," he said, checking out the space as he went in to kiss her on the cheek.

"It's all Remy," Meredith said, smelling his aftershave and feeling the slight roughness of his morning-old stubble.

He smiled. "It's good to see you."

She played with her hands, not sure what to do with them. Should she fold them in front of her, or hold them across her stomach? Did she just look completely stupid no matter what she did? She decided to clasp them together and rest them against her dress.

"Did you find the information about the conservation helpful?" he asked, getting right to business.

A heavy feeling washed over her, disappointment along with the same cut of sadness she felt the night he canceled their dinner.

"Quinn," she said, not caring if it was the right moment or not. "Are you here just as my attorney? Or did you come to see me too?"

He stared at her, and the silence was deafening.

"Because I don't think I can keep being your client if we can't be friends," she said. She felt horrible, but it was too hard seeing him and feeling something for him, with him being the old, cold Quinn.

She didn't want to spill her feelings, but Meredith was fifty. She didn't want to waste any time being uncomfortable around people in her life.

"Meredith," he said.

She waited for him to say something, to explain, but he just stood there staring at her.

"Right, well, I have an auction to sit through," she said, as people mulled around the barn. She began to walk away.

"Meredith," he said, grabbing her clasped hands and stopping her from walking away. "I can't stop thinking about you."

"What?" she said, her heart stopping in its tracks.

"I think about you all the time," he said, not letting go of her hand. "And I wish I hadn't freaked out, but I did. I didn't want to start something and get attached and then have everything fall apart because I'm stuck in some law office working all the time."

"You didn't even want to see if it would work," she said. "You just decided it couldn't."

"I know I'm going to be a miserable human being working for my father-in-law."

"Then don't," she said. "Don't work for him."

"I can't afford college, even if Kyle doesn't use his money to buy the boat." Quinn huffed. "I took a job from my father-in-law under the promise that he'd pay for Kyle."

So that's what it felt like to have her heart crushed. She looked down at their hands.

Quinn entwined his fingers into hers. "But what if we did try being more than just attorney and client? I mean, maybe, if you're up for it, we could try seeing each other on the weekends."

Her heart skipped a beat as she looked up at him. "I'd really like that."

He nodded. She could feel his heart pounding inside his chest when he said, "Meredith?"

"Yes?" She looked up at him, waiting for him to say something.

And with a small tug into his arms, he dipped her down and kissed her. He held her against him as the whole barn spun underneath Meredith's feet.

When he brought her back to her feet, he said, "I've wanted nothing more than to do that for ages."

She smiled. "I've been waiting for you to kiss me for ages."

And with that, he kissed her again.

CHAPTER 37

*C*ora showed up first, then Ryan and Muriel drove up together without her boyfriend, which couldn't have been better in Meredith's opinion. All three had showed up before the auction started, and it felt like old times with all of them together right away.

"Muriel got lost seven times," Ryan had complained.

"Oh my goodness, you'd think he'd be happy since he didn't have to pay for any of the gas," Muriel had shot back.

"It's good to see you guys!" Meredith had said, hugging each of her children a little tighter and longer than usual.

During the auction, Meredith and the family sat on the side of the barn away from the buyers as Greg, along with a woman who wore a very posh designer dress, started the bidding for the pieces they'd put up for auction. She hadn't noticed until Remy whispered in her ear that the governor of Maine sat in the crowd bidding on Jacob's harbor painting.

Jacob's pieces went for prices Meredith couldn't fathom. Never in a million years would she believe anyone should spend that kind of money on a painting, but there were over seventy-five people who had been specially invited to attend and more than willing to pay. Greg kept hitting the gavel at numbers

Meredith could only imagine, and she lost track of how much had been auctioned off in total.

In the end, all the paintings went for more than their asking price. Greg's buzz, networking, and word of mouth had paid off just like he said it would.

Meredith was thrilled.

She could have even saved the house in Andover if she had just waited long enough, but she didn't have any regrets. Not with Quinn standing on the side, staring at her with that look in his eyes. She loved the feeling she had when he looked at her like that. Like she was the most beautiful woman in the whole room.

He smiled at her when she looked back at him when the last painting came up.

It had been the one of the boat in the harbor. The one she had offered to Quinn, but he hadn't taken.

"We'll start the bidding at twenty-two hundred. Twenty-two hundred," Greg said, echoing the number to make the buyers certain of its price.

A man in a flannel lifted his paddle.

"Is that…?" Meredith whispered to Remy.

She nodded. "Yes, it's the news anchor from NBC."

Meredith giggled at the idea that Ron Humphries was sitting in her barn buying one of her father's paintings.

"Do we have a twenty-five hundred?"

"Ten thousand," a voice called out.

"That's the governor!" Remy hissed in Meredith's ear. "He wants it for the mansion."

"Fifteen!" the news anchor shouted before grinning at the governor.

The governor crossed his arms over his rather large belly and said, "Twenty."

By the time the two gentlemen stopped bidding, the governor won the painting at fifty-six thousand dollars.

Meredith almost threw up from the anxiety of the whole thing.

"Will they have to pay that?" she asked Remy, who laughed at the whole scene.

Greg looked as though he wasn't at all surprised.

The whole family took pictures with the governor and Ron Humphries. Greg and the group of art collectors and buyers mingled in the barn under the twinkling fairy lights.

Meredith's children all stood with her as Quinn came up to her again and kissed her on the cheek.

"Quinn, these are my three wonderful children, Cora, Muriel, and Ryan." She stood like a proud momma showing off her chicks.

Quinn held out his hand to all three.

"Quinn is a special friend of mine," Meredith said, then she smiled at him.

Cora lifted her eyebrows when Quinn turned to greet Muriel and Ryan, and Meredith smiled at her eldest. She wouldn't hide her feelings. If her daughter wanted to know how she felt about Quinn, she would tell her. Meredith was done holding in her feelings for fear of upsetting anyone. Now she was going to be open and honest no matter what.

Meredith could feel herself blush as Remy gave Meredith a little jab in the rib and said, "You two look really good together."

She *felt* like they were good together. Did she officially have someone special? Like a boyfriend?

People mingled around the barn, drinking champagne and having hors d'oeuvres. A string quartet played softly in the background. The whole time, she noticed Quinn stealing glances at her.

Was she supposed to ask Quinn to go steady? At fifty? What did people do when they were falling in love for the second time?

She shook her spinning thoughts away and took his hand into hers. That's what felt right. Quinn holding her hand.

"Want to take the kids to the festival tonight?" she asked him. "After the blueberry picking, of course."

The side of Quinn's mouth perked up. "That sounds great."

It didn't take long for Ryan and Kyle to start talking about fishing. Ryan's face lit up as Kyle told him about Jacob's boat. He didn't even pay attention to his mother holding another man's hand. "And you catch lobsters with it?"

She turned to Quinn and said quietly, "I want to give Kyle the boat."

Quinn shook his head. "I can't have you just give it to him."

"I want to do that for him," she said, looking at her son and Kyle talking. "Besides, that way he can use his money for college."

Quinn stared at her. "Are you sure?"

She nodded. "Nothing would make me happier than to give Kyle his boat."

"I think Jacob would've been very happy to know what you've done with everything," Quinn said.

He squeezed Meredith's hand before letting her go to greet Gordon.

"You must be Meredith's dad," he said, shaking Gordon's hand with both of his.

"You must be Quinn." Gordon gave a little wink at Meredith.

She looked right at Remy, who smiled back at her. She had spilled the beans about Quinn.

When they all walked out of the barn, Quinn took Meredith's hand again.

"What if the money from that painting that the governor just bought could be Kyle's college tuition?" she said. "I know that's what Jacob would've wanted for him."

Quinn shook his head. "I can't take your money."

Then she stopped, holding him back as the crowd went ahead. "This is what Jacob would've wanted for Kyle and for you and for me."

"I don't know, Meredith, it's too generous," said Quinn.

"Think of it like a scholarship. Kyle could be the first Jacob O'Neill scholarship recipient?" she said, begging silently for him to stay in Blueberry Bay with her.

Quinn looked into her eyes, holding her hands with his. "I

can't thank you enough, Meredith. Ever since you came into my life...it's been better. You make me happy. And it's been a long time since I've been happy like this."

Meredith laughed, placing her hands on his face, pulling him closer to her. "You make me happy."

"I want you to be part of my life, Meredith." He stood inches away from her. His breath warming her lips. "I want to be all in."

She kissed him right then. "I want to be all in, too."

And Meredith had never been happier.

CHAPTER 38

$\mathcal{M}$eredith watched as people paid Ginny and the rest of the Queen Bees to go through the blueberry fields and pick their own. Dozens of families walked through the rows of blueberries, and all of them passed through the barn to look at Jacob's art that Meredith had kept up for the public.

She and Remy sat at the entrance and asked for donations only. "All proceeds go to local scholarships."

A woman walked up to Meredith with her three young daughters.

"Are you Meredith Johnson?" the mother asked.

"I am," Meredith said.

"Do you still teach?" the woman asked.

Meredith must've made a face giving away her complete confusion, because the woman answered before Meredith had to ask what she meant.

"Piano? Do you still teach piano lessons?" the woman asked.

"I did," Meredith said.

"I've been looking for a piano instructor for my daughters for a while, but I can't seem to find someone," she said. "Carolyn said you used to teach lessons."

"Yes," Meredith said.

"Would you consider starting lessons with my girls?"

Meredith looked down at the three young girls and smiled. "I'd love to."

The girls looked up at their mother in delight. And Meredith felt excited about the possibility of teaching again.

"Why don't you come by the house next week and we can set up some times," Meredith said.

"That would be fantastic!" the mother said, shaking Meredith's hand.

When the Queens closed the fields for the day, Meredith and Remy closed the barn up as well.

"There's easily over a thousand dollars in here, probably more," Remy said as she collected the donation money.

"You ladies did great!" Ginny said, walking through the barn, which was still decorated for the auction, but without the chairs and the people, the space looked like a rustic art gallery. Just how Meredith imagined Jacob would want to share his collection of Blueberry Bay. All the paintings Meredith and Remy had set aside were of the small town and its community.

"Maybe we could make this as a community space," she said to Ginny. "A place where we can hold Queen Bee meetings and art lessons and poetry readings and, well, anything."

Ginny clapped her hands together as she heard the ideas coming out. "That all sounds wonderful!"

Meredith then held Ginny's arm, making sure she understood the next part. "I want to make the fields all conservation, where no one can come in and build on the property, and the blueberries can live another ten thousand years."

Ginny wrapped her arms around Meredith, sweeping her breath away by her strength. "I sure love you girls."

Remy put her arms around both and hugged them too.

"Remy?" a voice said from outside the barn.

Standing on the path from the house stood Joe. He didn't

wear his usual fancy business suit but a casual outfit and a baseball cap.

"Joe?" Remy let go of them. "What are you doing here?"

Joe walked closer to the barn.

"That's Joe?" Ginny whispered to Meredith.

"Mm-hmm," Meredith said, wondering if she should lead the ladies away, tell the lingering crowds of blueberry pickers to give her sister and her estranged husband some space.

"I thought I'd come up for vacation," he said to Remy, but he clearly hadn't taken a vacation in a really long time, because Joe looked completely out of his element. "I've missed you so much."

Remy stood there, not moving, not saying anything, not giving any sign of her feelings whatsoever. Joe looked at Meredith, who shrugged.

"I'm sorry," he said to Remy.

"Where are you planning on staying?" Remy asked, her voice the exact same as it had been while hugging Meredith, but her body had stiffened.

"I rented a cottage down the road," he said, jabbing his thumb behind him.

"Right," she said. "Then what are you doing *here?*"

He stood uncomfortably in front of everyone. "I thought I'd ask you to the festival."

Meredith hadn't seen a romantic movie in a very long time, but she knew it when she saw a man begging for his wife back.

"Aw," Greg said, holding up his champagne glass. "He did come."

"Let's all go downtown to the festival and let Remy and Joe have a minute," Meredith said to the group. "We have to check out the baking contest. Remy put in her blueberry cake."

"She'll surely get a place for her cake," Gordon said, standing with his grandchildren.

"Want to walk?" Quinn asked Meredith.

She liked the idea of all of them walking but didn't think Gordon could make it that far.

"What if I drive the old timers and you all walk to town?" Ginny said, hitting her elbow into Gordon's stomach. "Want to hitch a ride with me?"

"I'd love to," Gordon said, walking toward Ginny's car with Carolyn and two other Queens. Gordon looked like he was in heaven when they took off.

"Where will I meet him?" she asked Quinn.

He held her close to him as they walked toward the path. "They'll be just fine."

Meredith kept her hand in Quinn's the whole way to town. They stayed behind the kids as they walked through Jacob's property, down the sandy path, in between the rose bushes, and over the hill, walking along the beach, then going back over the cliffs to the harbor and town below.

Cora walked with Muriel as Ryan and Kyle led the way, talking about the boat and fishing.

"Kyle's going to take us out tomorrow to fish," Ryan said to Meredith once they reached town.

"That sounds like fun," Meredith said, holding Quinn's hand comfortably in front of the group.

"Are you guys going to come?" Kyle asked.

Meredith looked to Quinn and smiled. "We'd love to."

The whole town of Blueberry Bay went to the festival, which had been set up along Main Street all the way to the park and to the pier. Booths with different kinds of crafts and foods were set up on both sides of the streets. Quinn led the way, holding Meredith's hand, and walked through the crowd to the baked goods tent.

"Remy's cake is over there," Quinn said, pointing to the other side of the tent.

"Oh! I see it," Meredith said, wondering if she looked as happy as she felt.

"I sure do love blueberries," Quinn said, smelling the air inside the baked goods tent.

"Hmm," she said. "They are so sweet and good."

Quinn stopped suddenly in the middle of the tent, taking his arm and wrapping it around her waist. "I bet if we created a blueberry honey treat, we could get a ribbon just for creativity."

She smiled at his idea. "I love it."

He kissed her, right next to Linda's blueberry scones and Fred's barbeque sauce.

"We could start on that right away," he said.

"Does that mean you're staying?" she asked.

He nodded. "I mean, if Kyle has a scholarship to college."

She kissed him again, wrapping her arms around his neck, and he lifted her off the ground.

"You're making me happy," she said, as he held her up, kissing him.

Quinn slowly brought her feet back to the ground, resting his eyes on her. "You're making me really happy too."

After the fireworks, they all walked home, the kids hurrying ahead to the cottage to eat the leftover blueberry cake.

Everyone sat out on the back deck with blueberry cake and vanilla ice cream.

Meredith sat next to Quinn as her children all told him and his family stories of growing up in Andover down the road from their grandparents. Stories of Meredith acting like the over-the-top involved mother. They told stories of Gordon's mishaps and they all laughed, even Meredith.

Remy and Joe sat together, snuggling up against each other on the couch next to Cora, while Ryan and Kyle sat with Quinn at the table, planning out their fishing excursion the next morning. As Quinn explained the different areas of Blueberry Bay, he kept stealing glances at Meredith as she talked with Gordon and Ginny, who had hit it off right away.

Meredith thought things couldn't get any more perfect at that point in her life. As she looked around the room, grateful for the people that sat among her, she couldn't feel happier.

When everyone started getting tired and left the porch,

heading for bed, Quinn said goodbye and whispered into her ear, "I'll come get you when it's ready."

"You better," she said, as excitement swept over her.

When Gordon headed upstairs, he told Remy and Meredith he was proud of them.

"You girls did a very good job today," he said, before heading to bed.

Remy and Meredith kissed him on the cheek.

"Thanks, Dad," Meredith said, as she hugged him goodnight. "I'm so glad you're here with us."

"Me, too, sugarplum," he said, then gave her a wink. "Me, too."

Meredith stayed up as everyone headed to bed and sat on the porch, sitting under a blanket. She looked up at the sky and out at the water, listening to the waves crash into the shore.

"Thank you, Jacob," she said. She had never been so grateful for having Jacob as her father than she was at that moment. "Thank you for everything."

That was when she heard his footsteps coming up the path.

"Hey," she said as he came up to the back porch.

"Hey," Quinn said, flashlight in hand. "You ready?"

She looked out at the beach, and she could see a bonfire already lit by the water's edge. "Are you finally going to tell me the myth of the Blueberry Bay mermaid?"

"Only those who live here can know the legends," he said, holding open the door for her.

She stopped as she passed him, kissing him, and said, "Then I guess you'll have to tell me," before walking toward the sandy path through beach roses and blueberry bushes.

"What do you call this beach?" she asked Quinn.

"Whatever you want to call it," he said. "It's yours."

She laughed at that. It was hers, but really, it was all of theirs. "What about The Queens' Beach."

"You'll never get rid of them if you name a beach after them," he said, kissing her hand.

"What if I want them to stick around?" This made Quinn

laugh as they walked down to the beach. Meredith had no trouble finding her way down now.

Quinn had a blanket and a basket set up in front of the fire. He opened the lid and pulled out a bottle of red and two cups. "I even have some marshmallows."

He pulled out two sticks as well.

"You thought of everything," she said, impressed.

He poured two cups, and they sat down in front of the fire. She snuggled deep into his arm, letting the crackling fire warm her cheeks. Then she pulled out the piece of sea glass she had carried with her since he'd given it to her that day.

"You kept it?" he said with a smile.

She nodded and turned to face him. "I'm ready to make my wish."

She put it in her palm, closed her eyes, and made her wish. Then, she took the piece of sea glass and threw it as far as she could into the dark water.

I hope you enjoyed *The Cottage on Blueberry Bay!* The next book in the series, *The Market on Blueberry Bay*, focuses on Remy and her journey of self discovery and happiness. Click HERE to read it now!

If you'd like to receive a FREE standalone novella from my Camden Cove series, please click HERE or visit my website at ellenjoyauthor.com.

Click HERE or visit ellenjoyauthor.com for more information about all of Ellen's books.

Cliffside Point
Beach Home Beginnings
Seaview Cottage
Sugar Beach Sunsets
Home on the Harbor
Christmas at Cliffside
Lakeside Lighthouse
Seagrass Sunrise
Half Moon Harbor
Seashell Summer
Beach Home Dreams

Camden Cove
The Inn by the Cove
The Farmhouse by the Cove
The Restaurant by the Cove
The Christmas Cottage by the Cove
The Bakery by the Cove

Prairie Valley Sisters
Coming Home to the Valley
Daydreams in the Valley
Starting Over in the Valley
Second Chances in the Valley
New Hopes in the Valley
Feeling Blessed in the Valley

Blueberry Bay
The Cottage on Blueberry Bay
The Market on Blueberry Bay

Beach Rose Secrets

ABOUT THE AUTHOR

Ellen lives in a small town in New England, between the Atlantic Ocean and the White Mountains. She lives with her husband, two sons, and one very spoiled puppy princess.

Ellen writes in the early morning hours before her family wakes up. When she's not writing, you can find her spending time with her family, gardening, or headed to the beach. She loves summer and flip-flops, running on a dirt country road, and a sweet love song.

All of her stories are clean romances where families are close, neighbors are nosy, and the couples are destined for each other.

Made in the USA
Monee, IL
12 October 2024